D0627522

HARD RAIN

HARD RAIN

IRMA VENTER

TRANSLATED BY ELSA SILKE

This is a work of fiction. Names, characters, organizations, places, events, and incidents are either products of the author's imagination or are used fictitiously. Any resemblance to actual persons, living or dead, or actual events is purely coincidental.

Text copyright © 2012 by Irma Venter
Translation copyright © 2020 by Irma Venter
All rights reserved.

No part of this book may be reproduced, or stored in a retrieval system, or transmitted in any form or by any means, electronic, mechanical, photocopying, recording, or otherwise, without express written permission of the publisher.

Previously published as *Skoenlapper* by NB Publishers in South Africa in 2012. Translated from Afrikaans by Elsa Silke. First published in English by Amazon Crossing in 2020.

Published by Amazon Crossing, Seattle

www.apub.com

Amazon, the Amazon logo, and Amazon Crossing are trademarks of Amazon.com, Inc., or its affiliates.

ISBN-13: 9781542018005
ISBN-10: 1542018005

Cover design by Shasti O'Leary Soudant

Printed in the United States of America

For Anneke and Erika

PART ONE

ALEX

1

If your job is to hunt down chaos, you become familiar with noise. And squalor. Crowds. The middle of nowhere. If you report the news long enough, sooner or later you'll end up in a place where you think no one can survive and nothing ever happens. But you'll be wrong. People carry on with their business, and nowhere is just another place to do exactly that. Maybe it's even easier, because there are fewer people who see. Who remember.

There are many such places in the world, not all of them bad. Some are among the most beautiful places I know. A few miles north of Port Nolloth, just before you reach South Africa's border with Namibia, if you keep the sea on your left, fixed west—everything else gradually disappears, until there's only you and the silence.

It's the same when you drive into the tall dunes even farther north, beyond Walvis Bay, into the Namib Desert.

And then there's this place in Tanzania, somewhere between Arusha and Dar es Salaam. Not a place with a name; more just a huddle of dwellings, like lost cattle in tall grass.

Of course there is a bar. The middle of nowhere always has a watering hole.

The occasion is a wedding, and I find myself standing in the shade of an azure-blue hall, beside a peeling, hand-painted Coca-Cola sign, watching the passing parade of family, friends, and curious children. The beer in my hand is lukewarm, and the sun is scorching.

I don't know why I felt obliged to be on time. People are bustling, carrying food, chatting, comparing dresses and hairstyles. And the pastor will clearly sit and drink tea under the umbrella trees for another hour or so.

It's the kind of day when time doesn't matter.

I turn away, looking to make myself useful. Maybe someone needs help with the chairs or the drinks.

The first thing I notice is her hair: black and abundant. She gets up from the fallen tree she's been sitting on in the small clearing in front of the hall, grips the Nikon camera between her legs, gathers the curls into her hands and ties them up behind her head. Her purple T-shirt proclaims that Dr. Seuss is always right. She's probably six feet tall, her body that of a swimmer—willowy and lithe, her shoulders broader than most people would consider attractive on a woman.

And me? I know in the blink of an eye. That's how it is. That's how you fall in love: in a flash. In less time than it takes to draw a breath.

How utterly bizarre.

I walk up to her and clear my throat, hoping she'll look up.

It works. Her eyes are blue. Closer to violet, in fact.

The beer is in the way, so I move it to my other hand. She does the same with the Nikon. It's a fluid, practiced movement, as if the camera with its gray lens weighs nothing. She shakes my hand. Her skin is cool, despite the day's searing heat.

"Alex Derksen," I say.

"Ranna. I thought I was the only one crazy enough to cover this part of the world. What are you doing here?"

"Is it that obvious I'm a journalist?"

She waves two fingers in the air, a multitude of silver bangles shifting up her arm. "Your eyes keep on weighing the scene, looking for an angle. Condensing it all into three hundred words or less." She laughs. "I've been watching you for a while."

Is that a compliment? I hope so.

She switches off the Nikon, then switches it back on. "You haven't said why you're here."

Something about her faint American accent jogs my memory, but I don't know why.

"Same reason as you."

"A photo?"

"A story. Same thing, isn't it?"

I run my hand over my jaw and wish I had shaved this morning. I need a haircut as well; my hair is curling on my neck.

I sip my beer and try not to stare. Her restless, suntanned hands keep touching and letting go, fidgeting with her hair, the camera. Fine muscles ripple along her arms every time she rotates the lens. But most of all it's her eyes that hold my attention. She blinks slowly, deliberately, as if she's taking photos and storing them. As if it's important to remember everything.

Suddenly her hands stop moving. She laughs as the silence between us persists. Swinging the camera over her shoulder, she leans forward and whispers, "It's your turn to say something."

"Sorry." I shake my head, embarrassed. "I write a lot better than I speak. Wait till you see me at a computer. At least sixty words a minute."

The wind has picked up. Fine dust swirls and eddies around our feet. She moves her sunglasses from the top of her head to her nose. Reverses the process. Her eyes look searchingly into mine.

"Who do you work for?"

"AP."

"Ah, the wires. Figures. The papers don't bother much with correspondents these days."

"You sound upset."

"Aren't you? The Internet, Instagram, and Twitter have taken over the news cycle. People can hardly concentrate on anything longer than a hundred and forty characters. And I can't tell you how many of my shots have been canned because a photo of Duchess Kate in a new dress will get more hits and sell more copies."

I raise my beer in response. "True." I've never worked beyond the borders of South Africa before, but after almost fifteen years I know the news business well enough to realize what she's saying is correct.

"How many photos have you shot?" I point at the expensive Nikon hanging by her side like an AK-47.

"Hundreds. I don't keep track."

"How many have they used?"

"A few. That I know of."

"Where?"

"I'm a hired gun, so in various publications. The *Washington Post*, the *New York Times*. One or two in the *Independent*."

She turns to retrieve the half-full beer next to the log where she was sitting and takes a few sips. A small boy dressed up in a striped suit and tie trots by, carrying a can of Coke as if it were a small treasure.

"And you?" she asks. "How many stories?"

"About ten or so."

"Ah, fresh meat."

"I arrived last month."

"You'll learn. No one gives a damn about what happens in Africa, no matter who's writing the story."

I shrug. "I suppose I can't argue with that. Except when there's a bombing, or when the American president or a Hollywood celebrity arrives on a visit. Or if it's about AIDS or Ebola. Some terrible disease usually beats everything else. Sometimes even the Duchess of Cambridge."

She laughs as if she believes me but gives no reply. I notice where her gaze is lingering and turn away. I know what's coming.

"You couldn't have gotten that here. A month isn't long enough."

Most people take a bit longer to mention the L-shaped scar under my left eye.

"It's an old injury. An encounter with a tractor. It's nothing," I lie.

She shakes her head, a crooked smile on her lips, as if she knows all about the stories you tell when you don't feel inclined to explain.

I like her even better.

Before I can ask how she ended up at the wedding, I have to jump out of the way of a beat-up white Isuzu truck heading straight for us. On the back a gaggle of women in peach-colored dresses laugh raucously.

Ranna is still rooted to the same spot. The rusty pickup idles a hand's breadth away from her body.

"Hamjambo. Habari gani," she greets the women.

She puts down her beer and kneels in the dust, the ground neatly swept this morning for any errant leaves. Click-click-click goes the Nikon.

One by one the passengers climb down, careful not to spoil their outfits.

"Another one, Miss America!" shouts the oldest of the women when she's finally on solid ground. "But just wait first."

Ranna nods.

The woman, probably in her fifties, motions for the driver to leave before positioning everyone for the picture. At last she's satisfied and takes her spot at the center of the group.

She motions with her head for Ranna to go ahead.

Click-click-click.

"You'll give it to me later?" she asks, running her hands over her shiny black hair.

"Of course, Hadhi," answers Ranna. "You look lovely."

The woman tugs at her dress and smiles proudly. "It's a very special day."

2

Much later that evening I find out how Ranna and I ended up at the same wedding. And that we can speak to each other in Afrikaans, though her *g*'s and *r*'s tend to be a little softer because she's been away from South Africa for so long. It explains why her accent rang a bell in the first place.

Ranna's friend Hadhi Batenga is the mother of the groom. Hadhi's son—her firstborn—is marrying a doctor with a practice in Dar es Salaam. Hadhi owns the building where Ranna rents an apartment. She calls Ranna Miss America because Ranna's South African mother and Israeli stepfather moved to New York years ago, in search of the bright lights and the relative safety the US offered. "And the dollars, of course," Ranna joked when I asked.

I was invited to the wedding because I wrote an article about Hadhi's future daughter-in-law and the HIV/AIDS clinic she established for sex workers. It was my first article after arriving in Tanzania, and it appeared on page twenty-eight of the *New York Times.* I was as proud as if it were my very first story in print. At last my name had appeared in the bible of journalism.

I know I haven't exactly been working hard since my arrival, yet I wonder why I haven't run into Ranna before. But it's good that I met her today, I think—at a wedding.

As the evening progresses, I drink too much and eat too little. I chat with the other, mostly older guests, who complain that the white wedding is too Western and modern, but my eyes keep singling out Ranna's tall, restless figure.

At the end of dinner and three lengthy speeches, I watch as she dances with Hadhi, Ranna's hands on the much shorter woman's shoulders. They keep throwing glances at the bridal couple and laughing.

Ranna told me how happy Hadhi is to see David married at last. Neither Hadhi nor David's brothers thought he would ever pluck up the courage to pop the question. David has never been in a hurry. Hadhi worked hard to put her oldest through university in the UK, and finally, almost eight years later, he graduated with a master's degree in economics.

Ranna's boots step carefully around Hadhi's elegant black shoes. Around and around in the brown dust. Suddenly she looks up, her eyes even bluer than I remember.

"Take a photo!" she calls, as if she knows my eyes will be on her.

She dances three more steps and turns, putting her arm around Hadhi's shoulders and drawing the older woman close.

Click goes the Nikon I've been holding for her. Click-click.

"Another one, another one!" a voice cries.

It's Hadhi's youngest. The boy, clad in David's old suit, has been struggling all night to keep the too-long sleeves out of his food. There's a clear family resemblance among the four boys. They're all tall, slim, and broad-shouldered.

He hurries across to Hadhi and Ranna and stands in front of them, his hands making peace signs. I take another photo. And more, as people keep joining them.

Later, I'll display the last, happiest picture on my desk. "How to Survive Being a Correspondent in Africa" would be the title of my attempt to describe that near-extinct species to green journalism students.

Fall in love, I would write. *With the country. With the people. Maybe even with someone extraordinary.*

Never expect it to be like home.

Home will never be the same again.

3

When the sun rises, I'm still awake. I came home at three but couldn't fall asleep. My thoughts kept returning to Ranna and the wedding.

Perhaps I should go for a run. It always helps clear my mind.

As I'm putting on my running shoes, I remember the Springbok Radio serials my grandmother was addicted to when she was still alive and the romance novels she devoured over vacations.

I've never believed in love. Or, as Ouma would say, True Love, with capital letters. It was fine for her, I always thought, because my grandfather died seven years after their wedding, and she never remarried, despite there being no lack of suitors on her doorstep.

I've never shared her view of love. If your earliest memory is of your father beating your mother so that she can barely walk, you don't believe in True Love. In love, maybe, if you're lucky. Or maybe just in a body, any body, to make the nights shorter and the silence more bearable.

And that's the problem.

All of a sudden, just because I've met a beautiful woman, I'm all set to forget about my father, my mother, and the farm. All I want to remember is an old lady touching my shoulder, telling me that someday everything will become clear to me—even the thing between my mother and father.

She called it love; I call it chaos.

I'm familiar with chaos. From an early age I learned to spot its approach from a distance. It's what kept me safe. Continues to keep me safe. If I could anticipate my father's rage, I could make myself scarce before it boiled over. Sometimes I could even defuse the situation.

I pull on a clean T-shirt and tie my apartment keys to my shoelaces, then begin to stretch.

The problem is that when I look at Ranna, all I see is chaos. She hides her emotions, tries to blend in with the people around her, but inside there runs a taut steel wire, as if she's waiting for something to go wrong.

I wonder what kind of trouble could possibly sneak up on her here in East Africa, but then decide that it isn't my problem. The only job I have to do is a three-mile run through downtown Dar es Salaam in under twenty-three minutes.

My first appointment for the day is in the city's central business district. The reception area of Lion Mining is all chrome and glass, as can be expected of a mining company listed on the Canadian stock exchange. The CEO is still in a meeting, which means I must obey one of the first rules of news gathering: wait.

I lean back in the uncomfortable chair and stretch my legs, still feeling the burn from this morning's run. The vinyl upholstery squeaks as I settle into the noon sun. A secretary, one of two, looks up and makes an irritated sound at the back of her throat. I give her a half-hearted smile. She ignores it, raises her eyebrows, and turns back to her computer.

When my phone rings, she shoots me a venomous glance.

"Derksen."

"Alex?" It's Ranna.

"Yes?"

"Feel like supper?"

I turn away from the secretary who gave me the angry look. Cover the phone with my hand. "Always."

"Choose a place."

"You know Dar es Salaam better than I do."

"Just say Dar. Fine, make it Hardings."

I know where that is. "Sounds great."

"See you at seven."

There's a moment's silence.

"And, Alex," Ranna says, laughing, "bring some more words. For a journalist you're pretty stingy."

As the line goes dead, I turn to find the same irritated secretary tapping her foot next to my chair. She motions me toward the CEO's office. "Mr. Paulson will see you now."

Hardings' yellow neon sign flickers in the muggy evening air, as if someone had just switched it on a moment ago. I push open the door and look at my watch. Quarter to seven. Early again. A bad habit in this place.

A man in a white New York cap with a neck like a tree trunk is sipping his beer at the bar as if it's lukewarm water. In one corner a middle-aged woman is eating a hamburger. Except for the two of them, Mkwepu Street's favorite haunt is deserted.

A waitress in a tight blue T-shirt looks up from her newspaper as I enter. She motions from behind the bar that I can pick any of the thirty-odd wooden tables. I choose one in the farthest corner with a view of the door, then sit down below a sign that promises two Heinekens for the price of one on Monday nights.

Inside Hardings, it's only a degree or two cooler than the February heat outside. A ceiling fan slashes feebly at the hot air. To my right is a newish air conditioner that will probably only be switched on later, when the tourists arrive. Sweat is pouring down my back. Why did I choose, and iron, a long-sleeved shirt for tonight?

I look at my watch again. Three minutes later than a moment ago. The music changes from Ali Kiba to Elton John. The smell of fried food drifts from the kitchen.

The waitress saunters to my table. "What can I get you?"

"A Kilimanjaro, please. No need for a glass."

Nine minutes to seven.

The beer she places in front of me a while later is ice-cold. Fine drops have condensed on the outside of the bottle. I look at the man in the white cap, who is still sipping his warm beer. Saying "please" must have done the trick.

I down the Kilimanjaro, banishing the heat for a moment or two. The man in the cap raises his beer in a respectful salute when I smack the bottle down on the table. I signal for the waitress, who is back behind her paper, to bring me another. She nods and smiles for the first time.

I lean back in my chair. Maybe this will be my lucky night.

Everyone looks up when she walks in. Even the waitress, who obviously knows her. Ranna said "Hardings" the way other people say "home."

I don't have to look at my watch to know she's late. It's half an hour after my first beer, and Hardings has filled up with every imaginable accent and color. It's rowdy and disorderly—which is how the photographer likes it, I guess.

She sits down, briefly laying a hand on my forearm. "Sorry I'm late."

She doesn't mean it, but the smile is real.

She smells of lemon and cinnamon. And something else. Smoke. Not cigarette smoke. Something more pungent. Pipe? Cigar? I can't place it, but I don't want to waste time guessing. What does it matter? She's here.

"What are you drinking?" I ask.

She points at the Kilimanjaro in my hand. "That looks good. Is it cold?"

"Ice-cold."

"Then I definitely want one."

She turns to beckon to the waitress, but the short, buxom lady in the blue T-shirt is already behind her.

"Maggie! Nice to see you again." Ranna takes the woman's hands in her own. "How are you?"

"Fine." The waitress gives her the broadest smile I've seen tonight.

"And your brother? Is he better?"

Maggie gives a relieved sigh. "Yes. He'll be back at work tomorrow."

"I'm so glad."

"So am I. Running this place alone is killing me. What can I get you? The usual?"

"A beer tonight, please. Same as his."

Maggie frowns. "You know how drunk you get on beer. Remember the headache?"

Ranna winks. "Who says I'm going to get drunk? Besides, this is a decent guy. Can't you see? Look at his shirt. He'll make sure I get home safely."

Maggie weighs me with her eyes. Then she laughs as if she doesn't believe Ranna, shakes her head, and turns to go.

I'm not impressed. I take a critical look at my green striped shirt. Decent? Is that what I want to be? I knew I should have worn something else.

"Don't look so annoyed," Ranna says, as if she can read my mind. She takes the bottle out of my hand and downs half the beer in two gulps. "It's good to be decent. Very few people are decent."

"Depends on what you mean by decent."

She thinks for a moment. "It means you'll put me to bed without getting in yourself."

"Then I'm not so sure I want to be decent."

I watch as laughter spills over her lips, along with the last of the beer. She stems it with a quick hand. "That's not a very decent remark."

"At least we agree on that. So I'm not so decent after all?"

She's about to reply, but something, or someone, behind me distracts her. She tosses the thick black curls back over her shoulders and cranes her neck to see past me. Her blue eyes, paler tonight against her white T-shirt, turn into searchlights, only to fade with something like disappointment. At last her gaze returns to me.

I turn, but all I see is a sea of people. Was it someone she knows?

She puts down the empty beer bottle with a loud enough noise to get my attention and fiddles with the label at the bottle's neck.

"I know people." She carries on as if there was no interruption. "You can object as much as you like: you're a decent man. Something happened to make you that way. Something that chewed you up and spat you out a long time ago, and it's too late to do anything about it now." She lets go of the bottle and trails a lazy finger along my forearm. "And no, there's nothing wrong with being softer, either. Softer sleeps better. I can promise you that."

"I suppose softer is okay." I think for a moment and decide to forget about the people behind me. "And so is decent."

She laughs. "Well, why are we arguing then? How about another beer?"

"Done!" Ranna shouts.

She slams down the bottle on the table. It teeters to the right, then the left, but stays upright. The German tourists next to us, all sporting stiff broad-brimmed hats and light-brown hiking boots with clean soles, applaud enthusiastically. They're leaving for the Ngorongoro Crater tomorrow.

I down the last of the Kilimanjaro and hold the cold bottle to my forehead, where a headache is lurking. "You win. Again."

She holds out her hand. "That'll be five dollars, thank you very much."

"You're cleaning me out. Whose idea was it to play for money, anyway?"

"Well, why don't you win it back? Winner of the next race takes all." She points at the pile of crumpled bills in front of her.

I count the bottles to her left. Nine. Most men would be on the floor by now. I'm on eight beers, and it's more than enough. Sounds are coming to me dimly, from a distance, and there's a sour taste at the back of my throat.

Where's Maggie? Maybe she can help.

I turn, spot her behind the counter, her shoulders stiff under the blue T-shirt. She looks at Ranna, then at me. Her expression says she doesn't want to know. She takes the yellow cloth that's draped over her shoulder and begins to polish the beer glasses lined up in front of her.

I turn back to our table.

"Ranna," I try to say over the drone of voices. Then louder: "Ranna, no! Come on. Time to go home." I run my finger across my throat. "Enough."

Instantly her smile vanishes. Her eyes turn an icy blue. "I offer you a chance to win your money back, and you chicken out?"

"Yeah. I don't want to drink anymore. Let's go. I'll take you home."

"I'm not going anywhere." She motions for Maggie to bring her another beer, but the waitress shakes her head, pointing from Ranna to me.

I get the message. The photographer is my responsibility.

The German tourists look upset and start to grumble as if I'm spoiling their fun for wanting to take Ranna away.

I ignore them. Tomorrow they'll be gone, and we'll still be here. Besides, I like Hardings. I don't want Maggie to ban me from the place.

"Why do you want to go on drinking?" I hang my head in a show of defeat. "You beat me hands down. I give up."

Ranna presses her lips together. Then she leans across the table and smiles broadly. From ice to water in one unpredictable second.

"What do I win?" she asks.

"A week's beer money." I point at the pile of bills on the table. "And someone—a decent guy—to walk you home."

"You said you're not decent."

"I lied."

"Is that a habit of yours?"

"Lying? Only out of decency. Like any good Afrikaner boy."

Her laugh comes from a place deep inside her throat, and I can't get enough of the sound. She gets up quickly, sure-footed, as if she's been drinking orange juice. Then she stops and tilts her head, deciphering the music in the background.

Turn up the volume, she motions to Maggie. This time the waitress obliges.

Ranna's hips, clad in tight blue jeans, begin to sway. The movement is hypnotic.

"I adore Angélique Kidjo." She pulls me to my feet. "Come, dance with me. Just for a minute. Then we can go home. Swear."

I wonder if I still know how to dance, but the promise of her body against mine is too tempting to refuse.

On the small, crowded dance floor at the back of Hardings I try to draw her body to mine, but she evades my hands. She raises her arms, shakes her hair back over her shoulders, closes her eyes, and starts moving to a rhythm my beer-fogged mind fails to grasp.

I remain still, staring at her, until finally she calls me closer. I put my hands on her hips, where I can feel her pulse, warm and rapid. Instantly I forget everything I said about going home.

We leave Hardings in the early morning. There's been a shower, bringing relief from the night's heat. The clouds have drifted away, and the clear, bright sky is flush with stars. Nights like these almost make me homesick for the farm.

Behind me Ranna is counting her steps. "Seventy-one. Seventy-two." She stops when her phone rings.

I turn when she doesn't answer the call. She's standing motionless on the poorly lit sidewalk, her long fingers pensively stroking her lips, as if she wants to erase the fear I can see hiding there. She's staring at the cell phone in her hand.

"Aren't you going to answer it?"

"It's the middle of the night. It's got to be a wrong number."

"But you're awake, aren't you? And what if it's a story?"

She returns the phone to the pocket of her jeans. "I'd rather talk to you."

She comes up beside me and links her arm through mine. We walk on in silence.

I know I should ask, but I don't want to. It's like knowing you're going to lose someone, yet still getting up every morning as if nothing is wrong. Or like calling your mother and talking about the weather, or the article you're working on, or the busy lambing season, but never your father.

You don't want to know. You silence the voices in your head. Because you know it's usually only a lover—past or present—who will call at three in the morning.

Someone forgot to switch on the air conditioner in the conference room, or maybe, like Hardings, the Skylark Hotel is saving money. The air in the long narrow room is so stuffy I battle to keep my eyes open. For the umpteenth time in the hour since I sat down, I yawn.

"Stop it," says the man next to me.

Tom—Tomboy, Tom Pom—Masterson freelances for a few publications, including the *Guardian*. Because of his name and the chest hair that spills over the top button of his shirt, he has to sing "What's New Pussycat?" at every foreign correspondents' Christmas party. It helps that he has a good voice, of course. Anyway, that's what I've been told. If I'm still around at Christmas, I'll probably find out whether it's true.

He runs his hand over the blond stubble on his chin, over his nearly bald head and sunburned neck. His eyes blink rapidly. Stop. Blink again. It's an irritating habit that makes it hard for me to look him in the eye.

He gives a long yawn. "See? It's contagious." He looks at his fake Rolex. "How long have we been waiting?"

"Fifty-three minutes," I say. "For the minister of health to come and open a brewery, because the president is in China. Am I the only one to find it ironic?"

To our right a number of journalists, mostly from the local media, are milling about. I'm here because I have nothing better to do. More than any other profession, journalism understands the value of the comparative degree.

"How long are we going to give the man?" Tom scratches his dry scalp with the chewed end of a pen. It grates like sandpaper. "I'd give anything for a beer. You?"

I look at the assembled audience, mostly factory workers in overalls and yellow T-shirts, hovering near the cases of beer stacked in the corner. From time to time, two bulky men in dark suits stop someone from pinching a bottle. The beer is for later, and probably the only reason anyone would be prepared to listen to a long list of boring speeches.

"I think it's going to be a long wait, Tom."

My nose picks up Ranna's scent before I see her. I register the elusive citrus fragrance combined with what I suspect is Cuban cigars from last night. It makes the hair at the back of my neck stand on end. Her unhurried approach is accompanied by the faint crackle of static electricity generated by her long blue skirt.

Finally her black Doc Martens reach us and come to a halt. "I can't believe you actually thought they'd start on time," she teases.

I wave a greeting. "I was optimistic. What time did you get up?"

She smiles, her eyes bright. She shows no sign of last night's heavy drinking. "An hour ago. Don't worry, you'll get the hang of it. Helps if you have a favorite dala dala taxi driver who goes out of his way to pick you up."

Tom swings his pen in her direction. "It's not as if you sleep much anyway."

"You leave my sleeping habits alone."

She sits down beside me, leans over behind my back, and runs her fingers over the Englishman's head. "You're getting lazy. When you first came, you used to shave your head every week."

He ducks to avoid her hand. "And when you first came, you were just about engaged. And look what happened to you."

"Engaged?" The word is out before I can stop it.

Ranna's lips become a thin line. "It was a long time ago. And it's nobody's business."

Tom laughs and turns to me. "I forgot: Ranna never talks about what happens between the four walls of her bedroom. And you can imagine how busy it gets in there."

"Did you get up on the wrong side of your empty bed this morning?" Her words are light, but the tone is frosty.

Tom squares his shoulders, but before he can reply, the heavy wooden doors swing open. A man in a gray suit walks in and holds up his hand for silence. The air conditioner springs to life.

The minister and his entourage take their seats.

I battle to focus for the duration of his thirty-minute speech. *Nearly engaged.* What did I expect? A woman like Ranna is bound to have a past. And what makes me think there's no one in her life at present? I've done absolutely nothing to find out. Or maybe I prefer not to know.

Last night she kissed my cheek at her front door to thank me for walking her home. There was no offer of coffee. What more do I need to know?

5

The minute I park behind Hardings the rain starts to pour down. I make a futile dash for the door underneath the yellow neon sign.

I'm soaked to the skin when I walk in. "Hi," I say, but Maggie doesn't reply, shaking her head disapprovingly at the muddy footprints I leave on the floor. Another black mark behind my name. She hasn't forgiven me for Ranna and the beer.

I wrestle through the crowd to reach our table. Maggie's handmade "Reserved" sign stands guard, so she can't be too upset. I sit down, tug at my wet T-shirt, and nod at the man in the white cap, who's in his usual spot at the counter.

Cheers, he salutes, raising his beer.

It's ten past eight. Must Ranna always be late?

I ask the people at the neighboring table for their newspaper and page through it distractedly. Fifteen minutes later Maggie brings over a Kilimanjaro without being asked.

As I'm finishing it, she puts down another one. "Would you like something to eat?"

"No, thanks, Ranna should be here soon."

"Ranna and time aren't exactly on intimate terms, you know. You may have a long wait ahead of you."

"Fine." I give in. "Medium-rare steak and salad, please."

When Maggie brings the food, I discover how hungry I am.

After a while she fetches the empty plate and shoots me a sympathetic look, as if I should know better than to think Ranna would show up—never mind on time.

She's right. Bloody wishful thinking. "May I have the bill, Maggie?"

"I'll bring it."

I'm counting out the money when the tall, slender figure appears in the doorway. From where I'm sitting her rage is apparent. She looks like a caged animal, hurt and defiant.

Ranna's eyes search out Maggie's. Maggie shrugs, motions with her head in my direction, and gestures something I can't make out. Ranna pushes her hands deeper into the pockets of her wet jeans and brushes past the bodies blocking the bar counter.

I smell a strange mix of sweat and lemons as she approaches. And something else, something familiar.

The metallic smell of blood.

My eyes search her khaki photographer's vest and white T-shirt, but I don't see anything.

"Hi. Sorry I'm late."

There's no regret in her voice.

She shifts her weight impatiently when I fail to react. Wipes her eyes and shakes the rain out of her hair. "Are you angry?"

"Yes."

"Then why are you still here?"

"I have nothing better to do." I get to my feet, suddenly furious. "I'm here because I wanted to see you. Fuck this, Ranna, find someone else to mess with."

I reach for my car keys but stop when she puts her hand on mine.

"Please," she says, almost inaudibly.

"Please what?"

She mumbles something I can't make out.

"Please what?" I repeat. "What do you want me to do?"

"Sorry." She pulls her hand away and jams it into the pocket of her jeans.

"That's all? That's all you've got?"

"What more do you want?" Her voice is raw and harsh. "What is it with men? Are we married? If there hasn't been a honeymoon or a ring, I don't owe you a thing. And even then . . ." She looks away.

"That's not what this is about. It's about common decency. You could have called to tell me you'd be late."

"Decency," she snorts. "The other day you didn't want to know anything about being decent."

My hand closes around her upper arm. I don't want her to run away before I've had my say. "Yes, that's what it's called: decency. Good manners. Consideration. All those things the grown-ups are always going on about. Ever heard of them?"

She jerks her arm out of my grip. My eyes fall on the deep red stain on my palm.

"You're bleeding."

"It's nothing."

I manage to suppress a sarcastic laugh. "Yeah, right."

I try to open the vest, but she pulls free, steps back, and shakes her head, eyes blazing.

"For goodness' sake, Ranna! I don't want to hurt you. If you don't want me to take a look, let me take you to the hospital."

"No."

"Ranna."

"No. I'm not going to the hospital. It's nothing."

"Are you at least going to tell me what happened?"

She shrugs. "It's a long story."

"I have more than enough time. As you can see."

"It's a longer story than you can possibly imagine." She bites her lower lip, as if overwhelmed by emotion. "Anyway, it's in the past." Her voice grows softer. "Let it go now, please."

A light blinks on in my mind as two seemingly unconnected thoughts connect. I trust their origin. They come from that place deep inside where sometimes you just know.

"The man who called the other night? Our first night here. It was him, wasn't it?"

Her eyes dart past me, toward the bar, the door. She says nothing.

"Ranna."

"What are you talking about?"

"The first time we were here. The call while we were walking home. The one you didn't want to take."

"What about it?"

"Was that him? Was he the one who hurt you?"

I try to take her arm again, but she steps away from me. "I'm going home."

"What?"

"I'm sorry I was late." She makes a half-hearted attempt to smile, turns away.

Dumbfounded, I watch her retreating back as she fights through the Hardings crowd, slips through the open door, and melts into the warm, unremitting rain.

There are many ways to fall in love. Suddenly. Slowly. Patiently. Excessively. Destructively. Obsessively. Love has more sides than any other emotion. More shapes and facets. More deaths, apparitions, and resurrections. It reaches farther forward and farther back than any other emotion. It has more history and future woven into it than hatred, fury, and insanity combined. It always wants more. Demands to remember more. Insists on digging up things that belong to the past. Yet it also wants to forget. Forgive. Ignore.

You know more about it than about any other emotion, yet you also know less. And if it's honest and raw and not premeditated, it always catches you off guard.

That's what Ouma, my grandmother, told me just before she died. When she abruptly announced on her sickbed that it was time to leave. That she was glad she was finally joining my grandfather on the other side. And on a wet, stifling February night in a bar in Dar es Salaam, I understand exactly what she meant.

6

It's still raining the next morning. It's coming down even harder than last night—hard enough to wake me. It reminds me of things I've long been trying to forget.

When I was six, I woke up one morning to find our house on the open, arid plains, just before you reach the small town of Vanrhynsdorp, surrounded by water. For a child used to bleak desolation and a father who let fly with his belt if you dared water your mother's roses at her request, it was strange to see so much water in one place.

At that age I had never even seen the ocean, though it wasn't far from where we lived. But if I'd had to imagine the sight of that blue expanse, it would have resembled what I saw that morning on the farm. Water everywhere. In the normally parched, struggling flower beds. In the two-track road leading to the sheep kraals. At the back door, where I would wait for my father to stop yelling before sneaking into the kitchen to warm up my supper, exhausted after my cross-country run.

That cloudburst would result in a great flood in our part of Namaqualand. Almost like the deluge that swallowed Laingsburg some years before. But, unlike our neighbors, we didn't lose everything, only enough for my father to become even more embittered and my mother even more withdrawn, her footsteps through the house growing increasingly soft, more tentative.

I had thought it impossible that she could tread any more lightly, but I was proved wrong the day I told my father I would be leaving the farm to study journalism at Stellenbosch University.

That day was different, however. Her footsteps might have been silent, but her heart was filled with joy. Her mind sang. She didn't say anything, but I could see it in her eyes. I would get away. I would escape.

I get out of bed. Shake my head as if it will rid me of the memories. It's of little use thinking about the past. It would be much more productive to try and figure out what happened to Ranna last night. I might even be able to do something about it.

Maybe she has calmed down by now. Maybe I should phone her and ask her what's wrong. Who hurt her. Why she refused to do anything about it. Such complacency seems completely out of character for someone like Ranna.

I know I'm supposed to still be angry at her for being inconsiderate, but am I? Or am I more upset because she didn't confide in me? Because there may be someone else in her life?

Oh, fuck it. Stop thinking.

I walk to the small kitchen and switch on the kettle. I stare out the window of my third-story studio apartment as I dial her number. The phone rings seven times before an electronic voice instructs me to leave a message. I end the call and put the phone down. Pick it up again. Make another call to her number.

My fourth call remains unanswered. It's half past six. In a few hours some cabinet minister or other is going to address the media about the budget. Will Ranna be there? Should I wait to see whether she shows up, or should I knock on her door and check whether she's okay?

As usual, the voice of chaos drowns out every other, saner answer.

I knock on Ranna's blue front door, tentatively at first, then more insistently. There's no sound from inside her apartment. All I can hear is the monotonous drumming of the rain on my jacket, deafening inside the black plastic hood that covers my head.

In the flower bed under the blue window frame, the muddy water is ankle-deep. I look for the shallowest spot to place my feet. I wipe the window and cup my hands on either side of my face to protect my eyes from the relentless, driving rain, but I see no movement inside. All I can make out is the vague outline of a couch. A kitchen counter. Books. Nothing more.

What should I do next? What is plan B?

Hadhi.

I go to the front door of the long, narrow house divided into four apartments. I knock. The door opens almost immediately.

"Hello, Hadhi." I throw back the hood and move closer to the door to get out of the rain.

Without a word she steps back, staring at me as if she's trying to place me. Finally she points at me with a crooked forefinger. "You're Miss America's friend. Alex? Your photos are beautiful. David framed the one of all of us on the dance floor for me."

I nod and remember to smile. When a strange man knocks on a woman's door in the early morning, he's obliged to be friendly.

Hadhi looks at her watch, as if she suddenly remembers it's not even eight o'clock yet.

"Are you looking for Ranna?" She puts her hands on her hips, ready to scold me for disturbing the photographer at this hour.

I hold out my hands, palms up, to show that I come in peace. "I'm glad you like the photos. I . . . Is Ranna still in bed?"

"I wouldn't know. It's very early."

"You haven't seen her this morning?"

"No. I've been cleaning since five. I get a new tenant today. Why don't you knock and find out for yourself?"

"I did, but no one opened."

"Then she's probably not there." Hadhi sounds annoyed. "Or she doesn't want to see anyone."

"I'd like to make sure," I say. "I need to speak to her urgently."

Hadhi frowns. "I don't think she came home last night, but I may be wrong. I don't keep track of everyone's movements. And she sure doesn't sleep a lot." The frown is replaced by a worried look. "It's unhealthy to be alone like that, without children or family. Especially for a girl her age."

I wish I could tell her about last night. About the blood and Ranna's arm. About her trapped, stubborn eyes. Perhaps Hadhi knows something that could help me. But I don't say anything. I don't want to sound the alarm for no reason but my own paranoia.

Hadhi tugs at the brown-and-white dress straining across her generous hips. "And there's something dark in her eyes. Some kind of unhappiness, as if she remembers too much. Bad things."

"When was she last here? Do you know?"

Hadhi shakes her head. "I haven't seen her for a long time. Day before yesterday?"

"Not since?"

"No. As I've said, I'm not always here, so I wouldn't know. I leave at about eight. I live next door." She waves her hand at the smaller white building to my left. There's no dividing wall between the two houses.

"But I did see a man sneak out of her place a while ago," she adds. "A pale man in a brown safari hat. About two or three weeks ago, I'd say."

I feel instantly resentful, though I have to admit that my response is irrational. There's nothing between Ranna and me. Just this thing, this feeling. The way she looks at me. The way I feel when she does.

I shake my head, annoyed, and stare at my feet in the mud-covered boots that were brand-new when I left Johannesburg. So this is how a teenage boy feels. I've completely forgotten.

When I look up, Hadhi seems amused. "So she's got to you too," she remarks dryly.

"What do you mean?" I feign ignorance.

"You all look the same when you first arrive here. Happy, then angry. And then disappointed. *You* never even got around to being happy."

"We *all*?" I sound angrier than I mean to.

Hadhi steps back, her hands back on her hips. She blinks a few times, suddenly on guard.

"I'll tell Ranna you were here," she says and steps back, her back stiff.

"Can I leave her a message? Somewhere she'll find it?" I call out before she can close the door. I step forward so that most of my size elevens are parked on her white tiles. "I'm worried, Hadhi. That's all, I promise. Just like you. I saw Ranna briefly last night. I think she was hurt. She was bleeding."

She studies me for a moment, then shakes her head. "Like I said, people keep to themselves around here. Ranna comes and goes without telling anyone her business. She doesn't socialize here. Push a note under her door."

"I will." I step back into the rain. "Thanks, Hadhi."

She nods but her hand remains on the doorknob. Her eyes are clouded. She seems to be weighing my sincerity, deciding whether I really care about Ranna.

"Bleeding, you say?"

"Yes."

"Badly?"

"Her arm. Badly enough."

"Maybe you should make sure she's not there. She may not have locked her door."

We're both silent for a moment. Then Hadhi waves a stiff goodbye.

"Thanks," I say before she closes the door.

I've known Ranna for less than two weeks, but I know she'd lock her door. She's not stupid. If my suspicion is right, Hadhi will be heading around the back of the house at this very moment to unlock the apartment.

I also know without a doubt that I should let the whole thing go. If Ranna finds out I broke into her home, this will be over before it has begun—whatever this is.

But there's something else I know: if you chase stories long enough—if you hunt chaos—you learn to trust your instincts. And my gut is telling me something's wrong.

I wait on the sidewalk, giving Hadhi sufficient time to unlock Ranna's apartment. No need to rush the woman. I watch as an old, dented Datsun and its three passengers slowly turns the corner, then hurry to the second bright-blue door in the row of apartment entrances.

I hope I'm wrong about Ranna. With any luck, she's safe and perfectly well.

Before I even touch the door, I see it. I don't know why I didn't notice it before. Despite the rain, there's a rusty-red smear at the lower end of the metal doorknob—like something from a Kandinsky painting.

It's easy to remove. I rub it between my thumb and index finger. Smell it. Is it blood?

Cautiously I test the doorknob. To my relief it moves under my fingers. The door opens noiselessly.

My breathing accelerates, then slows and becomes regular, as always before a big story, when the adrenaline makes way for self-control.

I enter, then stand completely still. "Ranna?"

Nothing. No sound or movement.

Water from my shoes and jacket forms a puddle on the floor. I place my shoes just inside the door, with my coat on top. I'll clean up later, even if it means using my T-shirt.

Inside the apartment it's airless, as if the place has been closed up for days.

I've never been inside Ranna's apartment before. Hardings is no more than half a mile away, and the one time I was here I said goodbye at the front door.

The place is in a state of organized chaos. Does it always look like this, or has someone been searching for something? There are two dirty mugs on the floor beside a brown leather couch. Judging by the pillow and pale yellow blanket, someone spent the night on the couch.

There are piles of papers and books everywhere, threatening to topple over. I estimate that there are two thousand books or more. They're stacked against the walls, next to the TV, and behind the couch. Hardcover spines stand in double rows in two bookcases in the living room.

I crouch beside the tower closest to me, scanning the titles. *Zen and the Art of Motorcycle Maintenance. The Secret Life of Bees. Advanced Quantum Physics. Domestic Violence: How to Survive.*

Interesting topics, especially the last one.

I stand up straight. Where does she find so much time to read? Has she truly read all these books? And more importantly: Where do I begin to look for something that will tell me what happened to her?

It can't be all that hard. I take two steps forward. Her apartment is actually one room—a living room, bedroom, and kitchen combined, with a bathroom hidden in a corner behind my back.

I rock back on my heels. From my position next to the couch I can see the sink in the bathroom. There's something in it—a red T-shirt, hastily peeled off and discarded? A few inches to the right, and it would have landed on the floor.

I approach, careful not to make a noise. I can't afford to draw attention to my presence. I don't want Ranna's neighbors to know I'm snooping around in her apartment.

The bathroom door creaks when I push it wider open. I stop. Try again. It swings open silently.

I was wrong about the T-shirt. It's white. I hold it up to the light that falls through the bathroom window. There's a bloodstain on the left shoulder, like a rose in full bloom. And there's a tear in the fabric, as if it was slashed with a knife. I push my index finger through the hole. It would take a sizable knife to make a gash this length.

How serious is Ranna's injury? I thought it was just a nick in her arm.

Then again, is this even her T-shirt?

I shake it out. She wears her T-shirts tight. It could easily be hers.

Where is this damn woman?

I put the shirt back into the basin and walk to the kitchen. There has to be something more, something that will tell me what happened.

I open the fridge. The battered off-white Kelvinator is almost empty. On the counter lies a loaf of dry bread. The sink looks equally sad. It contains a fork, a teaspoon, and five mugs, all of which hold the remnants of coffee. Strong coffee.

Strange medicine for someone who suffers from insomnia. Or perhaps she feels a need for caffeine. Maybe she's too scared to sleep.

I turn and take another look at the book-filled apartment. Not a purse or cell phone in sight. No sign of her bulky military wristwatch or the numerous silver bracelets she likes to wear.

Does it mean she's okay? Or does it mean someone made off with everything, including her?

I check my own watch. I'm not going to find any more answers here. And if I don't hurry, I'm going to be late for a press conference Joburg insisted I cover. I'll come back later today. Maybe make a few phone calls. There is no way I'm just going to let this go.

The press conference at the Plaza Hotel is already in progress when I arrive, but for some reason the subject under discussion isn't the budget.

I slide in next to Tom Masterson, just in time to witness the minister of finance shake his head in irritation.

"What's going on?" I whisper.

"The—what happened to you?" Tom points at my wet shoes and muddy jeans.

"Long story." I motion at the podium. "What's this all about?"

"Blame him." Tom inclines his head toward a journalist from the local *Daily News* sitting diagonally in front of us. "He wanted to know what would happen if it keeps raining like this."

"It hasn't been raining that long, has it?"

"Apparently parts of the countryside are flooded."

"Oh. What does the minister say?"

"Listen. Here it comes."

"Fine, let's talk about the rain." The bald man in the neat blue suit speaks heatedly. "Let's ignore the much more significant problem of the budget deficit." He takes off his glasses and wipes the sweat from his brow with a white handkerchief someone to the right of the podium has handed him.

"It's too early to say whether the rain is going to be a problem," the minister says. "As you all know, we have long rains and short rains every year, and this year the long rains have come early. They don't usually set in before March, so we're not used to seeing them in February. And the rainfall has been a bit heavier than usual, but what can we do about it?" He pats his chest with his open palm to illustrate his frustration. "All we can do is wait and see what happens. Maybe, if we're lucky, it will stop raining earlier than usual. That's also a possibility."

"So the government isn't seeking international aid just yet?" the man from a local paper, the *Daily News*, persists. "Two people died yesterday when their motorcycle was swept away."

The minister wipes his brow again, gives an exasperated sigh. "Every life is precious. That's how it's always been, and that's how it will stay in Tanzania. But what happened yesterday was an accident. I know, because I spoke to the police myself. Those men crossed the river where they shouldn't have. The bridge is a mile downstream, but they were in a hurry. My point is: Why should we apply for international aid at this stage? There's no crisis at present, and it's no use meeting trouble halfway."

"So you're not even slightly worried?"

The minister's mouth becomes a thin line. He seems about to lash out angrily when his gaze falls on Tom and me, and he coughs uneasily.

"We'll keep a close watch on the situation," he says, assuming a more reasonable tone. "We may decide that it's a good idea to alert the international community early on, just in case things go wrong. You never know. The weather is remarkably unpredictable these days."

Next to me Tom writes everything down. It has been one of the better press conferences of the past few weeks. Two stories for the price of one: the budget deficit and a looming natural disaster.

I look around the room. I seem to be the only one battling to focus. For a while now my pen has been moving of its own accord. *Situation. Aid. Go wrong.*

Go wrong.

Where is Ranna?

She's not among the huddle of photographers in the corner aiming their lenses at the minister like an impatient firing squad, waiting for him to stop talking. By now they've grasped that the bigger story is out there. Photos that can change the world. People battling to see another sunrise while the rain keeps pouring down. In here, there's a lot of talk, as if you could sidestep death by devising a three-point plan.

Along with the smell of sweat and last night's alcohol and moldy suits specially dusted off for today's event, there's something else in the air. Somewhere in the midst of everything, only barely discernible. If you lift your nose slightly, like an eager predator, you'll be able to identify it as the smell of anticipation. Of something about to happen.

8

Tom holds the Marlboro between his thumb and index finger. He drags on the cigarette, exhales. Looks around for an ashtray, then tips the ash in the fronds of a dried-out fern. The drone of voices around us abates as the members of the media finish their tea and coffee and leave.

I want to ask him, yet I don't. How much will I be giving away if I speak to him?

At last I give in to the need to know. One day it will probably be the end of me.

"You don't happen to know where Ranna is?"

He raises a quizzical brow, blinks rapidly. Again. There's an inscrutable expression in his eyes.

"So you've got a thing for her as well now?"

First Hadhi, now Tom. Why is everyone harping on the same string? I open my notebook and pretend to look for something. "I just want to know where she is, that's all. There's something I want to ask her."

Tom seems unconvinced. He stubs out his cigarette in the fern's soil as one of the hotel's managers approaches, shaking his head reprovingly.

"Sorry! I didn't know I'm not allowed to smoke in here."

As the manager stomps off, Tom turns back to me.

"There isn't a single journalist in this room who hasn't asked me that question. Except Gerald, maybe." He motions at a muscular guy with a crew cut. "And only because he's gay."

I knew it was a bad idea to ask Tom about Ranna. "Forget I asked."

He laughs and holds up his hands. "Don't let me upset you, Alex. She's one of those women who drives guys nuts. But she'll grow old alone. Men are too much work for her. Too much everything. She feels trapped, then she runs away. End of story."

"I'm worried about her, that's all."

"She can take care of herself."

"I know, but still . . ."

The Englishman is silent as he gives me a searching look. Is he looking for confirmation that I'm telling the truth?

"She and I have been friends for a long time. Years," he finally continues. "Don't take this the wrong way, but she's going to fuck you up. Let it go. Don't get involved. Look for someone else to pass the time with while you're here."

"Do you know where she is, or don't you?"

"Yesterday she was fine."

"So you saw her yesterday?"

"Yes."

"When?"

"Late afternoon."

"And she was okay?"

"Ye-e-s." Tom stretches out the word. He frowns. "Why?"

If what Tom says is true, then whatever went wrong must have happened in the few hours since he last saw her and my encounter with her at Hardings. Or could Tom have been involved?

I study the bald journalist with the nicotine-stained fingers. No. Ranna is taller than him, and he's probably right: she can look after herself. She's the kind of woman who knew how to make a fist and throw a punch by the time she went to nursery school.

"Alex." Tom speaks again. He takes the Marlboros from his shirt pocket, reconsiders, and puts them back. "What's going on?"

I sigh impatiently. "I don't have time to explain. Do you know where she is, or don't you?"

He relents. "Try the road to Korogwe. She said something about a butterfly migration. That's all I know."

9

Korogwe is a long way to the north. I've been driving for more than two hours before I come across the first butterflies. A few miles farther along, the scattered clusters of white turn into swarms of fluttering insects, oblivious to their surroundings, blindly following their instincts.

I know I'm supposed to write up this morning's conference, that I can't simply abandon everything and chase after a woman as if I have nothing better to do, but the realization doesn't make me turn back to Dar. Instead I follow the swarms of butterflies as if they're bread crumbs, constantly on the lookout for Ranna's white Land Cruiser.

It's hard to find a single vehicle among a horde of others. I try and locate her car between the multitude of shops, dala dala taxis, motorcycles, cattle, and goats at the roadside. I see nothing. Then, just as the patched, tarred road has taken me through a village and spat me out among the hills, I spot her 4x4 under a giant acacia tree.

I draw up behind her vehicle. Something doesn't feel right. The door on the driver's side stands ajar, but there's no sign of Ranna.

I jump out. The muggy air hits me between the shoulders like a wet fist. I jog to her car and look inside. Nothing. I close the door. There's blood on the door handle, just as there was blood on her front door this morning.

I turn and search for the flicker of a lens in the afternoon sun that occasionally breaks through the heavy gray clouds. Listen for the creak of the worn leather boots she wears in the field.

Nothing.

Then I hear it. Click. Click-click-click.

I veer sharply to the left and run into the long grass.

Click.

Deeper into the grass. Faster.

Click, click.

Then I see her. She's squatting on a red sleeping bag in the veld, her camera turned skyward. Click. Click, click.

Relief floods me like cool water. I almost laugh, but Ranna's voice brings me to a halt.

"Stop right there if you don't want to get hurt." She speaks in a low voice, her back to me.

I stop in my tracks, boots parked in a muddy puddle.

Click. Click. Click.

Shadows move across her face, the folding and unfolding of hurried wings, like the fluttering pages of a book. I look up. Hundreds of butterflies are passing overhead, white specks against the overcast sky. Some fly into my face, my neck.

Impatiently I brush them off. "Are you okay?"

She lowers the camera. Her eyes move from the butterflies to me. "Why wouldn't I be?"

I gesture over my shoulder at her car. "The blood?"

"I scratched my finger and it bled. Mosquito bite." She holds up her ring finger. A scratch runs down the right side. "Nothing serious."

She raises the Nikon. Click. Click, click, click, click.

I want to move to the right, get closer to her, just to make sure, but I stay where I am.

"Can I move now?" I ask at last.

She lowers the camera, straightens up, turns to me. There are mud stains on her elbows and on the knees of her jeans.

"What are you doing here, Alex?"

"You weren't at the press conference."

"So?"

"I was worried about you after last night."

She straightens her shoulders, her eyes suddenly a sullen dark blue. "Forget what happened."

"As simple as that?"

"Yes."

"You were bleeding. How do I forget that?"

"Same as when you've written a story. It's not your blood, so it's okay."

"What's that supposed to mean?" A warm breeze stirs up a few stray leaves around my feet. "That I don't care?"

"I've read your stories. You keep your distance. Always. Like the article on the HIV/AIDS clinic. It's very good, informative, but in a clinical way."

"What do you want me to do? Break down every time I write about death?"

"I suppose you're right. Keeping your distance is one way to survive." She takes aim at me with the camera, takes two photos. "Or, rather, it's how one learns to survive. Who taught you to survive, Alex?"

Typical of Ranna. Attack is the best defense.

I refuse to play along. "I care about you. I care about what happens to you. It's all that matters. Stop being so difficult."

There's a moment's silence, then she throws back her head and laughs.

Startled butterflies flutter up in the air.

"Was that a declaration of love?" she asks.

I shrug, tired of being cautious, of measuring and weighing my words. "Call it what you like." I turn, not waiting for an answer. Not wanting to see the pity on her face.

I head for my Land Rover as fast as I can through the tall grass and search for the keys in vain.

I'm still digging in the pocket of my jeans when the rain starts coming down, hot and heavy, as only tropical rain can fall. Within seconds I'm drenched.

Did I drop the keys somewhere? I punch Ranna's Land Cruiser door with an angry fist. "Fuck." Kick the wheel. "Fuck everything."

At last I find the keys in the long grass.

I drive off without looking back. I'm hardly in second gear before the first butterflies land under my windshield wipers like crumpled bits of paper, just like discarded love letters.

On my way back to Dar I write the morning's article in my head. It's better than thinking about Ranna. Tom was right: the woman is trouble. In capital letters.

When I reach home, I piece together a story on the budget and the rain in fifteen minutes. I send it off without reading it again.

The words flicker on my screen a few minutes later: *How big will this story get?*

Jasmine, the news editor.

The budget? I type intentionally.

No, the rain. Will it turn into a disaster?

I almost laugh. The chances are good that Tanzania is going to be flooded. It's chaos all over again, breathing down my neck. I came to Dar es Salaam bored with Joburg, and I ran into another mess headfirst. I just don't know whether it will turn out to be Ranna or the rain.

Or both.

Probably, I write back.

> *Can you handle it?*

> *Of course. Why do you ask?*

For a few minutes nothing happens, then the words come back: *Because your stories sound different from when you were still at the paper. Maybe the heat is making you soft.* ☺

That's not what Ranna said. According to her, I don't care. Who's right—Ranna or Jasmine?

What does caring sound like? I ask.

In my mind's eye I see Jasmine laugh. She's a rotund woman with a huge fear of small spaces and an obsession with Madonna.

> *You're starting to write about people, not names. How long have you been there?*

> *A few weeks.*

> *Hmm. Who is she?*

I don't know what to say, so I ignore the question and shut down my laptop.

But the truth doesn't always need a voice. Sometimes it waits where you left it, without anyone having to acknowledge it. Quietly and indisputably. And, above all, patiently.

10

Ranna calls two days later. Two days during which I grow steadily angrier because I've let on how I feel about her.

At first I don't want to take her calls, but I give up the fight after she's left the fourth message of the morning and my phone promptly rings again. I push my laptop aside. The story can wait.

"Bloody hell, you're stubborn," I begin.

"Well, we must be made for each other then, because you don't give up either—in spite of all the rumors about me. In spite of *me*."

Her tone is light, but I suspect she's working hard to keep it that way.

"Don't you have anything to say?" she says softly when I fail to reply. My mind is locked on "made for each other."

"How about a beer at Hardings? Things are a bit hectic at the moment, but next week is fine."

"Alex. Don't be like that. I'm sorry I didn't call before. I had to clear my head. You know, sort out a few things. Sometimes I also have to think things through. Believe it or not."

"What kind of things?" I run a frustrated hand through my hair, then get up and walk to the kitchen to make a cup of coffee.

"Just things."

"You see, Ranna, that's the problem: there are so many *things* you don't talk about. Like your near engagement. And I still don't know how well you and Tom know each other."

"Yes," she answers simply.

"Yes what?"

"Yes to the beer at Hardings. See you tonight at six."

She ends the call before I can tell her to go to hell.

Ranna arrives at Hardings before me. *You're ten minutes late,* she indicates, pointing at her watch, smiling.

Ten minutes? I shake my head, annoyed. I tried to be even later, but before I knew it I was parking behind the bar.

Hardings is still fairly empty, with only three of the tables occupied.

Ranna gets up, inviting me to sit in the chair opposite her.

She's the first woman I've ever met who's tall enough to look my own six feet in the eye. Tonight her gaze is unwavering, though her hands betray her anxiety.

"I was afraid you wouldn't come."

"I nearly didn't," I lie.

She gestures again for me to take a seat, but stubbornly I remain standing. She looks down at her boots, which are surprisingly clean despite the rain that's still coming down. When she looks up again, her eyes are glistening. She gives an embarrassed laugh and runs her hand through her hair.

"I would've deserved it, you know. If you hadn't come."

"Yes, you would've."

She hesitates a moment, then places one hand on my shoulder and the other on my chest, almost as if she's pushing me away while drawing me closer. "I'm sorry."

"Yes?"

"Are you really going to make me beg?"

"Yes." I stare at the bunch of office workers in the middle of Hardings, celebrating what seems like a birthday.

"Why?"

She sits down. I finally give in and sit down as well.

"Because I'm angry, Ranna."

"And you want to restore the balance?"

"What balance?"

She raises the cheap whiskey tumbler and empties it. "My mother says that's what my stepfather does when he forgets their wedding anniversary. She's always late, no matter where they're going. He gets her back by 'forgetting' their anniversary. She says he does it to show her she's not the boss."

"Sounds like a power struggle."

"Maybe it is," she agrees. "Sometimes I think that's what every relationship is, except when the wife meekly accepts the role of cooking and cleaning and bearing children. Things like that." She runs out of words.

"Are they still alive? Your parents?"

She toys with the empty glass. Shuffles her feet and parks her boots between mine. "Why are we talking about them here in Dar es Salaam, where it's seventy-five degrees out there and tomorrow the rain may wash all of us away? New York is a long way from here. A lifetime away."

She takes my hands in hers. "I'm sorry, Alex. Really." She glances over her shoulder to see if anyone is watching, then leans across the table and kisses me gently, briefly, on my cheek.

"Alex. Please. I'm sorry."

I move my hands over hers, wrapping my fingers around her slender wrists. I imagine I can feel the blood and whiskey pulse through the veins knotted across her hands like a river delta. The whiskey that, just like beer, can't silence anything, no matter what people say. I wonder whether she knows it.

Clearly I'm not the only one with ghosts.

"Please," she says again. "I don't know what decent looks like anymore, but I know I want it. I want you."

I'm at a loss for words. There's a rush in my ears. Something kicking inside my chest. I bring her hands to my lips, but she hurriedly pulls them out of my grasp. Makes a fist.

"What? I thought . . ."

"Not here."

"There's hardly anyone here." I try to make a joke. "You can't already be ashamed of me."

She shakes her head, laughs. "No, man. Maggie frowns on bad behavior in Hardings." She gestures over her shoulder to the woman behind her waiting impatiently to take our order.

"Tell me what happened that night when you came in here bleeding." I put down my knife and fork and push away the empty plate. Maggie's chicken curry is a winner.

Ranna turns in her chair, resting her back against the wall. She scans the crowd almost nervously, chewing on her bottom lip. "It's someone I once knew—slept with." She corrects herself quickly, as if she has remembered she's supposed to be honest.

"Slept with, or still sleeping with?" I want it to sound like a question, but it comes out wrong. Somehow the words have hardened into an accusation.

She clasps her fingers together. "Slept. Definitely. Totally. I promise."

Her words come out in a rush, as I have come to know happens when she feels unsure.

I breathe more easily. When you write news stories, you know the value of the past tense. Of over. Murder. Drought. Kidnapping. War. Finished. Written off into the past tense and its lies, its euphemisms and misrepresentations, its seduction of perfection or despair—but still finished.

"What happened?"

She shrugs, as if the answer is obvious. "He didn't want to hear . . . accept . . . that it's over. I've been trying to get rid of him, but he won't listen."

I lean forward on the table, raising my voice so that she can hear me over the din in the bar. "Have you been to the police?"

"No."

"Why not?"

"What difference would it make?"

"He might stop bothering you."

"Nothing could have stopped what happened."

A waitress hurries past our table, her tray laden with empty beer bottles and glasses.

"You must report him. It's important. The police can arrest him. Keep him away from you. Stop it from happening again."

Future tense. The weight of possibility. Uncertainty.

For a moment she seems to consider my words, but then the possibility is gone, cloaked in the stubborn resistance I've come to know so well.

"Nothing will stop him."

"Who is it?"

"No one."

She clenches her hands into fists in her lap. Closes her eyes for a moment as if she doesn't want to see me. Around us people are laughing and talking, competing with the loud eighties music pumping over the speakers. Behind me rapid-fire French mingles with the gentle inflection of Swahili.

"Ranna. Please. Why not? What's going on? What aren't you telling me?"

"There's nothing to tell. It's just . . . nothing," she says. "It's unimportant, really."

"I can't help you if you don't give me more information."

She laughs. The hollow sound is unexpected. It bounces off the walls and faces around us.

"I've never asked for your help." She looks down at her hands. "I'm just asking you to love me. No, not even that. I'm asking you to slowly, very slowly, consider whether you *can* love me. Why do men always want to pretend the two things are equal? It's not the same at all. Loving and helping are two completely different things."

"Ranna—"

"Leave it." She fires the words across the table. "He's gone. It's over. I don't want to talk about it."

"But you said he'll never go away."

"Everyone gives up at some point. He's no exception." She waves away my concern. "It's not important anyway. What matters is you and me. Nothing else."

11

When I meet up with Ranna again, it's still raining. She sent me home last night, even though I promised to sleep on the couch just in case this mystery guy came looking for trouble again, but she refused.

The new day is as hot and humid as yesterday. The fetid smell of the city is in my nose—a mixture of wet earth, unwashed bodies, and garbage left out too long. The street hawkers are standing around restlessly. Everything is wet: their wares and the street corners where they usually set up shop. The muddy water makes it hard to see where the street begins and the once-dusty pavement ends.

The passersby keep looking up at the sky, as if they're expecting a catastrophe. I wonder how many of them went to bed soaked to the skin last night.

Ranna, Tom, and I are waiting for the general manager of Lion Mining in front of the Plaza Hotel. The company promised to show us from the air where the rains have left their mark. One of their gold mines has been flooded, and three neighboring villages have been cut off from the outside world. It worries them that the government has not yet requested international aid.

I check again that I've got my wallet. Notebook. Pen. Spare pen. I had to get up at four to file a story, and I'm not properly awake yet.

Last night Ranna and I talked till late. I couldn't make sense of everything she told me, but I know one thing—no, two: she said we should take it slowly—very slowly.

No problem there.

The second thing I find a bit strange. She doesn't want anyone to know about us until we're sure things will work out. Apparently it's the only way my reputation will remain intact. She's had too many relationships that came to nothing, and even though she feels differently this time, people won't see it the same way. There will be gossip, and that's the last thing she wants.

I disagreed at first but gave in after a while. I'll do as she asked. But not for long. I refuse to run around as if I'm having some sordid affair.

At least I know now that she's not married or involved with anyone else.

I rub my eyes and suppress another yawn, the result of only three hours' sleep. Ranna didn't get much more time between the sheets, yet she looks fresh and relaxed. She's standing in the gentle drizzle, taking photos of a middle-aged woman with a red umbrella feeding a stray cat out of her handbag. The woman looks up and smiles, as if she has some unseen bond with the photographer.

Ranna nods almost imperceptibly, her eyes gentle. She studies the Nikon's screen and looks pleased as she wipes strands of hair, studded with misty raindrops, from her face.

"Nice shot?" I call.

"Yes." She walks up to where Tom and I are hiding from the rain near the hotel's entrance and holds up the camera for my inspection.

It's remarkable. The woman's face is raised as if she's listening to something. She looks pensive. Tired. It's the perfect frozen moment. Unfortunately, it's worthless to Ranna's employers. It lacks any news value.

Next to me Tom steps on his cigarette butt. He runs his hand over his freshly shaven head and looks from me to the camera. Then he looks at Ranna. "Are you still working on that exhibition?"

When she fails to reply, he lights another smoke. "Surely you have enough photos by now? When can we see them?"

Ranna tugs at the hem of her black T-shirt and wipes the rain from the Nikon's screen. "Someday."

It's news to me. "Exhibition?"

Tom hisses smoke through his teeth. It disappears against the gray clouds behind him.

When Ranna doesn't say anything, he answers. "She wants to exhibit all her work. Not just the murder-and-mayhem shots. The moments, the people. All the photos those guys in London and Washington consider unimportant."

I turn to Ranna, my eyes questioning. She shrugs and rests the Nikon against her thigh. "He's right," she admits.

"Do you remember that photo you took in Paris?" Tom asks. "When the two of us covered that absurd presidential scandal?"

"The immigrant boy from Mali who stole the loaf of bread?"

"That one. And the one of the white woman from Joburg and her young Algerian lover who pitched their tent at the Eiffel Tower in protest against the way the police treated him? The woman with the Karl Marx tattoo on her back. Remember? She said she had it done years ago as a fuck you to the South African National Party and the so-called communist threat."

"She was beautiful."

"She was sixty-two." Tom takes a long drag from his cigarette. "And she came on to you like a horny cougar. Just think of the photos if you'd been game." He winks at me. "Perfect gentleman that I am, I even offered to take them."

"In your dreams, Tom. In your fucking dreams." Ranna raises the camera and snaps him as he grinds the cigarette butt under his heel.

He sticks a good-humored middle finger in the air, wipes his hand across his chin, and smiles, as if the memories please him.

At that moment it strikes me: Tom is in love with Ranna.

I'm about to ask about the history between them when my phone rings. It's Alan from Lion Mining.

"I'm afraid we have to call off the flight," he says. "We can't go anywhere in this rain. We'll try again tomorrow. The forecast says it might clear a little for a few hours."

"Can't we make another plan?"

"Driving is out of the question. Too dangerous."

"Okay, then," I say, disappointed. I promised Jasmine the story. "I'll tell the others. Same place, same time, tomorrow?"

"Yep. I'll pick you up in the Landie and take you to the airstrip. Sorry, but there's nothing I can do," he says, before breaking off the connection.

I put my phone away and turn to the other two. "Bad news. We're not flying today."

Tom's face darkens. "Why not?"

I point at the sky. "Guess. And sorry, but my contacts don't go as high as that. Alan says tomorrow, same time, same place."

Ranna sighs resignedly. "Probably just as well." She swings the black backpack off her shoulder and puts away her camera. "What do we do now?"

"Don't know about you two, but I'm going back to bed," Tom says, annoyed. "So much for Africa not being for sissies. The rain isn't so bad. Nothing compared to London."

He waves and walks away. "See you tomorrow."

"Bye," Ranna says. "Enjoy your nap."

She looks at her watch and turns to me. "Let's go for a beer."

"What's the time?"

"Almost ten."

"Why not?"

12

The rain steps up its fury as we get into the taxi. It streams down the buildings and the dala dalas as if someone has turned on a tap. People scatter through the ankle-deep muddy brown water, looking for shelter.

On a narrow pavement up ahead a man in a black suit aims to jump across a large puddle. A white Nissan pickup brakes sharply for a woman and her child and drenches him from head to toe. The suit steps into the road, cursing. Three of the words are familiar to me by now. Our taxi driver mumbles and steers around him. Ranna laughs, her camera capturing the moment.

At the turnoff to Hardings Ranna taps the driver on the shoulder. She's changed her mind and signals for him to turn left. To her apartment.

"What's up?"

"I'll make breakfast. Unless you really want to go to Hardings. It will be dead quiet this time of the day."

Five minutes later we stop in front of her place. I pay the driver while Ranna makes a dash for the front door, her backpack tucked under her shirt.

When I enter the musty room I avoid her eyes, afraid mine will reveal that I've been here before. I prop my backpack against the wall and stand around uneasily as she moves past me to switch on the air conditioner.

The double bed, the worn leather couch, the TV, and the thousands of books are all still there. I try to look at everything as if I'm seeing it for the first time. And in a way I am, now that I'm no longer worried about her.

There are large and small books, thick and thin ones, philosophy textbooks, detective novels, travelogues, sci-fi, and photo books. There seem to be even more than I recall. In the kitchen, even the salt, pepper, and other spices stand on stacks of books.

The couch is still being used as a bed. There is one empty mug on the floor, at the end where a pillow lies. A single white sheet is the only bedding. No sign of a duvet.

I notice there's a time switch on the lamp next to the couch.

My eyes automatically travel to the sink in the bathroom that contained the bloody T-shirt. Today there's nothing except the faint smell of bleach.

"Sit," Ranna says in passing. "I forget you're so polite that you'll wait for an invitation."

I follow her around instead. In the kitchen she takes two beers from the fridge, holds one briefly against her forehead and passes me the other one. Then she goes over to the couch and sits down with a contented sigh. She gives me a slightly embarrassed smile when I sit down next to her. I push the pillow into a corner and, for want of a coffee table, balance the beer on a stack of books. If the bottle leaves a stain, it will be one of many.

I point the beer at the disorganized library around us. If there is some order to how the books are stacked, I can't see it. "How do you travel with all these books? Do you pack them every time you move? Or do you simply start a new collection?"

"They go along. All of them. They're like my children. I'm on eight crates now. I use the same movers every time. I think they have a standing bet on how many crates it'll be the next time." She shakes her head. "My mother tells me to buy a Kindle, but I don't know. There's something about paper, you know? Stories and photos that can't be removed or deleted. You should understand. When you've set something down in ink, it's permanent. People quote it as the gospel truth. On paper you can live forever."

She puts her beer on the floor, takes off her boots, and swings her legs up onto the couch. She leans back and pulls her left leg up under her chin. Her right foot comes to rest on my thigh.

My eyes take in the black hair without a trace of gray and the fine lines around her mouth. The soft light falling through the window behind her. The books. The walls.

Something isn't right. Is it possible? Especially after what she has just said?

I move her foot out of the way, get up. Turn slowly. "But there are no . . ."

She runs her hands through her hair, tucks a few errant strands behind her ears. "I know."

"Why not?"

Her face is calm, stripped of emotion. "I have enough trouble sleeping. When I'm here, I want to forget."

"Not even of the good things? Like the woman and the cat? And what about living forever?"

"Well, living forever may not be for me."

She picks up the beer and sips from it, and I know it's the only answer I'll get. She has nothing more to say on the matter.

I sit back down beside her. Drink my beer slowly and stare at the bare walls. Ranna the photographer's walls are white and stark and empty.

I don't know when it happens, but I fall asleep. Suddenly, like a child, without considering where I am.

I wake up from hands tracing the outlines of my body, touching me as if they want to touch me again. As if it matters what I think. What I feel. What's under my skin.

Too afraid to open my eyes, I feel Ranna's hands move cautiously to my neck. Across my face. The realization is overwhelming: Her hands are uncertain. Ranna's confident, eight-photos-per-second hands are uncertain. Maybe even afraid.

I feel her lean forward. She kisses me slowly, as if I might break in two. Her mouth is soft and her breath smells of beer and peppermint.

"I know you're awake."

I keep my eyes closed, in case it's a dream. "Says who?"

She laughs. "You're holding your breath."

I don't tell her I've been doing it all along, since the first time we met, as if I still can't believe my eyes.

When at last I look at her, I know she can see it. She sees everything.

She draws a breath and kisses me again. Harder this time. I'm wise enough to know it's the end, and the beginning, of everything.

13

The next day I'm sitting at the open door of Lion Mining's aging Puma chopper as it speeds away from Dar. We're half an hour north of the city, on our way to Kibakwe, but already the damage from the rain is apparent. The grassy plains move past beneath my feet, one scene exactly like the next.

Water. More water.

I take a few photos for Instagram, signaling to Ranna to look at the devastation below, but she shakes her head and occupies herself with the Nikon. Tom ignores me as well.

Heights have no effect on me, but for Ranna it's quite the opposite. That's why she's sitting at the back, near the vomit bags the French pilot, cursing steadily, has tossed back with one hand as she pushes the Puma in against the wind with the other.

In a few minutes, when we're hovering over the water, Ranna will have to move forward and take her shots as if she has no fear. The *New York Times* and the *Guardian* have no use for fear. They want brave, insightful photographs of the devastation brought about by too much rain.

And I, who always attract chaos, must look and listen and write. About every emotion and sensation. Like five years ago in Alexandra, near Joburg's high-rises, when the Jukskei River flooded its banks and swept away a nursery school and 71 squatters' shanties.

And here I am again. Water. Too much water.

Life repeats itself relentlessly.

The pilot looks over her shoulder and holds a thumb in the air to indicate that she'll hover while we get our shots. I signal that I understand and beckon Ranna closer.

The earth underneath us is covered with muddy brown water. To our right, a few cattle and their herdsmen are stranded on an island created by the rain. Next to them I can see the battered roofs of a cluster of huts, everyone who used to live there hopefully already evacuated.

Neither the cattle nor the boys seem perturbed. Merely surprised at the sight of the metal dragonfly overhead. Were they left behind to look after the village's most precious asset?

I turn back. Where's Ranna? Still fidgeting with the Nikon.

I beckon to her again, point to the space between my legs. When at last she shuffles forward, I see her detach from the fear. Her expression becomes serene, her eyes a dark, intense blue.

She sits down next to me and motions for me to put my arm around her waist. I do as she asks. She slides down and wriggles herself in between my knees, signaling that I should hold her more tightly. Then, with the monotonous whop-whop of the chopper drowning out every other sound, she leans out through the door.

And even farther.

I dig my heels into the Puma's steel belly. Under her T-shirt, the muscles of her back are knotted at first, then they relax as she forgets about me.

I know better than to be afraid on her behalf. Ranna is who she is, and expecting her to change would be pointless.

Hours seem to pass before the pilot taps me on the shoulder. *Bring her back,* the woman gestures.

I begin to pull Ranna back inside. She fights me at first, then surrenders.

At last she's sitting beside me again. The steel cable inside her is taut. Her flushed throat and the smile around her mouth, filled with life, betray the adrenaline rush.

I've never seen her more beautiful.

She shouts something, but her words are scattered by the drone of the chopper's ascent.

"What?" I shout back.

Her lips form the words again, more slowly this time. I smile when I understand.

"I love you too!" I shout, and know without a doubt that this is one of the best days of my life.

The adrenaline lasts all the way home. Wet through, we duck into Ranna's apartment. She struggles with her boots and finally kicks them off. The wet jeans are harder to get out of. She curses under her breath as the material stubbornly clings to her skin.

I interrupt her attempt to undress and turn her around to face me. I draw her close, kissing her shoulder where the tanned skin shows through her blue shirt. Then higher up, on her neck. She moans, long and deep. I pull her hips closer and feel her hunger take over, her mouth seeking mine.

She fumbles for the buttons of my shirt. Loses patience. "Dammit." She rips one off. Another.

I understand. I know about now, not later. Later dissolves in time. In perhaps. In maybe. Now is all that really exists.

She tugs at the top button of my Levi's. My breathing quickens. I grow hard. A sound escapes from her throat. She pushes me deeper into the apartment. Up against the corner cabinet. The bookcase next to the TV. Equally impatient, I spin us around so that her back is against the books. I hoist her up against me. She pulls away and tears the shirt from my body.

Now.

With one hand I search for her jeans. Struggle with my own. Give up. Lower her to the floor and peel off her wet jeans completely so that she can step out of them. Then my own. I lift her again, my hands around her waist. She wraps her legs around my hips. Her nails dig into my back.

Around us books fall to the ground. *Primal Fear. The Mating Habits of Butterflies. The Dream Taker.*

Inside.

Now.

Now.

Now.

14

The weather, like sports and movie stars, is always news. Everyone wants to know whether tomorrow will be hot or cold, even though there's nothing they can do about it. Some of the worst days in history have been those when the weather headlined the news. Days and names no one will ever forget.

The Indian Ocean tsunami of December 26, 2004. Hurricane Katrina. Japan's 2011 tsunami. They made the front pages every time.

When the temperature in Oudtshoorn rises to 116 degrees Fahrenheit and six people and 130 ostriches die of heat exhaustion, it's news. When it snows where it hasn't snowed for a hundred years, it makes the papers. The same when it hails. When the wind blows. When it doesn't rain. When it rains. And rains. And rains.

When the first villages were flooded days ago, the story was hidden on page six in the local papers, eclipsed by stories of a minister's unruly illegitimate child. When the flood was on its way and it seemed as if Dar es Salaam was going to be swept out to sea, the story moved from page six to the front page.

The day before yesterday, when three British tourists and a journalist sent word to London by email that they were stranded in Zanzibar, the country's tourist island paradise, it made headlines in four overseas newspapers and on eleven websites. Not even Lion Mining has managed that.

And then it happened. The thing that changed everything. The thing that made everything worse. Chaos.

The flood reached Oyster Bay, the beach resort of the Dar es Salaam elite. The three-story vacation home of IT billionaire William K. Jones III was swept into the sea, along with three other houses. Within thirty-six hours a CNN correspondent was reporting from the scene. After all, Billy Jones was an American citizen—and not just any American citizen. He was the man who discovered how to make a computer work at six times the normal speed. Moreover, he was an eligible bachelor with a bad-boy reputation and a long line of A-list women in his wake.

A day later his body washed up on the beach. It topped the news cycle everywhere.

The rain fell unremittingly, as one by one newspeople began to arrive at the waterlogged airport. All the newspapers and TV stations without correspondents in Tanzania were sending in their staff. The town was suddenly teeming with journalists, camerapeople, and photographers with hungry eyes.

But even before the first plane ungracefully skidded to a halt on the wet tarmac, Ranna and I were there. We were the ones to discover the body, after all.

We're collecting seashells, walking slowly, our jeans rolled up, like children or old women during long, rainy June vacations on the West Coast. As if it really matters. As if it's a competition. Ignoring the bad weather, we sift through the wet sand in search of the perfect shell. The one that has managed to survive the churning waves.

Earlier this morning, out of pure boredom, we had decided to come to the beach. Ranna closed her book and said you can only read and watch TV for so long.

It's Sunday, and we're the only people on the wide, sandy expanse. The beach is empty, and the thatched huts where the sunseekers can usually be found are deserted. The fishermen's dhows lie tied up, the never-ending rain too much for even the most fearless among them. The sea is dark, unlike its usual bright-blue color, the normally calm water turbulent.

Ranna is forging ahead in the drizzle like an explorer, a dim figure in the gray morning light, hell-bent on success.

"Got it!" she calls. She turns, looms suddenly in front of me, her left fist clenched. "Close your eyes."

I do as I'm told. She places something in the palm of my hand. It's cold against my skin. It smells of the sea, of a woman.

I open my eyes and look at the white shell with the little face carved on it. "Looks good." I turn it over. There's a chip on the underside, but I don't point it out to her.

"Hey! You were supposed to keep your eyes closed." She smiles. A proud, pleased smile, the black curls windswept around her face.

As the rain begins to come down harder, I put the shell in my pocket and pull my jacket more tightly around my body. But Ranna opens her arms wide to embrace the rain and starts to run, faster and faster, as if we're at the end of the earth and she's about to jump off the edge.

She's flying. She takes off, leaning into the wind, and I watch her body strain against the drenched T-shirt.

Then, just past the rocks, I see her recoil. Like a question mark and an exclamation mark combined. As if she can't believe her eyes. Ranna, who has seen everything.

"What is it?" I hurry toward her, jumping over rocks until I'm standing next to her, breathless.

I draw in a sharp breath. "What the hell?"

She doesn't say a word.

I look from the dead man to Ranna. She's watching the broken, pale body at her feet with a strange expression on her face. After a while I identify the emotion: she wishes she had her camera with her.

But, because she didn't want to cart it along in the rain, it's in the Land Cruiser, which is parked a good half mile away.

Later I would understand that she wasn't looking for her camera after all, but a back door. A way out.

The waves push the man to shore, until he's lapping against our feet with the tide, a tuft of brown hair showing on the back of his head. On his neck is a faded tattoo. Something Celtic. I lean forward to get a better view. Three interlaced circles signifying eternity.

I close my mouth, but it's too late. The stench has already settled at the back of my throat. It slides down to the pit of my stomach, and I take an involuntary step back. I draw a deep breath before moving forward again. When I kneel beside the body, my knees sink into the soft sand. Ranna stands rooted to the spot.

"Help me," I say.

"Why? There's nothing to see. He's dead." She looks at me as if I'm stupid. "Half of him is . . . missing."

I ignore her while I struggle with the man's bulky figure. I don't say it, but I'm trying to turn him around to see who he is. Perhaps we know him. He's lily-white, so he's probably not from Tanzania.

I grab hold of his black shirt, dig my heels into the wet sand, and struggle to my feet. At last I'm looking at the remains of his face. I don't recognize him. I place my fingers at his throat. His skin is an icy wet rag, moving under my fingers as if it's no longer a part of him. His hair is slimy and sparse. Ranna was right: The sea hasn't spared him, especially not his face. Neither have the fish.

I feel along the length of his body. There's no jewelry or wallet to make it easier to identify him, though the tattoo may help.

Next to me Ranna begins to move away carefully. The sand sucks at her boots, as if it wants to keep her here. There's an expression almost like grief on her face.

My eyes go from her to the man. "Do you know him?"

She nods slowly, her face blank. "I don't know. Maybe. It's hard to say. I think I photographed him once for *Time*."

"*Time*?" That means he's a well-known figure.

I look at the man again. Maybe . . . could it be? Impossible.

I turn back to her. "Are you okay?"

"Yes." Suddenly she sounds afraid. Not the emotion I expected.

"Are you sure?"

She looks away from the body, at the sea, at me. Then she turns and walks briskly away.

"Stay there. I'm going to fetch my camera!" she calls over her shoulder just before she disappears around the rocks.

15

"You go first."

"What?" I shake my head, but not because of what she said. Ranna is much too calm—almost clinically so—for someone waiting at a police station. She seems almost used to the situation.

It feels as if a different person is seated next to me. The impassive woman of the beach is gone. When she returned, camera over her shoulder, I wanted to comfort her, but her body was hard and stiff, like lovers' rigor mortis.

The police station is in a frenzy, people scurrying past, the discovery of a potential VIP calling all hands on deck. The uniforms dumped us at the end of a long, dimly lit corridor. Told us to wait for a detective who will interview us as soon as possible.

I rub the palms of my hands together. Unlike Ranna, I'm finding it hard to stay calm. This side of a story is unfamiliar to me. I write the news. As a rule, I don't make it.

"Will you cover for me?" She speaks again. "Just for a few minutes."

"Are you kidding me? Where are you going?"

She holds up the Nikon. "I want to send the photos through." She points at three uniforms drinking coffee in the corner, the end of a long shift etched on their faces. "One of those officers is a good friend of the guy from the *Daily News*. He'll definitely tip Patrick off."

"And where are you supposed to have disappeared to?"

"Flu. Asthma. You'll think of something."

"I'm not going to lie to the police."

"It's no different from lying to anyone else," she snaps.

"Sounds like something you do all the time."

"Lie to the police or to other people?"

"Ha-ha, very funny. Both."

A door creaks open at the end of the hall. A plainclothes policeman steps out, glances at us, and then retreats back into the room.

She takes her car keys from her pocket. "Is everything always black or white with you?"

"There's very little in between. And what there is is man-made."

"That's where you're wrong, Alex. There's an entire universe in between. A fucking abyss. And one day someone is going to push you off the cliff."

"I'll refuse to jump."

"Good luck." She slings the camera bag over her shoulder. Her hands are clenched into fists, a certain indication that she's upset. Or scared. "I'm sure you've tweaked a few facts in your career. Add a little sensation, a little drama. It's no different."

"Photos can lie too," I retaliate. "What about the things you leave outside the frame?"

She knows at once what I'm referring to. Her back stiffens and her eyes become veiled, as if I'm the enemy. "You don't always have to show all the detail."

"Why not? Won't people want to know if something, or someone, removed a few of the dead guy's fingers?"

"It may have been fish. Sharks. Anything. The sea is wide and deep. Anyway, on one or two pictures it's clearly visible."

She can say what she likes, but I know it's not true. While we've been sitting here, I've looked at all the shots on her camera, and it seems she navigated around the hands, as if she didn't want to capture the missing digits.

"No one will want to publish such gruesome photos anyway," she continues. "You know that as well as I do."

I give up. "Go send your photos. I'll tell my part of the story and then go and file my own article." I lifted my phone. "I already sent through four quick paragraphs."

"Thanks."

She begins to walk away but turns and hurries back, smiling slightly, as if she wants to defuse the situation. She leans forward and kisses me briefly. "I owe you big-time."

The tall, thin, middle-aged policeman asks the same questions over and over. How did we find the body? Why were we on the beach? Where's Ranna? Why isn't she here? The only reprieve he offers is to urge me twice not to say anything about the dead man missing some of his fingers. He does so grudgingly, as if he hates asking me a favor.

I look at his graying hair, the knife-sharp nose and his eyes like mud—unfathomable and murky. While he speaks, I'm writing my article in my mind, the one that will appear on the front page of the *New York Times*, the one next to Ranna's photograph.

The one that will summon the rest of the world to Tanzania.

"You're in love with Miss Abramson." The words find their way into my consciousness.

I look up, into the dark eyes of Hamisi Bahame of the Tanzanian detective service. The Criminal Investigation Department. There's a smile on his lips, as if he knows my attention was elsewhere.

Was.

Of course a question like that would promptly bring me back to the cramped, windowless room at the police headquarters in the heart of Dar es Salaam. My watch tells me that the sun is probably setting outside, but in here no one would notice.

"What makes you say that?" I ask when he doesn't elaborate.

"The way you speak of her." He rubs his high forehead, his gaunt, clean-shaven jaw. "The way you say her name, as if you'd like to be saying it in the middle of the night instead of here." The hand with the long, thin fingers waves at the dirty carpet, the white walls, the single potted plant in the corner, begging for water.

"You should have been a poet," I scoff.

"You're not denying it."

I shrug, no answer within easy reach.

The policeman gives a slight smile. "If you love Miss Abramson, it means I can't believe a word you say."

"Why not? Everybody loves somebody."

He rests his chin on his hand and closes his eyes. The tea in front of him has grown cold. He offered me some as well, but I refused. I crave something stronger.

"Yes. Most people love somebody," he muses. "Somebody loved Billy Jones as well. Somebody has lost him. People who lose something want answers—it's one of the first rules of ownership. And Billy's people are rich. They have a lot of influence. They live in California somewhere, don't they?"

Definitely a poetic policeman. And a clever one. I don't reply. What can I say? Answers are his job. Telling stories is mine.

"Does this mean you're sure the man on the beach is Billy Jones?"

"Who's asking? You or the journalist?"

"We're the same person."

He moves the teacup toward me, draws it back. "We're still checking, but it seems likely. Two previously published articles mention the tattoo on his neck. And the one on his lower back. *Teresa.* His ex-wife's name. Everyone knows he's been in Dar for the past few weeks, just as everyone knows what he looks like. He was a regular at the clubs."

He takes the gift of confirmation away as quickly as he offered it. "But the official answer is that we have yet to confirm his identity."

"When will you be a hundred percent sure?"

The policeman shakes his head. He puts the teacup down. "This is my interview, Alex." He gives me a friendly, impersonal smile. His fingers begin to drum a slow beat on the wooden table. "Tell me about Ranna Abramson. Why isn't she here with you?"

"Why is it important? I can tell you what happened."

"It's important for a number of reasons. Billy Jones's family will want to know what happened. The American government will want answers. You must know they were one of his many clients."

"Look," I say slowly and clearly. "All we did was find Billy Jones's body. We went for a walk in the rain because we were fed up with being cooped up inside. With writing flood stories. It's not a crime. And like law-abiding residents, we immediately called the police."

The policeman's eyes seem to warm somewhat. "You're probably right. Let's hope you're telling the truth." He sips his cold tea. Pulls a face. "Besides, there's no reason to suspect either of you, is there?"

16

"Come over."

I'm instantly awake. Ranna's voice is thin and loaded with tension. Did things go badly at the police station? The only thing she had to do was make a statement on discovering the body.

I look at the faint yellow hands of my watch. Eleven. "I take it you had a rough evening. Did they keep you long?"

"Not really. I stopped for a beer, but Hardings was too busy. I couldn't think."

"And now?"

"Now I want you to come over. Spend the night. Be here. You. Your body. You know? Everything."

Everything. One of my favorite words. More so when Ranna says it.

She misinterprets my hesitation. "Must I spell it out more clearly?" Then, suddenly, her aggression fades. "Sorry, Alex. It's just . . . sometimes it's hard to forget it was a person. Someone who lived and dreamed. Not just a body. A photo. I remembered it when I had to tell that detective about the beach. Bahame?"

"Hamisi Bahame."

"Yes. Him."

I feel around in the dark and switch on the bedside lamp. Ranna sounds uncertain. Vulnerable.

"How well did you and Billy know each other? Did you really just do the shoot for *Time*?" I remember the expression on her face earlier. Her body language said she had lost something. Lost someone.

"Are you going to interrogate me as well?"

Maybe I'm wrong about the vulnerability. "I was just wondering. You don't have to answer."

I hear her open the fridge on the other end and take something out. Open it. A beer, probably.

"No. I'm sorry." She swallows twice, three times. "Of course you may ask. After the *Time* shoot, I photographed a few of Billy's parties. When he moved into his new house, on his birthday. That's about it. He was a fan. I made him look good."

She sighs, fumbles with something that crackles like plastic. "Well, sleep tight."

"No, wait." I sit up in bed. "I'm on my way. I didn't mean I don't want to come over. I just want to understand . . ."

"Why?"

"Yes."

"Why is it such a thing with you?"

Busted. "If I had to believe things happen for no reason, I'd go mad. Somewhere in this crazy mess there must be an explanation. A reason. A why. Cause and effect."

"Alex, stop thinking," she scolds. "Just for a moment. Get dressed and come here. I miss you. Please."

I do as she demands, taking a taxi to her apartment as usual because she still doesn't want everyone to know about our relationship. Besides, Hadhi didn't like me taking up her tenants' parking space.

By now I didn't even have to pack a bag. Everything I needed was at Ranna's place.

She opens the door before I can knock. Drags me inside.

She has a tattoo that begins at the bend of her leg, traveling all the way up her left side. She, the picture maker, has chosen to adorn her body with words. The flowing black lines of verse climb up her supple skin, circle her left breast, and lead to her heart. "Vroegherfs," by the well-known Afrikaans poet N. P. van Wyk Louw, is a lyrical lament about the change of season from summer to autumn. To the credit of my high school teachers I vaguely remember it being an intimate prayer for spiritual awakening. About stripping down to the bare minimum as time steadily moves by.

Ranna says it reminds her that nothing lasts forever. That the present is the only time that truly exists. That she should never forget where she comes from. Her mother may have forgotten—may have wanted to forget—but she hasn't.

New York is good, she says when I ask. Busy. Full. But it lacks the piercing blue sky of the Free State, or the last light of day settling over the sea at Lambert's Bay. Or the sound of women's voices on the side of the road while they're cooking mealies and vetkoek, or the happy laughter at a New Year's braai.

Even though she's spent three years away from South Africa, it's still her home, she says, her accent thick with pleasure.

I run my lips over van Wyk Louw, just like the first time her body froze under mine before spilling over. My touch makes her skin contract. She moans softly, draws me nearer. My fingers brush over the wound from the day her T-shirt was soaked in blood.

She draws in her breath and laughs in her throat. "There are better places to explore. You were doing so well a moment ago."

"I know."

She must have heard the light in the two words. She laughs again. "Don't get all cocky now. Remember, success lies in repeating the performance. Not in a single fireworks display."

I'm awakened by a soft voice. It sounds like chanting in a monastery—a lingering sound that insinuates itself everywhere.

I don't have to open my eyes to know that Ranna is still lying beside me. I listen to her name the stars she sees through the open window. "Sirius. Canopus. Orion . . ."

I listen until I fall asleep with her hand resting on my chest.

Later still, I wake up again and her place next to me is empty. I call her name.

"Yes?" she answers from somewhere in the room.

I roll onto my stomach and move to the edge of the bed. She's reading, two candles at her feet. Something is steaming in a mug beside her.

"Doesn't coffee make it worse?"

"It's tea. From the southern highlands."

"Why tea? Does it help?" I yawn.

"Always."

"What are you reading?"

She holds up the book. Stephen Hawking.

"Light entertainment."

She laughs.

I wonder if something is troubling her, but she looks strangely happy. As if nighttime agrees with her. I sigh and roll onto my back. "Wake me if you're looking for a different kind of therapy."

"I will."

Just before I fall asleep again, I hear her voice. This time she isn't talking to the stars, but to me.

"Alex. Promise you'll be careful."

"Careful? Why?"

"No reason. Just promise. And promise you'll tell me if anything weird happens."

"Weird?"

"You know what I mean. I don't want anything to happen to you."

"Nothing will happen to me," I say before I doze off, happy that she's reading here, close to me, and not on the sofa. As if she won't let me out of her sight.

17

The phone keeps ringing. I try to ignore it, but the silly tune bounces off the white walls of Ranna's apartment. I put the pillow over my head to escape from the noise.

She wakes up beside me, alarmed. Searches for the phone under a pile of clothing beside the bed. She looks at the Samsung's illuminated screen, swears, and throws it down. "Wrong number."

I remember a similar incident a few weeks ago, at the beginning of our relationship. After our first evening at Hardings.

"Bullshit." I toss the pillow aside, lean over her, and pick up the phone. The number is not displayed on the screen. "You don't even know who it is."

"Exactly. I've got the numbers of everyone I know on my phone."

The phone resumes ringing in my hand. Ranna grabs at it, but I hold it out of reach. She jumps out of bed swiftly, like a predator. Her white T-shirt rides up to reveal her taut stomach muscles. Her breathing is quick and uneven.

"If you answer that phone, you can pack your stuff and go."

"What's going on?"

"Nothing."

"You're lying."

She makes another grab at the phone, her clenched fist brushing past my nose.

"Whoa. Here." I hand her the Samsung.

She grabs the phone and throws it. It shatters against the wall.

"Ranna! What—"

"I said leave it. It was a wrong number. Can't you just leave things alone sometimes?"

I sit up slowly. What just happened?

"I'm sorry," I say cautiously. "I didn't mean to upset you."

She sits down on the edge of the bed. Her hair falls over her face, and for a moment she looks impossibly young. Slowly I move closer, as if any sudden movement might cause her to bolt. I extend my hand across the white sheet. A peace offering.

"I'm sorry," I say again.

"It was just a stupid phone call." Her eyes are a dark, inscrutable blue. "I said it's not important. Who knows how much time we have left? Look at Billy. At what happened to him."

She swallows. Breathes hard. Wipes the hair from her face. Uses one finger to draw an invisible line down my arm. Puts her hand in mine. "What does it matter, hmm? We're here. No one else. Just us. If you can't accept that, it might be better if you go home."

Two days later Hamisi Bahame calls.

Ranna is in central Tanzania to take new shots of the floods. I've stayed behind to write an in-depth article, before anyone else suddenly finds time to do it, about the response of developing countries to natural disasters.

Chaos can become boring. What recurs often eventually loses its impact, diminishes in perceived size and importance, even if it continues unabated. Shock, like love, can ebb away. What once moved the earth can become normal. Routine and predictable. Boring.

The rain and Billy Jones's death are old news, so I write about the lack of funds. About food and blankets piling up at Red Cross and

United Nations depots because no choppers are available to distribute the goods. I write about the lack of potable water despite the rain.

In every good story there's always a touch of irony, after all.

I answer my phone at the second ring. It's Hamisi.

"This is a surprise."

"Why?"

"I wasn't expecting to hear from you again." I press save and close my laptop.

"Why not, Alex?"

"Because . . ." My words fade away.

"Because you didn't know Billy Jones?"

"Yes. And you sure as hell wouldn't call me with a tip-off."

"Good guess. I won't, but I do have a few questions for you. I hear Miss Abramson isn't in Dar es Salaam at the moment."

"Yes, sorry. Work," I apologize vaguely on her behalf.

"Never mind, I'll speak to her later. In the meantime, there are one or two matters I want to clear up with you. I thought it might be better to do it while she's not here."

"What do you mean?"

"You'll see. I believe most of the foreign journalists are regulars at Hardings? Why don't I meet you there? Tonight. Half past five, before it gets busy."

18

"What are you drinking?"

"Castle. You South Africans make the best beer." There's the shadow of a smile around Hamisi's mouth. "But I'll pay for my own. Before I'm accused of improper conduct."

"As you wish."

I wave Maggie over. She eyes us inquisitively as she takes our order but makes no comment. The only other familiar face in Hardings is the man in the white cap, glued to his usual spot at the bar.

I don't want to spend the entire evening with the cop, unless he gives me a lead on Billy Jones's death. I haven't yet filed my Red Cross story.

"How can I help you?" I ask.

Hamisi takes his time pouring his beer into a glass. Tasting it. "Miss Abramson," he says at last.

"Ranna?"

"Ranna."

"What about her?"

Hamisi's eyes are fixed on the condensation dripping down the outside of the glass, staining the weathered wooden table. He looks cool in a perfectly pressed white shirt and neat black trousers. "What do you know about her and Billy Jones?"

"She took some photos of him. For him, if I remember correctly," I answer cautiously. "One of the photos was on the cover of *Time*."

"And that's all?"

"As far as I know."

"And your relationship with Miss Abramson . . . Ranna? How's that going?"

I consider my answer. What exactly does he want to know? Perhaps it would be better to act stupid.

"You'll have to be a bit clearer. I don't understand the question."

Hamisi takes another sip of his beer. Puts the glass down. Every gesture is noiseless, precise. I wonder whether he's married or living with someone. It can't be easy. The silence around him is almost absolute.

He tries again. "Do you and Ranna have a sexual relationship?"

"You seemed convinced I was madly in love with her the first time we spoke."

"Sex and love aren't the same thing. Men will sometimes do more for sex than for love."

I don't know what to say. He may be right.

"So?" he asks again. "Do you?"

"Yes."

"You must be pleased."

"What do you mean?"

"Nothing. I heard she can be rather standoffish. Or it seems so in public."

"Who told you that?"

"People talk."

I spin the beer bottle in my hands. Around and around. Did Hamisi speak to Tom?

"Well, yes," I concede. "It wasn't easy to convince her of my feelings. She's wary of relationships."

Hamisi rubs his chin thoughtfully. "That's not what I heard."

"You must be referring to her previous relationships."

"Among other things."

"Perhaps I should qualify: she's wary of long-term, serious relationships," I say.

"Ah."

There's a moment's silence. Maggie approaches before I've finished my beer, as if she wants to eavesdrop on my conversation with the policeman.

"Another one?" She holds out her hand for the bottle.

I nod. Hamisi indicates he's had enough. Maggie seems reluctant to return to the bar.

Hamisi takes a notebook from his pocket. He opens it at a page marked with a yellow Post-it note. "From what I can see, Ranna knew Billy Jones very well."

"What do you mean?"

"Just what I'm saying. Tom Masterson—you know him, he works with you—says Ranna was involved with Billy for about three months. The relationship ended only recently."

Blood hammers through my head like the stuttering traffic in the rain outside. The buzzing in my ears drowns out every other sound. I can see Hamisi's lips moving, but I can't hear a word he's saying.

I nod my thanks to Maggie as she puts the Kilimanjaro in front of me. I try to gain time by wiping the condensation from the bottle and tasting whether it's cold enough.

"Are you okay?" I see empathy in Hamisi's eyes but no surprise.

"A relationship?" I ask.

Was Billy Jones the man who called Ranna in the middle of the night after our first date at Hardings? But if so, what about the late-night call after his death?

"Yes, a relationship." Hamisi's empathy seems to have vanished, his voice curt and decisive. "She didn't tell you."

It's not a question. In fact, the policeman sounds smug.

No one told me, I think angrily. No one. Including Tom.

"When exactly did they . . . when did the relationship end?" Had I been trespassing on the IT billionaire's territory?

Hamisi pages through his notebook. "Tom was very clear about it. February the eleventh."

I sift through the dates in my mind. It's . . .

My expression must have given something away. Hamisi's eyes turn into sharp searchlights when I don't speak.

"Alex, is there something you're not telling me?"

"No." I speak calmly, as if I lie every day.

"If there's something you should tell me, you better do it now. Before you're so deep in trouble that you don't know how to get out again."

Hamisi stresses the word *deep*. He closes his notebook, his eyes fixed on me.

I manage to shake my head and give a half-hearted smile. I finish my beer in silence and beckon Maggie over. This time I order a whiskey.

Tuesday, February 11, was the night Ranna arrived at Hardings covered in blood.

"When did Billy die?" I speak at last.

Hamisi looks disappointed. "About the same time the relationship ended. Sometime in February. At least, that's what we think. The fish got to him, so it's hard to be exact. If he had been in the water a day longer, we might not even have known it was him. Fingerprints can be problematic when someone has been in water for so long. And DNA testing is a lengthy process, especially here. The tattoos helped with the initial identification, and of course Ranna knew who he was, but we had to request his dental records to make sure."

Exasperated, he drums on the table with his fingers. "Alex. Let me make it quite clear: don't keep quiet if you know something that might help me. Billy Jones had a family. A group of companies. He put food on the table for a lot of people, and he was murdered."

"Murdered? You guys haven't said anything about murder. Who's to say it wasn't just an accident? His home collapsed in the rain, didn't it? Maybe he was in bed when it happened."

The slight smile reappears. "A stab wound in the back isn't an accident."

"I thought the sea . . ."

"This may not be Las Vegas, Alex, but we're not completely stupid."

"That's not what I meant."

"Whoever killed him was angry. Very, very angry. Don't remain silent and be surprised if one day you also end up at the wrong end of that sentiment. No one in the Tanzanian police force would have any sympathy for you."

19

I take a roundabout route home. I need time to think about everything Hamisi said.

A pedestrian wags an angry finger at me when I turn a corner without giving her time to cross. I give a brief apologetic wave and drive on. My mind is on Ranna and Billy.

What the hell does Ranna think she's doing? Did she really think the police wouldn't find out about her and Billy? And how stupid am I?

I remember the day we found the body. Only now I grasp that she didn't really want to fetch her camera to get the money shot—she wanted to get away from me so that she could bring her emotions under control, before I realized Billy had been more to her than a photograph on the cover of *Time*.

Why hasn't she been honest with me? Was Billy the man who kept on hounding her? Who wouldn't leave her alone? He must have hurt her that evening in February. Did she fight back? Kill him?

There's only one way of finding out what really happened. I have to talk to Ranna. And I'd better find her before Hamisi drives her into a corner.

The next day finds me sitting on the steps at her front door, waiting. Hadhi brings me a pot of tea when I decline her offer of lunch. She gives me a worried look and mumbles something about Miss America.

I'm drinking the last of the sweet, milky tea when the drone of Ranna's Land Cruiser announces her arrival.

She laughs when she sees me. The laughter spreads from her mouth to the fine lines around her eyes. "I've missed you," she says as she walks up to me.

I would have preferred her to be angry with me for arriving unannounced. Upset. Anything but happy.

"Hi." My voice stops her before she can throw her arms around my neck.

"What's wrong?" She runs the palm of her hand across my cheek. "Darling. What's the matter?"

"How can you even think that?"

Ranna is angry. She's leaning against the kitchen sink. Her backpack lies at her feet, where she dropped it at the first mention of Billy Jones's name. Her right hand has a stranglehold on a half-full glass of water. Her knuckles are white.

"Is this how it works, Alex? You sleep with me and a few days later you accuse me of murder?"

The glass shatters in her fingers.

"Ranna! For fuck's sake." I try to open her fist to see whether she's hurt, but she pushes me away.

"Leave me alone."

She searches in a drawer, finds a dishcloth, and wraps it around her hand. Moments later blood begins to seep through the cloth. The two of us stare at it as if we've been hypnotized. It's her trigger hand. The right hand with the long, strong, sure fingers.

"Don't do what you always do. Don't run away. I'm trying to find out what's going on."

"Why?"

"Because it's important to me. I love you. Despite the fact that I may be rushing blindly into things." I want to say "stupidly" but swallow the word in time.

She blinks, as if I've caught her off guard.

"I want to know what happened that night you arrived at Hardings with blood on your clothes. You were hurt. Someone hurt you."

"And you think it was Billy?" She grimaces. "No, what you're really asking is whether I killed Billy."

There's a moment's silence—not because of what she said, but because of the way she said it. She said Billy's name as if she had known him much better than someone who had merely taken his photo.

"Why don't we start at the beginning," I say calmly, though I want to kill her for lying to me. "How well do—did—you know Billy?"

She peels the dishcloth from her hand and inspects the wound. It's still bleeding. She wraps it up again, this time more tightly. The broken glass is still lying at her feet.

"Ranna." I try again. "If you can't be honest with me, it's over. I must be able to trust you. You must be able to trust me. There can't be any lies between us."

"I don't lie. I just keep quiet about stuff." She tries to smile, but it's a feeble attempt.

"And keeping quiet isn't lying? Are we arguing about semantics now?"

"You're familiar with the weight of words." She crosses her arms. "You know, those things that you're not allowed to say but include in your stories anyway, because you want people to know. Because you want people to make certain deductions. Like when you don't say the man probably killed his wife, so instead you say the police are looking for him, because he could 'help them with their investigation.' Does that make you a liar?"

"Stop." I feel my hands clench into fists and stuff them into my pockets. "Stop your clever arguments. Tell me who Billy Jones was.

Who he was to you. Hamisi says you were in a relationship. Did I come between you?"

"Be careful of Hamisi. Can't you see he's trying to drive us apart?"

"Just answer the question. What were you and Billy Jones to each other?"

She runs her good hand across her mouth. Tucks her hair behind her ear. Closes her eyes. Opens them. "We slept together. For a few weeks. Nothing more."

"When?"

"Just before us."

"Why then get involved with me?"

"I was a distraction to Billy. Someone to pass the time with while he was here, away from everyone at home." The corners of her mouth turn down. "At first I thought it would be enough. An easy fling with no complications and demands, but it wasn't. I don't want to be anyone's distraction. I want more. I want that thing that takes your breath away. That hurts and makes you happy at the same time. Drives you crazy. Like when I met you. It happened so quickly I didn't know what to do with it."

My heart, that stupid tangle of blood and tissue that got me into this mess in the first place, can't help itself. It pushes all logic aside and tells me to stop right here. I don't need to know more.

Still I persist. "And then?"

"I told Billy I wanted to end it."

"And?"

"And what?"

"Was he angry?"

The words of Tank Oliver, my first editor, echo in my mind: Never ask a leading question unless you're looking for a very specific answer. A sound bite. A quote. A few useful words.

She stares at the blood on the dishcloth. Wraps it even tighter.

"Ranna. Was he angry?"

"Yes."

"Did he do something to you?"

"Yes."

"Did you defend yourself?"

She hesitates a moment. Draws a deep breath. "Yes."

20

Ranna dabs disinfectant on the cuts in her palm. Her hand has finally stopped bleeding. I cut strips of adhesive and fetch gauze from the bathroom cabinet.

We occupy ourselves with the mechanics of healing, as if it might make us forget the stuff we don't want to talk about.

"I didn't kill him." Ranna's voice is hesitant.

"Not even by accident?"

"No."

"What happened?"

"I told Billy about you. That I met you and that I liked you. It was before . . . before anything happened between us. He was furious." Her voice is tense. "He wanted to know who you are. How it happened. What he'd done wrong. In the end he went ballistic. He had a vicious temper. He could be totally unreasonable and crazy."

"And then?" My hands freeze around the gauze.

"There was a cheese knife in his hand. One moment we were drinking wine and eating cheese like grown-ups, and the next moment he totally lost it. I don't think he knew where he was."

"Did he stab you?"

"Yes. Just a flesh wound in my shoulder. I fled, but I turned at the front door and threw a vase at him. I was livid. I think it struck him on the cheek, but I don't really know. There was some blood, not much. I got into my car and drove off."

She takes a deep breath and continues more calmly. "I went home to clean off the worst of the blood before I went to Hardings. I wanted to tell you everything, but you were so angry. And then I got angry as well. The rest you know."

"Did you ever see him again?"

She shakes her head. "No. Not until the day we found his body on the beach. I didn't hear from him either—not even a phone call or an email. But I didn't find it strange because a few days later his house was swept away in the flood. I assumed he had enough on his mind."

"Why didn't you say anything? Why did Hamisi have to tell me?"

"Because I didn't want to be that girl. The one with the reputation. Especially not with you. And I hoped that night would remain a secret, that neither you nor Hamisi would ever find out." She pulls a face. "So, yeah, okay, I know I was naïve, and I know it's not the answer you're looking for."

She takes the gauze from my hand, soaks it in antiseptic cream, and scrubs the palm of her hand, screwing up her face.

"I'm not good with stories, Alex." She sounds bitter. Her eyes grow darker and her voice softer as if she herself is fading away. "I find it hard to talk about myself. When I was at school . . ." She stops talking.

"Yes?" I urge, gesturing for her to hold out her hand for the bandage.

"I attended nine schools. No one sticks around, despite all the empty promises to stay in touch. Everything gets left behind when you move yet again. And again and again. Your stories get lost in the packing and unpacking. In the feigned interest of people who know they can't invest in you because you won't be there when they need you."

"Sounds lonely."

"You get used to it." She bites her lip when I gently apply pressure on the bandage.

"So you don't talk. Not about anything?"

"No."

"Well, that will have to change, or it can never work between us. I must know what's going on inside that head of yours."

She makes no reply.

I take a deep breath. Hold her hand. Wait for the tension to flow out of it, but it doesn't happen.

"What did you tell Hamisi?" She breaks the silence.

"As little as possible."

"What do the police think happened?"

"That Billy was murdered. But they don't know exactly when and how he died yet. Apparently the warm tropical water does strange things to the human body. I hear through the grapevine that they're looking for the last person who saw him alive. Let's hope it wasn't you."

"I don't know if we'll be so lucky. I think it might have been me, and Hamisi is going to find that out pretty soon. He called this morning—he wants to see me tomorrow. He told me not to go anywhere over the next few days. I have to stay in Dar until he has completed his investigation." She tries to smile. "You should be glad. It means we can be together every night."

She makes a fist, then opens it. The bandage lifts on the left, unable to stick in the folds of her hand.

She looks at me with bright eyes filled with worry. "Do you believe me, Alex? About Billy? Everything?"

I don't hesitate for a moment. "Yes. Of course I do."

21

Hamisi Bahame is a determined man. I ignore his call the first and second times, chiefly because I'm with Ranna—first having coffee in bed, and later kissing her goodbye in the morning air, yet again heavy with rain.

When Hamisi calls half an hour later, I'm back at my place shaving. I'm on my way to a media conference about the first American and British relief teams expected in Dar.

Over the past few days the city has been invaded by every possible acronym and initialism. BBC. ETV. CNN. AFP. Apparently Billy Jones's death is also on the agenda this morning. It promises to be a busy day. Jasmine sent word that she's looking for my story ASAP.

"Hamisi must be taking this thing personally," I said to Ranna last night as we finished dinner. The police are evidently under great pressure to come up with something. Anything.

What I didn't say was what I've been wondering about ever since the invitation to today's media conference arrived in my in-box. What if it's announced this morning that Ranna is the chief suspect? What if a desperate Hamisi puts her name on the table? She'll instantly be without an income, at least until the investigation is completed. And the media will tear her apart. She'll get no special treatment because she's one of them—us.

As I'm looking at the screen, the phone rings again. Hamisi's fourth attempt. I wipe the last of the shaving cream from my face. "Morning."

"You're a difficult man to get hold of."

"I'm not crazy about phones. How are you?"

He ignores my question. "Will you be at the conference today?"

"I'm on my way now. Why?"

"Come and see me afterward. There's something I want to ask you."

"About?"

"Ranna."

"Why don't you speak to her yourself? Why do I always end up in the middle?"

"Because she refuses to speak to me. She just sits there and stares at my forehead." There's a hissing sound on the line, as if he's smoking. "Please. I'll meet you outside the hotel afterward."

I'm lucky to find parking almost right in front of the Skylark Hotel. I sprint the ten yards to the foyer, covering my head with my notebook. I head straight for the elevators. I know where the conference rooms are. The government has held three media events at the hotel in the last few weeks, and it's where most of the international journalists usually stay.

Inside the biggest of the conference rooms seven other journalists are already waiting. The walls are decorated with an array of African masks and wildlife photographs from *National Geographic*. Zebra and cattle skins lie on the floor.

The decor looks like something from a safari magazine for tourists.

Tom is talking to an attractive young brunette in a colorful skirt and leather sandals. She has a posh British accent and weary eyes. I can make out fragments of the conversation—malaria, flu, and natural remedies. When he touches her arm as if they're old friends, she takes a step back, drinks the last of the water from the bottle in her hand, and begins to rummage in her handbag.

"Sorry, I have to take this call," she apologizes, and hurries through the door.

Neither of us heard a phone ring.

"Don't say a word, farm boy," Tom mutters, avoiding my eyes.

"Wouldn't dream of it. I would also have tried if I were you. She's beautiful."

Tom runs his hand over his bald head. "Only if you don't have Ranna."

His words take the wind from my sails. "I thought we were being discreet."

"You are. Exceptionally so. Few people would guess you're together, but I know Ranna." He gives a vague smile, but his eyes remain somber.

"What's the matter? Are you going to warn me off again?"

He shrugs. "Nope. That would sound like sour grapes. It's your turn. Ranna and I hooked up a long time ago, and I couldn't make it work, so congrats."

"It was never a competition."

He wets his lips and blinks once, twice. "No. But I bet you feel as if you've won first prize."

I don't know about that. "What exactly did I win, Tom? I still can't work it out."

"What do you mean?"

"How much trouble did I win?" I finally ask the Englishman what I've wanted to know for a long time, though I planned to do it later, more privately. "Why didn't you tell me about Billy Jones?"

He gives me a quizzical look. "Tell you what about him?"

For a moment I wonder whether his surprise is genuine. Maybe he really didn't think it necessary to tell me.

"Why didn't you mention Ranna's relationship with him? You told the police, but not me."

"I can't lie to the police."

"But you can lie to me?"

"I kept quiet. It's different."

"You sound like Ranna. It's her justification for everything."

Behind us the doors open, and everyone is ushered to their seats. The conference is about to begin.

Tom shakes his head. There's a hard expression in his eyes. "I've known Ranna for a very long time, Alex. You'd be stupid to think I trust you more than I trust her."

"Fuck you too."

He holds up his hands. "Relax, buddy. You're a decent person, make no mistake. But Ranna counts for more in my world. I've known her for years, though we see each other only when we happen to be working in the same country. So do me a favor: forget this honor thing where men supposedly have each other's backs. I'm not that guy."

22

The vice president speaks briefly but forcefully. His hands measure out his sentences. He expresses his gratitude for the international aid received already and asks for more money, helicopters, food, and medical supplies. Behind him the chief of the Tanzanian Red Cross nods his head in agreement. The Mkondoa River is in flood and Kilosa is underwater. The army and Red Cross have relocated most of the residents to tented camps, but it's a struggle to keep the tents standing in the rain.

Cameras flash—Ranna's as well—and although everyone seems to be listening attentively, the air is filled with anticipation, as if the vice president's speech is only a prologue to the news everyone got up for this morning.

When Hamisi Bahame appears on the podium, the humidity seems to intensify. The heat becomes more palpable. The air-conditioning more futile. At last, the better, the bigger story that will get more hits. More readers. More likes and shares.

What a stroke of luck for the government that Billy Jones died while Tanzania is experiencing its worst rains in thirty years, bringing the world media to its doorstep to alert everyone to the disaster. Or maybe it calls for resentment instead, because why does one death seem so much more important than all the other lives threatened by the rain?

Hamisi raises his hands to silence the buzz in the room. He begins to speak, setting out the circumstances around Billy's death.

It's clear that the policeman doesn't want to be here. He speaks even more curtly than the vice president, if possible. His eyes sweep across the assembled journalists, then jump to the left of the room and linger, first on Ranna, then on me at the back.

I squirm in my seat. Why does he want to talk to me after the press conference?

"Do you have any leads?" asks a journalist to my left when Hamisi has finished. It's the woman with the posh accent Tom spoke to earlier.

"Several," he answers. "But there's nothing we can share with you at this time. All we can say with certainty is that he was stabbed with a short, sharp object. We are not one hundred percent certain whether it caused his death. He also had several broken bones. This may be due to the collapse of his home. His house was completely destroyed. It might have been due to bad workmanship or because it was built much too close to the beach. The problem is that it all seems to have happened more or less at the same time—the collapse of the house and his death."

"So it may not be murder after all?" The posh lady speaks again, quick to read between the lines.

"Anything is possible," Hamisi says reluctantly. "Including murder. All we can say with reasonable certainty is that he didn't drown."

"What about suspects?" asks Tom.

"There are one or two." Again Hamisi's eyes stray toward Ranna.

She keeps taking photos as if nothing else matters.

"Come on!" another British voice calls out sarcastically. The press tag around the woman's neck says she's from the *Times*. "You can't just stand there and not give us anything. Surely you've made some progress? Isn't it true that the American government offered help with the investigation?"

There's a buzz among the journalists in the room. It's news to most of them.

Hamisi seems to be weighing his options. "Yes," he admits. "Interpol and the FBI offered their help because Billy Jones was the leader of an international business conglomerate. We've accepted a degree of assistance. But it wouldn't serve our purpose to bring in hundreds of foreigners. We don't even have a crime scene."

"What kind of help did they offer?" I'm surprised by the sound of my own voice.

Hamisi tilts his head slightly, his brown eyes suddenly sharper. A slight smile plays around his lips.

"Forensics. Pathology. An expertly conducted postmortem to determine the precise cause and time of death. It appears to be of crucial importance."

Ranna swings her backpack over her shoulder. "Are you going to file?"

I jam my hands into the pockets of my jeans. "Not yet. I want to have a quick word with Hamisi."

"About?"

"The story," I lie. "The postmortem."

"Okay. Are you coming to my place when you're done? Or how about yours?" A thought seems to strike her. "I've never seen where you live."

"You haven't missed much. It's like a cramped torture chamber. I'll come and write my story at your apartment when I'm done."

"Sounds good," she says, but remains standing.

"What's the matter?" I check the urge to look at my watch.

"That woman from the *Times* wanted to speak to me this morning. About Billy. About how we found the body. She managed to cook up some excellent sources in a very short time."

"And?"

"I said no. Told her we cover stories, we don't make them. It's just a coincidence that we found him."

"Sounds like a good answer."

"She wanted to talk to you as well. I gave her a wrong number. She asked what you look like. I told her short and ugly."

"That should buy us a little time. And thanks for the compliment."

She smiles. "Don't mention it." She looks around for her sunglasses and uses them to push back her hair. "So . . . see you later?" Her voice is small and uncertain.

"I'll be there as soon as I can," I promise guiltily.

23

I follow Hamisi outside the Skylark. I'm not the only one. He walks as fast as he can, but the reporters follow him down the stairs to the foyer and through the hotel's revolving doors. Outside on the sidewalk he looks up, annoyed, then sighs and turns to face them.

"It never rains when you want it to. Okay, then. Who's first?"

When the last journalist has turned around and headed off, cursing, I approach. Hamisi clearly doesn't want to say anything more to the press about Billy Jones. His repeated "no comment" still hangs in the air when I step up to greet him.

"Alex!" He sounds relieved. "I hope you don't have a bunch of questions as well. Thanks for coming."

"It didn't sound like I could refuse."

He lights a cigarette and draws the smoke deep into his lungs. "I suppose you could have, but your curiosity and your feelings for Ranna wouldn't allow it."

"Careful. You don't always know what I think and feel."

"Let me guess: one day I'm going to pay for my arrogance?"

"Without a doubt."

"But until then we can assume I know everything?" His tone is light and mocking.

"If it makes you feel better."

The policeman considers his next words carefully. "You heard what I said in there. It's very hard to determine exactly how and when Billy Jones died. Almost impossible, in fact, though I did my best to put a positive spin on it."

"Is that where the FBI and Interpol experts come in?"

"Mm-hmm. A forensic pathologist on loan from the FBI. She's landing later today. I spoke to her on the phone the day before yesterday." He frowns. "She's not very positive she'll find anything new."

"But it'll make a good story for the media."

"The hounds of hell? I imagine so."

"Will you let me speak to her?" Thunder rattles above our heads. We shuffle closer to the protection of the building.

"Maybe. You're not really a suspect, so I suppose I could get you an interview. Dr. Julia Gomez." He grinds out his cigarette butt with the heel of his shoe. "Her services are free. Won't cost me a shilling. The US Department of Defense is highly upset about Billy's death. He was doing work of a sensitive nature for them. Something to do with their ballistic missile program. They're fearing the worst in terms of state security."

Hamisi lights a fresh cigarette. "Of course, they're always fearing the worst, but that's their problem. From where I stand, Billy's death seems personal. An act committed in anger, yet with precision. Remember his missing fingers? The thing we urged you and Ranna not to mention to anyone? If it hadn't been for that, I might have considered his death accidental, but those cuts seem too precise, like someone played with a very sharp knife."

He jabs a thumb against his chest. "So, while Dr. Gomez is conducting her investigation, *I* have to work out why someone wanted Billy Jones dead. And in order to do so, I have to find out more about his relationships with the people around him. His relationship with Ranna, to be more specific."

He stops talking, but the silence speaks volumes.

"You keep harping on the same string," I say. "But like I've told you before—I can't help you. Ranna says her relationship with Billy ended before his death. That's all I know. All I want to know."

"Even though he paid thirty thousand dollars into her bank account a few days before his death?"

"Yes." I try to keep my expression neutral.

Hamisi smiles smugly. He must have noticed the confusion in my eyes.

"It's one advantage of international collaboration, Alex. Ranna and Billy both have US bank accounts. And I've received certain information about them. Interesting information."

I shrug. "The money doesn't prove anything. She worked for him. She's a very good photographer. So what."

"Thirty thousand dollars' worth of work? Maybe. Or maybe she was blackmailing him."

"Why would she blackmail him?"

The first raindrops drift down from the sky.

"It's impossible to know every little detail of what goes on between two people, Alex. Most of the time we're just guessing, don't you think?"

I dig in my pocket for my car keys. "Why are you giving me all this information? What do you want me to do with it? Print it?"

Suddenly I'm angry. What's the policeman's game? And more importantly: What's Ranna's game? Why didn't she mention the money? Why didn't she tell me about Billy in the first place?

Hamisi looks past the anger and sees my conflicting emotions. "I must get Ranna to talk to me, Alex. Something's wrong, but she refuses to answer any of my questions. She might know something that could help the investigation. Things aren't looking good for her, and if you're honest with yourself, you'll agree. I don't have enough evidence to charge her, but I can't eliminate her as a suspect either."

"And you want my help? I can't *make* her talk to you."

"Maybe we should try something else, then." Hamisi steps on the cigarette butt. Looks up at the sky, shivers. Clasps his hands together as if he is cold. "Tell me what she's doing. What she did. Whether she's hiding anything. If you're convinced of her innocence, prove it. And if that doesn't work, I appeal to your survival instinct."

"What do you mean?"

"You really have no idea, do you?"

"Listen, get to the point—quickly. I'm tired of your bloody games."

Hamisi's eyes drill into mine. "Ranna got money from Billy Jones on three occasions. She was questioned by the police in two countries in the course of murder investigations. The victim on each occasion was a man she'd been involved with. Only, three years ago her name wasn't Ranna Abramson. It was Isabel Baker."

24

"I don't fucking believe it!"

I bang on the steering wheel in anger and frustration. Swerve around an old Peugeot that has broken down in the middle of the road. What else is Ranna hiding from me? What else is she blatantly lying about? Murder, lust, theft—she single-handedly takes care of all of the ten biblical commandments.

And yet I refused to help Hamisi. Why?

Maybe it's incredulity rather than reluctance. Or maybe pride. I just can't believe she has lied to me so often and so freely. Or, how did she put it? *Kept quiet.*

She has kept quiet about many things—more than Hamisi realizes. I remember the name Isabel Baker. It's well-known in photographic circles. Isabel Baker refused to accept the World Press Photo award. What kind of person says no thank you to the World Press Photo award? And why would you say no after you've taken the trouble to enter?

I wonder whether the answer hasn't just landed in my lap. What if you wanted to avoid the attention it would bring? Especially from the police?

Ranna Abramson and Isabel Baker have to be one and the same woman. Isabel took a series of photos of a fire that destroyed a children's home in San Francisco. Eleven children and one fireman died. It was big news in South Africa because one of the firemen in the photos was originally from the East Rand.

The photos were excellent—just like Ranna's.

I always assumed Isabel Baker was American. But Ranna has an American passport, I remind myself, although she's originally from South Africa. At least I know that about her.

I must find out what the hell is going on. The only way I can make an informed decision is by gathering more information. Anger will serve no purpose. No one knows that better than me. People disappear in anger. Everything disappears.

Hamisi mentioned Paris and San Francisco. Two men. Two murders. Three cash deposits from Billy Jones, but countless possibilities. Even Hamisi had to admit that.

The money could have been a gift from Billy, or perhaps a loan. Or Ranna might have done some work for him, and he paid her in cash to avoid putting it through the books.

Or Ranna might be a hit woman, and Billy paid her to get rid of the men. Maybe Ranna then killed him when he threatened to go to the police when she ended their relationship.

Or Ranna might be a serial killer.

One thing is certain, I promise myself: I'm going to find out exactly what Ranna Abramson is hiding.

Back home I make myself a cup of coffee and sit down in front of my laptop. I write my news stories and then start the search for Ranna Abramson and Isabel Baker.

It's surprising what people will post on the Internet. They'll give their names, email addresses, and details about their workplace, children, family, and friends. They'll announce on Facebook whether they'll be home for Christmas and broadcast their future plans on Twitter and Instagram.

It's easy to find information if you know where to look. You gather almost everything you need from résumés, CVs, conference attendance, employee registers, and company websites. Not to mention school and university reunion databases. No problem.

But after a two-hour search I have to admit that Ranna Abramson is the exception. Ranna, or Isabel, or whatever her real name is, is barely present in the virtual community. There are a handful of articles that speculate about where she might be at present, but besides those, it's as if someone has gone to a great deal of trouble to erase every piece of information on Isabel Baker.

A single reference to Ranna Abramson dates from about three years ago. The most recent murder, of Gerard Peroux, occurred at about the same time. In Paris.

Ranna is a photographer, but I can't find any photographs of her. She's not on Facebook, and evidently never supplied any of her employers' websites with a portrait shot. It also seems she never got a photo credit. Ranna Abramson remains firmly on the other side of the lens.

Isabel Baker lived in Paris. Before that, in San Francisco, where she was a freelance photographer. For two and three years, respectively. After Paris she vanished into thin air.

This means that Isabel must have changed her name to Ranna while she was in Paris. It's the only place where the two names overlap.

The only sign I can find of Ranna in Dar es Salaam is on the Facebook profile of Hadhi's daughter-in-law, who posted the photo I took at the wedding, the one of everyone together on the dance floor.

Slim pickings for someone who has been in the city for almost three years.

I sit back from my laptop, yawn. It's almost twenty minutes past midnight. I called Ranna earlier to cancel our date. My reasons weren't very convincing—too tired, too much work. And the hours spent at the computer didn't deliver any results. I'm no wiser than when I sat down in the early evening.

Hamisi's Interpol and FBI colleagues must have better sources. I still don't know anything about the money Billy paid Ranna. Besides the photo on the cover of *Time*, I haven't been able to find any connection between her and the IT magnate.

I'll have to come up with something. Use better sources than those available to Hamisi or Interpol or the Americans.

Perhaps it's time to call Sarah.

Every journalist has a little black book. Whether the information is written on paper or saved in an iPhone is beside the point. I consider myself old-school and, true to the way Tank taught me, I keep all my contacts in a small notebook. It's the size of my palm and contains all the numbers and email addresses I might ever need, including those of Sarah Fourie.

Sarah grew up in Pretoria West. In what used to be called Church Street, in a tiny apartment over a café that sold everything from washing powder to chewing gum. Her parents loved her dearly, but they couldn't understand how, since the age of nine, she could spend so many hours at the computer—which had taken them three years to save up for.

Her father, an official at the Department of Water Affairs, wished Sarah was more like his other four children. But his pale, thin daughter was not at all interested in the Springbok rugby team, fishing, the beach, or camping. She was hooked instead on Coca-Cola, nicotine, and white chocolate.

When Diederik Fourie's eldest son was suddenly awarded a university scholarship despite his mediocre grades, no one paid much heed. Nor were they unduly surprised when the city council paid a refund into the Fouries' utility bill after having overcharged them for years. It was only when Nellie Fourie opened the door one morning to take delivery of a brand-new living room set, which no one had ordered, that Diederik smelled a rat.

Still he remained silent. He had a feeling that his oldest daughter was up to something illegal on the computer she kept upgrading, but he hoped she was clever enough not to get caught.

But Sarah became a little too generous.

The judge agreed, and seeing that she'd just turned eighteen the previous week, he sentenced her to eighteen months in prison and ordered her to pay back the money.

There were mitigating circumstances. She was young, a first offender; her father had made an emotional plea on her behalf, and she had used the money to benefit her family, not herself.

It was true. Sarah had not spent a cent on herself, except to support her habit of six cans of Coke and twenty cigarettes a day.

I covered Sarah's trial and did a little more work than was strictly necessary. I wrote about poverty, white-collar crime, and blue-collar pain. About Sarah, the why and the how.

She tracked me down from prison—heaven knows who gives a hacker access to a computer in prison—and said she liked my story. Apparently I had been the most objective among all the sensation mongers. Pale, delicate Sarah is exquisitely beautiful, and a beautiful young woman committing a crime to help her family almost compares to the fourth marriage of an Afrikaans pop singer on the media Richter scale.

I did two exclusive interviews with Sarah. She promised to help me if I ever needed anything.

I've already asked her once, just after she was released from prison. My request wasn't perfectly aboveboard, and I insisted on paying her. I suffered no guilt about what we did. It was the right thing to do. Sarah helped me to track down a pedophile, and neither of us had any regrets afterward.

Sarah is smarter nowadays. Much, much smarter. Her family has a vacation home on the South Coast, and her youngest sister is a talented gymnast who regularly competes abroad.

I have no desire to find out how they can afford such luxuries.

25

The next morning I sleep late and do a quick run to the shops to stock up on supplies. Greeted with mostly empty shelves, I make do with what I can gather. Back home I call Sarah Fourie.

I can hear I've woken her up. She mutters something into the phone, coughs. The bed creaks as she rolls over. I look at my watch. It's late morning, almost time for her to get up, so I may as well continue.

"Sarah? Hello? Sorry," I begin cautiously. The short woman has a temper completely out of proportion to her length.

Again the creaking bed. A groan—hers, thankfully—or I'd immediately have put the phone down. "Alex. Dammit."

"Shall I call back later?"

I hear her sit up, stumble out of bed, stretch, and light a cigarette. Inhale. Open a can. Sarah has been trying to quit smoking for four years. Coke has never made the list of bad habits she feels the need to kick.

"Okay. Let's try again," she says at last.

"Hi, Sarah."

"Hello. What can I do for you?"

"I need your help."

She laughs softly, the sound grating in my ear. Over the past few years smoking has made her naturally low voice even huskier. "You never phone to say you're coming over for coffee. Why not?"

"Because you're too young. Otherwise I would've beaten down your door. You know that."

"You keep saying that, but I'm almost twenty-three."

"And I'm nearing forty."

"Nothing but numbers. Age doesn't have to come between us." She crumples the can, and I can hear the metal crack. "But okay. Let's talk business. I could do with a new fridge."

"How much is the model you've got in mind?"

"You don't necessarily have to buy a new one, but if you want to, why not? I'm game."

What she really wants to know is whether my request involves any illegal digging. Her fee always takes risk into account, and few risks are too great for her. I'm not quite sure that prison rehabilitated her in any way. It just taught her to be more careful about getting caught.

"Nothing too substantial . . . I hope." Clearly I don't know enough about Ranna to make any promises.

"Shoot."

I explain that I'm looking for information—anything she can find on Ranna Abramson, aka Isabel Baker, and the two murder victims connected to her.

"We can negotiate the fee when I'm done, but it will probably come to the same as last time. Maybe a little cheaper."

She stops talking. I can hear there's something she's not saying.

"What?" I try to keep my voice light. "Not a big enough job for you? Or not exciting enough?"

"This woman means a lot to you." She doesn't want to make it a question, but she can't help it.

I hold my breath, then let it out slowly. "Yes."

"If you're looking for this kind of information, she must be bad news. Drop her. Find yourself a Cape Town girl with a rich daddy. You know, one with an almost clear conscience and a tanned beach body."

"Can't."

"Why always go for the troublemakers? What is it you say? Chaos."

We both know what she's referring to. There was a night, two years ago, when we nearly ended up in her bed. The only thing that saved us was that she was too drunk to remember where it was, and I was too sober to take her to my apartment. Finally we sat drinking coffee at the Palace Hotel in Pretoria West until four in the morning. When the fog of alcohol lifted, we drove to our respective beds.

I shake my head as if Sarah can see me. Rub my stiff neck muscles, suddenly exhausted. I can't lie to her.

"You're right, Sarah. Chaos. Always bloody chaos."

26

I have to be patient, no matter how hard it is. That's what Sarah said. I must do nothing until she has gathered more information about Ranna.

But waiting is easier said than done. I feel as if I'm losing my mind, and it doesn't help matters that the woman from the *Times* keeps calling, wanting to know when and how we discovered the body.

Billy Jones seems to have risen from the dead and moved in with me.

And still the rain keeps falling. It's been weeks since I last felt the sun on my skin. The water has begun to rise in the streets and is starting to lap against Ranna's front door, as if her apartment is a ship that has run aground. Apparently Hadhi dropped off some sandbags early this morning. Just in case.

My studio is on the third floor, so I have fewer worries keeping me awake at night. But that doesn't mean I'm not also sick and tired of the rain. Ranna and I both are. We'll do anything not to have to see it. Stand in it. Do another story about flood damage and take another photo of drowned cattle.

The local papers are still faithfully covering the floods. Several places in Dar es Salaam already show deep scars. Four neighborhoods, 127 houses, and three bridges in and around the city have been washed away, and no one knows where the money to rebuild them will come from.

I close the newspaper, put it down on the stack of books next to the couch. I can't focus. It's early evening, and we've finished our dinner, having decided to stay in for the night. Ranna is in the kitchen, making coffee. Just like when she's cooking, her movements are brusque and impatient.

Water. Milk. Stir.

Her neck shows the reckless marks of my mouth, and I know my back looks even worse, her pent-up frustration scratched into my skin.

Wordlessly she puts the coffee in front of me. I sip, pull a face. She forgot the sugar. I get up to fetch it.

"Sorry," she mumbles from the couch.

I shrug, as if it's of no importance.

And it *is* of no importance, I realize. None at all. What's important is what's happening between us. The lies. The mistrust. The frustration seething just below boiling point.

Three days have passed, and I haven't heard a word from Sarah. No word from Hamisi either. As far as I know, Dr. Julia Gomez arrived some time ago. I left two messages on Hamisi's phone, asking for an interview with her.

I pour the coffee into the sink and sit down next to Ranna.

"Tell me about your parents," I ask.

Her eyes remain glued to the TV screen, where a man and a woman are steaming up the windows of an old Buick. "Why?"

"Because I'd like to know. I want to know why you drink your coffee bitter. I want to know whether you were too poor for sugar or whether you like it that way. Whether your dad lifted you up on his shoulders when you were young. Whether you got to see the world from above. Whether that was why you decided to be a photographer. When you decided you wanted to be a photographer."

"Because I like it that way. No. No. And no. When I was seventeen."

Her answers strike me like hammer blows. Each one precise and measured, in cold, neutral Afrikaans. It's the accent of someone who no longer comes from anywhere, but from everywhere. Not from Malmesbury, the Cape Flats, Pretoria, or the Richtersveld.

"Fuck it, Ranna. I asked you a few simple, innocent questions."

She turns to me, fire in her eyes. "Why are you always going on about the past?"

"Because it affects what's happening now. It affects us."

"Only if you let it." Her voice is still sharp, but her eyes reveal an unexpected softness. A plea.

I'm about to argue, but decide against it. Not today. It's not worth it. Maybe none of this is worth it. Not she, nor this thing between us that still doesn't have a name.

I get up, grab my car keys from the kitchen counter. "See you later. I'm going to Hardings for a beer."

"Maybe you're right!" she calls out behind my back. "Maybe we *should* let it go. Maybe this is a mistake. Wishful thinking. Nothing more."

I slam the front door behind me, furious that she can read my mind.

"Alex, you've got problems."

Despite having downed two beers and four tequilas, I recognize Sarah's voice at once. The tequilas were the result of Tom arriving at Hardings looking for a drinking buddy.

Ranna has called twice, but each time I silenced the phone.

Tom wants to know what's going on, and I ignore him with equal success.

"Hi." I turn my back on the Englishman. The last thing I want is for him to eavesdrop on the conversation and report back to Ranna. "What kind of problems?"

"This chick of yours is by no means kosher."

I struggle to hear. It doesn't help matters that John Lee Hooker is singing at the top of his voice in Sarah's apartment. "What . . . ?"

"I said . . ."

"Just hang on a moment. I'm walking out. And turn that music down. I know you like blues, but hell." I hold up my hand as if she can see me and slide off the barstool. "I can't hear a thing."

I walk out of Hardings and make my way through the tourists, high-class hookers, and hard drinkers milling about on the wet pavement, laughing and shouting to make themselves heard. I have to walk two blocks before their numbers begin to dwindle.

I stop in the entrance to a clothing store and put the phone back to my ear. The music is gone, the night quiet. "Okay, that's better. I'm listening."

"Isabel's father took his own life when she was eleven. He was a nasty piece of work. He beat the shit out of her mother, Karla, on a regular basis. The cops wondered whether Karla might have shot him—the papers suggested it—but no one could prove anything. Karla remarried a few years later. A wealthy surgeon, well-known in Jewish circles. Isabel moved to New York with her mommy and new daddy. It should have been a quiet, happy-ever-after life, but then Isabel began to work as a photographer. She was pretty good at it. In time she made a name for herself, but then the funny business started."

I hear the click of a mouse. And again. "First Isabel took her mother's maiden name: Baker. She said Kroon had been her father's name, and she wanted to forget him."

"Okay, nothing wrong with that." It doesn't sound so bad. On the contrary, it seems a good reason to change your name. One I can understand.

"Not so fast," Sarah says. "Things began to look dark for our Ranna."

"Yes?"

"She moved to San Francisco, still as Isabel. Her lover of a few months, Peter Fox, was murdered in his apartment. It was a few months after she had taken those pictures that won her the World Press Photo award. It looked like a botched robbery, but the cops weren't convinced.

Isabel moved to Paris. New life, new love—Gerard Peroux, a journalist. They got engaged. When he died in a car accident, Interpol took an interest in her. The driver who had caused the accident was never found. Isabel went missing and reappeared as Ranna Abramson. In Paris, briefly, then in Dar es Salaam."

"Shit." I move back deeper into the shelter of the store entrance as the rain starts drizzling down. Watch as a couple of women run to meet a taxi in the street.

"You can say that again," Sarah says. "Does this have anything to do with Billy Jones's murder?"

"How do you know about him?"

"It's made headlines over here too. You should know, you wrote some of the stories. And remember, we're talking about the man who rivaled Bill Gates with his open-source software. And there are rumors about billion-dollar contracts with the Pentagon. So of course I know about him. I just wish I knew more. The papers speculate that he was murdered in his lavish vacation home in Dar es Salaam just before the place was swept away in the flood. Apparently he was building a hotel in Zanzibar. Property development was one of his hobbies. Along with parachuting and playing Fortnite."

I should have known Sarah would fit all the puzzle pieces together.

"This girl of yours is bad news, Alex." She repeats her earlier warning. "Bad news in capital letters. She's a female spider. Mate and kill."

"But you said there's no proof she had anything to do with the deaths of Fox and Peroux. One was a robbery and the other a road accident."

I can almost hear Sarah shaking her head.

"The cops in Paris suspected her of Peroux's murder, but they had to drop the investigation for lack of evidence and motive. After that, Interpol flagged her. And the FBI, because she's an American citizen. No one has been able to prove anything, but there were definitely things that made the police wonder. One woman can't have that much bad luck."

"You're probably right. Thanks for the info, Sarah. I appreciate it. I'll deposit your payment in your account. I gave you three thousand last time—is it still okay?"

"For you, yes. But only if you promise to come by for a whiskey when you're back. And not at the Palace, like last time."

I ignore her smoldering tone. "Thanks. You've been a great help."

She gives an exaggerated sigh, then says, "Alex, I know you don't want to hear it, because it's clear this woman means something to you, but be careful."

I wake up in the middle of the night, rain streaming down the windows. My apartment is dark and airless, and I can smell the sweat on my own body. It's four minutes past midnight, and I'm gasping for breath. I had a dream, the kind I used to have as a child, but with a different set of characters. Ranna killed me with the knife I used to cut meat in her kitchen yesterday.

I lie back on the bed. The situation is absurd. Like a third-rate Hollywood movie. Why don't I just talk to Ranna?

Because she'll lie to you.

I want to ignore the voice in my head, but I know it's true. Ranna will say little or nothing, or she'll tell me to take my stuff and fuck off. She closes up as soon as I ask about her past.

And what about Hamisi Bahame? What if I tell him what I know?

But what do I actually know? And I have no proof. Everything I know points to possibilities. Circumstances. Nothing more. And none of it is likely to be news to him. Except perhaps that Billy stabbed Ranna with a cheese knife when she wanted to break off their relationship.

Or so she says.

Worst of all is that I suddenly understand why Hamisi believes Ranna might have killed Billy Jones.

27

Tom meets me for an early breakfast at the Skylark. He didn't ask why I want to see him, just told me on the phone I'd have to pick up the bill and warned me he was hungry.

He looks relaxed as he sits down opposite me.

"Morning. Sleep well?" he chirps.

"How can you be so perky after last night?" I touch the sides of my head, where a hangover persists.

"Tequila doesn't bother me. Besides, I left just after you and your phone did a disappearing act."

He doesn't sound angry, nor does he ask what happened.

I study his face and notice the crow's feet around his eyes. His forehead is a maze of lines. How old is Tom? Late thirties? Early forties? I know as little about him as I do about Ranna. He was born in Manchester, likes tequila, hates flying, and has been here for fifteen months. That's about it, and I doubt I'll ever know more.

We order coffee and the English breakfast. Tom didn't lie about being hungry. Halfway through his bacon and eggs he orders more toast. We eat overlooking the waterlogged street, full of sinkholes. The rain has left its mark on the hotel as well. Water is dripping monotonously into buckets, and large sections of the carpet in the foyer and dining room are soaked. The waiter says we're lucky to get breakfast. There's no electricity in the kitchen, and gas is only sporadically available.

We're still eating when the rain begins to come down again. When the waiter brings more coffee, he seems on the verge of tears. I find the expression on his face comical until I realize I'm equally fed up with the endless rain. How much is enough? More than enough? Haven't we passed that point yet?

Tom mops up the last of the egg yolk on his plate with a piece of toast and sighs contentedly. "So, what can I do for you? You sounded pissed off when you phoned."

"It's Ranna."

The Englishman laughs as if he should have known. "I told you she'll chew you up and spit you out."

"Everyone warns me against her, but no one tells me why."

"What happened?"

"There's a lot she's not telling me." I point at him, almost amused by the sudden pang of jealousy I feel. "Things I suspect you know."

"Yeah? Like what?" Tom's brown eyes deepen to an inscrutable black.

"Tell me about Isabel Baker."

He blinks a few times. He seems surprised that I know about Ranna's changed identity.

"Why did she change her name? You worked with her in Paris for a while. You must know something."

"If you don't know the answer to that question, I assume Ranna doesn't know you're here?"

"No."

Tom seems to think it over. "I don't know what I can tell you. If Ranna didn't say anything, she must have a good reason. Maybe she doesn't trust you."

His face is deadpan, but the message is clear: his loyalty to Ranna remains unconditional.

"Tom, there are things about Ranna that don't make sense. Things like her strange relationship with Billy. The money. The dead men. Even you must know that." I watch him carefully to see whether he knows what I'm talking about.

His eyes widen at my mention of the money, as if it's news to him, but he shows no reaction to the rest.

"Why do men die when Ranna is near? You know something, I can see it."

The shorter, sturdy man runs his hand over the stubble on his chin. Licks his lips, closes his eyes for a moment. Tilts his head to the left, right.

"I don't know much," he says at last. "Men become obsessed with her. She's like poison. Nicotine. A drug that will lift you up and throw you down. She gets in your blood and you can't get rid of her, and you don't know why. So men fall for her. They die. Maybe they stop using their heads when they're with her. Like you."

"Bullshit."

I sit back as the waiter clears our plates, brings another round of coffee.

Tom waits until we're alone again. "Come on, Alex. When's the last time you filed a decent story? Something worthwhile. Front-page quality. Hmm? Ranna's fucked you up completely. She's all you think about. She's made you lose your head. Before you know it, you'll be crossing a street without looking, and a bus will run you over. And then you'll be the next one gone."

"You sound as if you know what you're talking about. As if it happened to you as well."

He averts his eyes. "Of course I know, and I was the one guy who really should have known better. It's crazy." His index finger draws a circle against his temple. "We lasted a week, yet I still can't forget her. Every time I see the two of you together, I wonder what the hell I did wrong."

"Maybe you're the lucky one. You're still breathing."

"What happened to those guys were accidents, not murders. Ranna will tell you the same thing."

"That's not what the cops think."

"Why? What do they say?"

"They don't have the same high opinion of Ranna you seem to have." I beckon to the waiter and ask for the bill. "Not in the least."

Hamisi stares at me over his spectacles, his eyes inscrutable. The hands that have been flicking through a series of photos of Billy's body remain suspended in the air. Outside his office a man calls to someone, laughs.

I can't help thinking how he's part of this place. How it seems as if he belongs here. I always feel like the outsider, the unwelcome visitor, even at home. Maybe it's time to ask for a transfer. Or look for a new job. Chaos lives everywhere, after all.

Hamisi pushes his glasses up his nose, takes them off. "Say that again?" he says with the same surprise as before. He fumbles with the half-full pack of Dunhills in front of him.

"How sure are you that Ranna is guilty?" I repeat my earlier question.

"Guilty of what?"

"Stop the games, Hamisi. Please. Did Ranna kill Billy Jones? Do you have any proof? Evidence?"

He gathers up the grainy photographs. Stacks them so that they're lined up with the corner of his desk. Turns them over, as if he wants to give the mutilated body some privacy.

"Alex, there's something odd about Ranna, and you know it. Something isn't quite right. The name change. The men in her life who tend to die. Billy. The money. Too many bad things happen when Ranna Abramson is around."

"Maybe, yes. But that doesn't mean she killed Billy Jones."

The slight smile again. He picks up the packet of cigarettes. Puts it down.

"I can't prove anything yet, and maybe I never will," he admits. "The sea took its toll, so it seems no one can tell me exactly when Billy died. Not even our imported expert. The body was in the water too long. Neither can Dr. Gomez confirm that he was indeed murdered. He might simply have ended up in the water along with his house. The tides support that theory. There are some question marks regarding the fingers, but their disappearance might have been the result of nothing more sinister than hungry fish."

He shrugs, frowns. "All she could do was confirm what we already knew, namely that Billy didn't drown. So it doesn't matter whether I think it was murder. I don't know when he died, I don't know how he died, I don't have a murder weapon, and I have no idea where to begin searching for one. Billy's house, which was most likely the crime scene, was swept out to sea. I think someone was very, very lucky. I think someone got away with murder."

He adjusts the stack of photographs. "And yes, I must admit: there's no concrete evidence against Ranna. No one saw them together. Billy gave her money, but what does that prove? I hear he even left her money in his will, but enough to commit murder? It's no more than $100,000, and I can't believe Ranna was desperate enough to kill him for such a meager amount. I'd imagine he was worth more to her alive. I can't use the other men's deaths to prove she killed Billy either. It points to a pattern, but not to Ranna's guilt."

Carefully Hamisi smooths out the creases in his sleeves. Glances up at me. "That is, unless you've found out something that can help me. That's why I came to you right at the beginning. You look innocent and harmless, but you're wide awake. You notice things other people overlook. And I suspect you're not the type of guy to lie to yourself."

He sits back and waits for my reply.

He'll wait in vain. I think about Ranna. About what Hamisi may suspect but doesn't know with any certainty. The night at Hardings. The blood on her shoulder. The T-shirt in her sink. I think of her father. Of my father.

I breathe in. Out. I'm not going to be the one to give Ranna up to the law. No matter what she might have done.

"No, Hamisi," I say at last. "I know no more than you."

28

Hamisi is right. I don't lie to myself. Too many people do that, ending up in places they never intended to be. I put the cup of tea down next to the bathtub and watch Ranna shave her legs, but all I can think is that she's actually Isabel Baker. The famous photographer.

The question is out before I can stop it. "Why did you change your name?"

She freezes. Lowers her left leg slowly into the water. "Shall I ask how you know, or immediately put the blame on Hamisi Bahame?"

"You refused to tell him anything. Of course he's going to come and talk to me. He's a cop. He has to do his job."

"I talked to Hamisi, but he asked questions I don't have the answers to. I didn't do anything. If he thinks I did, he can arrest me," she snaps.

"Wait a minute." The conversation is taking a wrong turn. I'm not looking for an argument, just fishing for information. "This is not about your guilt or innocence, Ranna. Hamisi merely mentioned that you changed your name and asked me if I knew why."

I may not lie to myself, but it seems I'm quite willing to lie to other people.

She resumes shaving with long, rapid strokes. "I changed my name when I converted to Judaism."

"What?" It's the last answer I expected.

"Yes, yes, I know. It was a craze and it was soon over. My stepfather is Jewish. I felt it was something I could do for him after everything he had done for my mother and me."

"What did he do?"

"He took us to New York. Put me through college."

"And your father?"

"He's dead."

"How did he die?"

"Why are you asking all these questions, Alex?" She leans forward to turn on the hot tap, steam rising from her smooth, pale back.

"I wonder why anyone would say no to the World Press Photo award. The San Francisco fire was a huge story. The fact that there wasn't adequate water pressure to extinguish the flames, that it took five hours to get things under control. The children and the fireman who died. You documented it all."

"Exactly. All those children who died in the fire. Should I get an award for that? Should I be reminded every day how I heard them scream but took photos instead of helping?" She lifts her right leg out of the water and begins to shave it. "Maybe I thought changing my name would help. Maybe I hoped to start over."

She puts the razor down, picks up the cup, and sips her tea. "I don't want to be reminded of that day, Alex. I'll tell you everything you want to know about my past, but can we please just put this thing with Billy behind us first?"

There are many things I want to say, such as the fact that I know there won't be a later. Instead, I fish the sponge from the water and begin to wash her back. There's no need to point out there's a sheer drop ahead if everyone can see it coming. The same goes for the end of a relationship.

The rain keeps falling, and the periods of silence between Ranna and me lengthen.

Hamisi doesn't call again.

The police hold one last media conference. They ask anyone with information about Billy Jones's death to come forward, but no one does.

Dr. Julia Gomez grants two interviews. One to me and one to CNN. She explains why it's impossible to say exactly how and when the IT billionaire died.

Billy Jones's death is declared an accident. Most members of the international media go home; some stay, hoping for further developments. The rain washes it from the news cycle.

The day my interview with Dr. Gomez is published, the death count in the floods stands at 599 people and 987 head of cattle. Seventy thousand people are living in tented camps. My article is on the front page of three papers. The one I wrote about the floods has made page five in one daily and page thirteen in another.

Then, just like that, it stops raining.

I wake up next to Ranna one morning, and there's no water rushing down the windowpanes of her apartment. The air no longer smells musty and old. The sky is a clear expanse of blue, like the first day I got off the plane in Dar. The sun is shining. Birds still unfamiliar to me are singing as if they have rediscovered their voices.

In the days that follow, the stretches of water disappear. People who found shelter in the city return to their homes. The government thanks everyone for their help. The Red Cross warns against the spread of cholera, but announces that the situation is improving.

Hamisi Bahame invites me for one last beer at Hardings. He's throwing in the towel, he says, though he's still convinced Billy Jones was murdered. He tells me Ranna is still his number-one suspect. He warns me to be careful. America's Defense Department is nervous, and nervous people have long memories. Next time Ranna won't get away so easily, he says with conviction. There will be no flood to save her.

I assure him he's unduly worried. I'm on my way back to South Africa anyway. Going home. Without Ranna. No one can get through to her, and I'm tired of trying.

Her hand rests on my chest. She clenches it into a fist, as if she's angry. Then she opens it, as if she wants to let it go.

Close. Open. Close.

We're in bed in her apartment. It's early morning. I've buried my face in her neck one last time, speaking her name as I spilled into her body, something I don't usually do. Maybe I'm feeling sentimental. Maybe I'm screwed for life.

"You're not here anymore," she says softly.

I sigh. "You've never been here."

"That's not true. I was here. I am here. Look." She covers her eyes with her hands and removes them, like a child playing peekaboo. I don't laugh.

She rolls onto her stomach, away from me. I lean on my elbow, put my hand in the hollow of her back.

"Tell me. Tell me about your father. About Gerard. Peter. Billy." I finally ask what I've wanted to know for so long. "I keep waiting for you to say something, anything, but you don't."

She lies motionless for a moment, then turns onto her back. Searches out my eyes. "You've done your homework."

"I had to."

"Why? Are you scared I'll kill you too? Afraid you might be involved in some 'accident'?"

"I don't know what to think."

Her body stiffens under my hand. "But you *are* wondering if I might do something to you?"

She jumps out of bed when I don't reply.

"You don't know anything."

"Ranna, don't be silly."

Slowly I swing my legs over the edge of the bed, afraid that any sudden movement might upset her even further. "Help me understand." I catch her left hand in mine, hold it. "Ranna. Help me. Please."

"You wouldn't believe me if I told you the truth, just like every man I've ever tried to convince. Every detective and lawyer."

"What are we talking about? I don't understand."

She pulls her hand from mine and sits down next to me. Wraps her arms around her body. When she finally speaks, her tone is clipped.

"Okay, I'll tell you what you want to know. You're about to leave anyway. By now I know goodbye sex when I see it. I've just never understood how sad it is, because I'm usually the one handing it out."

"Ranna, I—" I try to calm her, though I have no idea why. She's right.

She silences me with open hands.

"There's a man," she says at last, speaking softly. "I don't know his name. I don't know who he is. Sometimes I imagine I see him from the corner of my eye. Short brown hair. At other times blond. Thin. At other times not. He's been following me since I was twenty-six—as far as I know. Maybe even longer."

"A man? Okay. And what does he do?"

"Kill everyone I love."

I lean back in surprise. "Everyone? Is that even possible?"

Her eyes widen at my reply. She jumps up and begins searching for her clothes. "You know what I mean. Men I love."

"How is that even possible?"

"Here we go. Same old questions I've heard a million times before."

She pulls on her jeans. The white T-shirt that hugs her breasts. Socks. The worn brown boots.

"Everyone I sleep with dies, Alex. And I keep running, but I can't escape. I've moved around so many times I've lost all sense of direction." She shakes her head, furious. "I spent three days in a prison cell in Paris after Gerard's death because I told the police everything and they didn't believe me. So I changed my name. Moved again. I thought it would be enough. And now? Now he's back. After almost three years of peace here in Dar. I really believed he was gone."

She thumps her chest. "Look at me, Alex. I'm the one person who knows everything there is to know about loneliness. About having nothing or no one."

I try to stop the deluge of words. "Ranna, I don't understand. Do you really mean this man kills everyone you have a relationship with?"

When I say it out loud, it sounds even more far-fetched. What if Ranna killed Billy, and this wild tale is her alibi?

"Yes."

"Why don't you talk to the police?"

"Weren't you listening, Alex? I tried! Gerard . . . we were engaged. I loved him. I told the French police everything, but they couldn't find any proof that my story was true. I don't go to the police anymore because I don't have a shred of evidence. At most I get a phone call in the middle of the night. He . . . this man . . . never says anything. Only when someone is dead, he'll speak. 'You don't deserve him.' That's all he says."

Next door Ranna's neighbors laugh. A car door slams.

"And his voice?" I ask. "Don't you recognize it?"

"He disguises his voice. You know, like in the movies. A low, metallic tone. These days anyone can buy those devices online."

"And the number?"

"The French police took the trouble to trace the number. It belonged to a coffee shop. They questioned the staff but found nothing out of the ordinary. To the French it meant I was lying, but to me it said he was too clever for them. How easy is it to use someone's phone?" She points to my Samsung lying next to the bed. "'Oh, sorry, my car broke down, do you mind if I use your phone to call a tow truck?'"

"Did the same happen after Billy's death? Did you get a call?"

I can see she doesn't like the answer she has to give me. "I haven't heard from him since Billy died. But I know it's him. And I no longer answer my phone if I don't know who's calling."

"How do you know he's involved in Billy's death then?" I insist.

"I see Hamisi didn't tell you everything. It's the fingers. Peter, Gerard, Billy—they were all found minus one or two fingers. Up until Billy I thought it was a coincidence, but now I know better."

"It could have been the sea. That's what Dr. Gomez thinks."

"It's the same pattern. And it's not just the fingers. This man orchestrates it so that I lose someone I care about and the police suspect me. There's always just too little evidence to charge me, but enough for the police to make my life a living hell and for everyone else I care about to take off. It means I have to pack up and start over in some strange country where nobody knows who I am. Every time." Her hands become fists, frustration etched on her face.

I go over the facts in my mind. Think of the phone calls she kept trying to avoid. The name change. Her wariness of getting involved with me. Tom's warning.

Tom.

"But Tom is still alive?"

She turns away from me, starts pacing the floor. "Tom was just one or two stupid nights. It was over before anyone knew about it."

Again she sits down next to me on the bed. Runs her hands over her face, her hair. "And then you came," she says quietly. "And I wasn't lonely anymore. Or alone. Just in love. And I forgot to be careful. It's been three years . . . I was sure I'd gotten away this time. I convinced myself the calls were really wrong numbers. It happens every now and then. For once I just wanted to be happy."

I nod slowly. "Okay. So Billy is dead . . . why am I still alive?"

"Because I was careful not to tell anyone about us, just in case. To hide you from the world as best I could. And I really thought that I was in the clear. I would never put you in danger."

She stares into my face, probably failing to find what's she looking for as her voice turns angry again. "Besides, I knew you wouldn't last. I knew you would pack up and go before we could draw attention to ourselves."

Her words sting, like they were supposed to do. I look down at my clenched hands. Force them open. "You don't act like someone who has a stalker. You sleep with your windows wide open."

"That's because I don't have a stalker. Only the men I love do." She's silent for a moment. "I wish it was me. I wish I was the one whose life was in danger, but I'm not. All I feel is guilt about all the men who have lost their lives because of me."

I still don't get it. "Why isn't it you?"

"What do you mean?"

"I don't understand," I try to explain. "A stalker fixates on a woman. He wants her. Physically. Mentally. It's about possession. Obsession. But this man . . . it's almost as if he's angry with you. As if you've done something to him and he wants to punish you. He doesn't take out his anger on you only once. He draws it out. Punishes you repeatedly. Is that what you're saying?"

"Yes."

"Okay." I consider her answer. "And how does the money fit into all of this?"

She looks at me as if I couldn't have said a more inappropriate word. "Money?"

"Billy Jones deposited money into your account on a number of occasions."

It's clear from the look on her face she had no idea I knew about the money.

"Billy was an old friend," she says finally. "He helped me start over every time. Until he began to want more, and I was too tired to fight it."

"More?"

"You know what I mean. I've told you." She stares at her boots.

"And the money just before his death?"

"It was in case I needed it. He was very angry when I met you, but he still loved me. He deposited money in my account one last time, in case I had to flee Dar."

I retreat from the edge of the bed, away from her, until I'm leaning against the wall, the sheets tangled between my legs, the plaster cool against my skin.

"Why are you only telling me now?" I ask.

She turns to face me. "I would have lost you. You wouldn't have believed me. Be honest: I sound like a complete nutjob."

"No. It sounds like"—I search for the right words—"a handy excuse."

Her eyes bore into mine, but this time there's no anger. Every emotion seems to have been extinguished, except one: defeat.

Or guilt, perhaps?

"You have a different story every time," I say. "First you don't know Billy. Then you know him. Then you slept together. Then he's actually just an old friend. Hamisi is right: I can't trust you."

"Hamisi? He knows nothing. Like every other cop, he sees only what he wants to see. And you? You're doing exactly what I expected you to do. It sounds so far-fetched that it must be a lie."

She gets up, her eyes wounded. Because she's been caught out?

"Go. I have work to do." She gazes past me at something on the wall.

"Ranna, please just give me something more . . . what he looks like, who he is. Anything. Give me more than these vague answers, these vague explanations. Surely you must have your suspicions about who it could be?"

"I really don't know. And it doesn't matter anyway," she says, and picks up her phone from the bedside table. "It's clear he's back. It's better that you go. He'll know about you by now."

She puts her sunglasses and wallet into her backpack. Retrieves the sunglasses and puts them on. Slings the backpack over her shoulder and walks out the door with long, purposeful strides.

29

Four shirts and three pairs of jeans will do the trick. The rest I'll give away before I get on the plane. I zip up the sports bag, open it again, and look at the collection of objects on the coffee table next to the couch I bought for a bargain at a secondhand shop. I walk over, pack the photo of Ranna and Hadhi at the wedding, but the seashell Ranna and I picked up the day we found Billy's body ends up in the trash.

Finally I make the call I've been avoiding all morning. "Hello, Ma. How are you?"

She's happy to hear from me, as always. "Fine, my boy. You?"

"Fine, thanks," I lie. "How's the farm?"

"We've had some unseasonal rains. We might see a few flowers in a while. The weather has been strange this year."

"Flowers? You can't be serious." They usually appear around September only.

"Would I joke about something like that?"

A beep warns me someone else is trying to get through. "Just a moment, Ma."

I hold up the phone to look at the screen. The journalist from the *Times* again. She's the second-to-last person I want to talk to.

I put the receiver back to my ear. "Sorry, Ma. I'm back." I walk to the bathroom. Grab my toothbrush. Shaver. "No wonder you've had rain. I'm coming back to South Africa."

"Really? When?"

She seems to cheer up instantly. I can almost see the hesitant smile on her thin face, the hands hiding in the white apron. I imagine her biting her lower lip, careful not to get too excited.

"I should be landing the day after tomorrow."

"So soon? Are you in trouble?" she asks, worried.

"No. Not at all."

She's silent.

I suppress a sigh. "I got a good job in Joburg, but I thought I'd come to the farm first for two weeks' vacation. If it's okay? I miss you."

"You know you are always welcome. It would be lovely to see you."

I can hear she's happy, and I know why. She misses me, yes, but my presence will also reduce the strain. Change my father's mood into something akin to two weeks of blessed peace—though it will hardly be more than a truce.

As soon as I leave, he'll start again. She'll have to travel a hundred miles to a clinic where no one knows her so that a newly qualified young doctor can tell her that she, Sophia Derksen, deserves better.

She'll nod submissively, say yes, and take the prescription for painkillers. Back home she'll swallow three at a time with tepid tap water and start to make my father's dinner.

PART TWO

RANNA

1

Emperor butterflies migrate more than eighteen hundred miles every year to survive the winter. Instinct drives them to where they must be. Where it's warm and the conditions for their survival are optimal.

That's what all the books say.

People call it the butterfly effect when they explain how one thing can influence a myriad others. How, when a butterfly flaps its wings in Dar es Salaam, something can happen days later in a different part of the world.

That's why I like butterflies. I know what it means to leave everything you know and love behind, just as I understand how one thing—one person—can change all your carefully laid plans. That's why I'm alone again, after all.

An invisible man has brought Alex and me to this point. An invisible man and my lies and silence. Can't deny it.

I only wish Alex could realize a miracle doesn't always mean a complete turnaround from certain death. An accident you survive. Cancer that goes into remission. Sometimes the miracle lies in what doesn't happen, in what is averted before it can happen.

If only Alex knew what didn't happen. If only he could understand that he has survived me. That I love him in a way that people like himself write stories about, and still he got away. Unharmed and unscathed. Un. Un. Un.

I down another tequila, without salt or lemon. It leaves a bitter taste at the back of my throat.

"Stay," I tell myself, staring at a group of tourists walking into Hardings. With the rain gone, the tourist trade has started to show some signs of recovery.

I fill the glass again, empty it. "Go."

By now the action is mechanical. Pour. Drink. I'm sure I'll have the answer by the time the bottle is empty. Should I stay in Dar, or start over somewhere else?

But is starting over worth it at all? He'll just find me and take everything away from me again. I've lost Alex. I lost Peter. I almost married Gerard, and Gerard wasn't Alex. Not even close.

I wish this fucking man would come out of hiding and face me, but he's much too cruel to do that. He has made me the loneliest woman alive. A woman whose guilt about everyone who has died keeps her awake at night. A woman who reads and reads and reads to silence the voices.

The tequila spills on the counter and on my hand.

"Stay."

I refill the glass.

"Ranna? What are you doing?"

The voice catches me off guard. It's soft and dismayed, but holds no judgment. Maggie.

"Can't you see?"

Go.

She puts her rough hands over mine. Maggie personally washes the dishes every night before she goes home. Hardings belongs to her brother, and together they care for two younger brothers and a sister. She's never explained what happened to their parents.

"All I see is that you're going to regret it tomorrow. And later." She sits down beside me.

"Later?" I fill the glass again.

Stay.

"Yes. When you remember the decision you made this way."

Of course Maggie knows what I'm doing. She always knows exactly what's happening in Hardings. You don't watch drunk people night after night without discovering why they want to get drunk. And she knows me. By now, after so many nights spent at this table, she knows me.

"Every decision I've ever made with my head has been stupid . . . senseless," I try to explain. I stumble over the words. Words aren't my thing. Neither is explaining. "I hoped . . . thought . . . it was time to try another method."

Maggie shakes her head. She rests her chin in her hand and ignores the man in the white cap beckoning her to bring him another beer. "Why don't you flip a coin instead?"

I could swear she's laughing at me. "This is much more fun."

Stay. Or is it go?

"You're confusing me," I say.

She fishes something from her jeans pocket. "Here. It's my lucky coin. A counterfeit five rand one of your compatriots left as a tip. He was arrested the next day on a charge of drunk driving." She nods, seems pleased. "Just outside this very door."

She balances the coin on her thumb. "Heads or tails?"

I put down the tequila, considering the movement carefully.

"Heads," I say. "Always heads. Do you know statistically you have a better chance if you pick heads?" I try to smile, but the tequila fills my mouth with the taste of bitter, burned almonds.

Maggie wags a stern finger at me. "You can say what you like, but if I win, you stay. If you win, you can run away again. I don't know who from or where to, but I don't suppose it matters anymore."

"And what if I *have* to run? If I have no other choice?"

Maggie's shoulders move impatiently under the T-shirt. "I've got news for you, Ranna Abramson. You can't afford to run again. You're falling apart, piece by piece. Too much of you will be staying behind."

I don't know what to say. Maybe she's right. Maybe not. A coin is probably no worse than a bottle of Olmeca.

Maggie tosses the coin and catches it. The man in the white cap calls her again but she ignores him. She slaps down the five-rand coin on the back of her hand and peers to see what it says.

"Tails."

I look at the silver coin resting on her hand. As easy as that. I empty the tequila bottle into the glass and down the contents.

"Stay," I announce.

Maggie gives a wry smile. "A new concept for you?"

"You have no idea."

2

I'm tall. It's a fact. That's why what happened to me has come as such a surprise. How did the man take me so completely by surprise? Why didn't I see him coming?

By the age of six I was the tallest child in my class. By the end of high school only the first rugby team's lock forward was taller than me. Standing at six feet one means I've always been able to see farther than most women, and I've never been ashamed of it.

My view has never been blocked by puffed-up chests and stubborn jawlines, nor by trouser legs and neat black lace-up shoes. I've always looked over the heads of other people. Without realizing it, I've always seen the world from a different perspective.

Luckily someone else discovered it too.

My frustration with putting words on paper meant that I almost failed languages in high school. Until one day the school psychologist told me to take photos in my head and write down what I saw. He said I had to capture a moment and think about what happened before that moment and what would follow from it, and then write it down. He understood that I have a visual memory. That I can visualize—remember—everything that happened in the smallest detail. The colors of a dress. A collection of items on a table. The expressions on people's faces.

The psychologist knew that I remembered too much and had trouble sifting through the memories. No one can write an essay like that, he said, and suggested I buy a camera and photograph the things that were important to me. To help me focus, to find a way to channel and use the constant stream of information I received.

I followed his advice. I took photos in black-and-white, sepia, and color. Of planes and buses and cars. Trees changing color in autumn. People. The sky and the gathering clouds. Hail and lightning and drought.

I graduated with an eighty-four percent average mark and left the country with my mother and stepfather. In New York I studied photography.

I imagined that I could see everything. That I could see more than most other people. Farther than most other people.

But I was wrong. After everything I had learned to be, after everything I had survived, I still didn't see the butterfly man coming.

Hamisi Bahame stands waiting for me at my front door. Hadhi must have served him tea. A white mug decorated with blue flowers rests in one hand and a cigarette in the other. He's smoking slowly and calmly, as if he has nothing better to do.

"Those things will kill you," I say, more cheerfully than I feel. "Chain-smokers are fifteen to thirty times more likely to get lung cancer."

"There are so many ways to die, I'll take the thirty times," he replies philosophically. He balances his mug on a flowerpot to shake my hand. "Sometimes you choose the most pleasurable way." He coughs from somewhere deep in his chest. "But I must confess, I don't know whether this is so pleasant anymore."

I unlock the front door and step inside. It's the first time Hamisi has been to my home. Before this, we met in a number of different locations. The first three interviews were at his office, then we spoke at a hotel, and last week at a coffee shop. Every time I've had very little to say. Nor did I ask for a lawyer to be present. I've learned that silence is better. And a lot cheaper.

I'm not surprised that the policeman is still chipping away at Billy's murder. Nor am I surprised that he is making no progress. The man is too clever. So I've been waiting for this day. Waiting for dogged, determined Hamisi Bahame to come to my apartment, desperate for answers.

Hamisi is hovering at the front door. I can't help but smile. He reminds me of Alex.

"I didn't know you were such a polite man," I say.

"You've never given me a chance to show you."

"If you say so. Come in. It's too hot to be outside."

The rain has given way to Dar es Salaam's usual blistering heat. I open the fridge and study the contents. Except for two Kilimanjaros, it contains one egg, the last of the milk, and three apples. Time to go shopping.

I lean over the fridge door and offer my second-to-last beer to the tall, thin policeman with the vigilant eyes.

"Thanks." He offers me the mug in exchange. "Will you give this to Mrs. Batenga? Tell her it was lovely."

He twists the Kilimanjaro's neck. "May I have a glass, please?"

I take one from the cabinet behind me. He pours the golden liquid so that just the right amount of foam is lying on top. Hands me the empty bottle to throw in the trash can behind me.

"If you're drinking, I presume you're here on your own time?"

"Yes." He thinks for a moment. "No one knows I'm here. As far as the police commissioner is concerned, the case is closed. Billy Jones's death was an accident. Best to move on and get the tourism industry going again."

It's the first time he has acknowledged it to me, and not just muttered the words at some press conference or other. I want to feel relief, but I can't help wondering what he's doing here.

"Please sit." I point to the single couch.

Hamisi shows no surprise at the sight of all the books—unlike Alex, who couldn't stop staring. The books are one reason why I don't allow people into my personal space. That, and the fact that my home is the one place where I can still exercise a degree of control.

Hamisi looks for a place to put down his beer, then gives up.

I sit down on the couch beside him. "What can I do for you?"

"Tell me."

"Tell you what?"

He gives an exaggerated sigh. "I can't take the investigation any further. I keep on running into dead ends. No one can work out when and exactly how Billy died. And there is an inordinate amount of people with a motive to get rid of him. He had so many enemies, it's a wonder he reached forty."

Hamisi draws a deep breath, as if he's trying to control his temper. "Tell me something I don't know, Ranna. Or do you prefer Isabel?"

The name is like fingernails on a blackboard. "Ranna."

"Okay then, Ranna. I suspect there's something you're not telling me. Something important. It's like this bright orange elephant standing in the room." He gives me an exasperated look. "Talk to me. Please."

Of all his words the last salvo hits me the hardest. I have never once heard Hamisi Bahame plead or seen him annoyed. Not even when I sat in his office, refusing to talk. Or when the woman from CNN cornered him and stuck a microphone in his face, implying he was incompetent.

"People close to you are dying, Ranna. Why? Why did you change your name? Don't tell me again it's because you didn't like the sound of Isabel. Or because you converted to Judaism. I bet you've never even seen the inside of a synagogue."

I study the policeman. He looks awkward on my couch, as if he is stranded here against his will. His heels keep tapping impatiently on the tiled floor, his hands clenched around his beer glass. I almost pity him.

"I didn't kill Billy Jones."

"That's what *you* say."

"It's the truth, but you don't want to hear it."

"No." The single word is like a gunshot. His jaw works as if he's masticating his answer, trying to make it softer. "No. I mean, you're right. I may not have wanted to hear it before."

"And now you're suddenly prepared to listen? Why?"

"Something's wrong with this case. I've been missing something from the start. There's something more, something else. I know it. You must help me. I *must* know what happened."

I search his dark eyes to see what has changed. I see visible anger and doubt—emotions Hamisi Bahame must hate, I think.

"Do you know it's the first time you've given me a chance to tell you my side of the story without simply assuming I'm guilty?"

He nods self-consciously. "I was surprised when Alex phoned me from the airport last week to say he's on his way home. I was so certain he loves you. Did he go away because you're guilty? Because you confessed your guilt to him? But here I am. Doesn't it say something?"

So, Alex is gone. Dead and buried. Thousands of miles away. Sometimes it's the same thing.

"Ranna, please. Help me understand what happened."

"I have nothing to confess," I say stubbornly.

Hamisi drinks the last of his beer, then shakes his head. "I'm not talking about confessing. Just tell me."

"Tell you what?"

"Tell me why it's not you. Tell me who it is."

"You won't believe me."

"Please," he begs more urgently. "You must tell me what you know."

I can see he really wants to know. He's every bit as adamant as Alex was.

But will he believe me?

3

Unlike Alex, Hamisi listens as if every word I say may be true. Perhaps I wasn't patient enough with Alex, or perhaps love makes you too jealous and insecure to listen properly.

"It sounds like this invisible man is beginning to move closer to you. His patience is wearing thin," Hamisi remarks when I've finished.

"*If* what I say is true," I scoff. But my eyes well up because he doesn't dismiss my story outright. I wipe at the tears. It's ridiculous to be so grateful—to a cop, for heaven's sake. In Paris, talking to the police didn't do me any good. It would serve me well to remember it.

Hamisi drinks the cup of tea I made while I was telling my story. I had to keep my hands busy because I couldn't bear seeing the inevitable skepticism in his eyes.

"There's a certain logic to what you are saying," he says.

Again the burning tears. I haven't cried for three years, and suddenly I can't seem to stop. What has Alex done to me?

Hamisi looks away, as if he's giving me time to pull myself together. He strokes the bridge of his nose. His chin. When he speaks again, he chooses his words carefully, as if he's unsure of my reaction.

"But I can also understand why Alex didn't believe you, Ranna. You get many types of stalkers, and very few of them understand that what they're feeling isn't love but hatred."

"Probably," I agree reluctantly.

"Have you gone back far enough into your past to try and find out who it might be?"

"That's another reason why I don't sleep at night."

"And?"

I push all thoughts of Alex aside. "Where do I start? With a fellow student in my second year who wanted to photograph me in the nude? With the man I dumped because he kept wanting to know exactly where I was and what I was doing? What if it's the guy who made my coffee in New York every morning and I never took notice of him? Or one of the people in my photos? Or what if it's one of my father's relatives? Or maybe Alex? You?"

Hamisi smiles wryly. "You could be right."

He finishes his tea. I again notice the clean, neatly trimmed nails, the elegant long fingers.

"Why don't you make a list? If you can't sleep anyway, try making a list of everyone you can think of. Everyone who was . . . or is . . . just a little different. A little off and strange." He thinks for a moment. "Men *and* women. You never know. I'll help. Bring me something to work with. A list of names. People who keep popping up, even if it's on the periphery of your life."

"I've been through this a million times before."

"But have you ever had a policeman on your side?"

I swear there's a hint of amusement in his eyes. "No."

"Well, what have you got to lose? Think about it."

"Why do you want to help me?"

"So many whys." Again the wry smile.

"It's important. I'm here with you and not behind bars because I've learned not to trust people like you. Cops get an idea in their heads, and then they don't let go. So I have to know. Why do you want to help me? Maybe this is just a clever trick to get information from me. Information to arrest me for Billy's murder—despite the fact that I'm innocent," I hasten to add.

He takes a moment to answer.

"Things aren't always as they seem, Ranna. It's one of the lessons I've learned the hard way. So, if you say a man is following you, murdering every man you love, you might just be telling the truth." He searches for the pack of Dunhills in his shirt pocket but jams it back when he remembers where he is. "I think it's a lead worth following. All things are possible where human behavior is concerned. Every single thing you can think of and then some."

He gets up, suddenly in a hurry. Motions at the kitchen. "Shall I put the cup in there?"

"I will." I finish my tea. "You hate cases like this one, don't you? Unsolved. Full of riddles."

He remains quiet. I take his cup from him. His dark eyes reveal nothing.

"What makes you lie awake at night?" I try again. "Cases like this?"

"Ghosts," he says cryptically. "Old and new ones."

He closes the door behind him when he leaves. Gently and politely, as if he's afraid of waking someone.

I watch through the kitchen window as he adjusts his tie, then bends down to wipe his shoes with his handkerchief. With long, careful strokes he irons out the wrinkles in the sleeves of his neat white dress shirt. Then he looks up and waves goodbye, as if he knew all along that I was watching him.

I meet his gaze and smile as if we're old friends.

Something about the thin, wiry policeman gives me hope. Makes me think he may find the answers if I give him enough time and space. But I still don't know whether I can trust him.

On the other hand, it may be time for me to trust someone again. I didn't trust Alex enough, and look at the price I've had to pay.

What if I could get Alex back? What if I could finally identify this phantom figure? If I could track him down and . . . And what, exactly?

I groan at my daydream and turn on the tap to wash the dishes.

4

I spend a sleepless night thinking about the list Hamisi wants me to draw up. People who keep popping up in my life. Who surface repeatedly. Who fits that category?

No one I can think of. That's what happens if the main theme of your life has been running away from everything and everyone.

No, wait, that's not quite true.

My mother is ever present.

The sigh slips out before I can stop it. Damn. Is that the best I can do?

I roll over on my other side. Moonlight seeps through the blinds onto the floor. The light is almost as strange as the silence. After the recent rains the night is suddenly quiet, the sky open and filled with stars, the air clammy and hot once again, just like the day Alex decided to leave.

Alex. Sometimes it's better simply to forget.

Focus, Ranna.

Tomorrow's photo shoot. A cabinet minister will be supervising the last of the emergency supplies being handed out. I wish I could find something more interesting to document.

Sometimes I miss my life. What my life could have been.

No. Back to Hamisi's list.

My mother.

The guys who move my books.

Ah! Why didn't I think of them before?

Tom.

No. Dar is only the second place where the two of us have worked together. And he's a good friend.

Hadhi.

No. Nothing strange about her. And, besides, I met her here for the first time.

Hamisi meant people who regularly turn up, everywhere, all over the world. People I see and speak to. Send emails to. People I tell what's going on in my life, even if it's no more than a cryptic message these days.

I kick the bedding aside. I'll fetch pen and paper and make a list. Maybe Hamisi is onto something.

Two hours later I have a list of names. It's not very long.

In fact, it's upsettingly short.

Six names. The sum total of the meaningful relationships I have managed to build over the past few years. A manifestation of my loneliness, in black and white.

Or am I not digging deep enough?

But what if there is nothing deeper? What if my stalker is nothing but a figment of my imagination? Maybe Billy's death was an accident after all. I haven't heard from the man since Billy washed up onshore. There's been no phone call. No contact.

Maybe Alex was right. Maybe I've completely lost touch with reality.

The next morning my first appointment is at a government building in the inner city, where the president expresses his thanks to the international community for their support. He's polite, with not much more to say except that Tanzania is working on a plan of action in case of future disasters. The woman from CNN, who stayed behind hoping to dig up more information on Billy's death, asks why the government didn't do it a long time ago. The minister replies that Hurricane Katrina proved that no one is ever truly prepared for a disaster of such magnitude.

The TV journalist seems surprised at first, then breaks into a smile. The president smiles with her, but there's no mirth in his eyes. In the photo I take, his eyes are dead and expressionless. He lost two sisters in the flood.

As I'm flipping through the photos on my camera after the conference, Hamisi walks up to me. "Good pictures?"

"You should instead ask whether anyone will be interested in using anything I've taken today. I've sent hundreds of photos in the past weeks, but lately very few have been used. All that is left of the floods is a lot of white noise from aid organizations. The US probably wouldn't even have bothered with donations, if not for Billy."

I erase a photo. Another one. How did I get the light so wrong?

Hamisi leans over my shoulder to see what I'm doing. "What makes you keep one and not the next?"

Why is he talking about photos while both of us are wondering about the list? I look up, irritated, then understand what the policeman is doing. The CNN journalist is standing a few feet away. She knows Hamisi and must have heard the rumors that I was his chief suspect until very recently.

"It's about the emotion in the photo," I reply. "About some invisible thing becoming visible. A moment that captures an entire chapter in history and sums it up. Shock because shares have crashed and pensions have been wiped out. Grief because someone has died or something valuable has been destroyed. A moment of victory."

The woman steps closer. She's pretending to page through her notes, but in fact she's tilting her head to listen to our conversation.

"Makes sense." Hamisi looks at the journalist and flashes me a helpless smile. *Call you later,* he gestures with his hand at his ear.

I decide I've waited long enough. "I've got that list you asked me for."

Hamisi's eyes widen. The CNN journalist's eyes become question marks. I search for the paper in my backpack, fold it once, twice. Put it in his outstretched hand.

"Ah," he says, pretending to be surprised. "That was quick."

"Trust is a strange thing. Especially when you're in a place where you feel you have nothing more to lose."

The journalist shuffles a step closer.

"Never a good place to be." Hamisi waves the paper in the air as if it's a white flag. "I'll do my best."

He turns and walks away.

Exasperated, the CNN woman pushes back her dark hair. Her eye catches mine.

"Boo," I say softly, just loud enough for her to hear.

She hurries away, her mouth a thin, angry line.

5

"Your list is incomplete."

"Impossible." I roll out of bed, yawning. Look at my watch. It's almost seven in the morning. I've been expecting Hamisi's call for two days.

"Ranna, it is." Hamisi drags at a cigarette. It sounds like static on the line. "You have to think. *Really* think. Who always knows where you are? Where you're going? It could be obvious, or really obscure. Think of the people who are always there. Around you. In the real or virtual world. Email, Twitter, Snapchat, Facebook, all those things people go crazy for these days. Think of relatives, friends, colleagues. Don't try to play detective and think logically about who it could be. Leave that to me."

"I did think about it. And I'm not on Facebook. Or Twitter."

"Then you must think again."

"Why?" I walk to the bathroom, tie my hair back from my face.

"It's not *my* life being ruined."

"Your empathy moves me. Deeply."

"Sarcasm won't do you any good," he says calmly.

"Fuck it." I turn on the tap, rub my face with cold water.

"Do it, Ranna. I refuse to remain in the dark about Billy Jones's killer."

"Why?"

"Why what?" He drags at the cigarette again, blows out the smoke with a hissing sound.

"Why can't you live with secrets?"

He doesn't answer.

"Hamisi?"

"My wife."

"What about her?"

"Nothing," he says, and hangs up.

It takes two days and two nights—time during which I sleep very little—to compile a new list. When I've finished, I phone Hamisi.

"What?" he mumbles sleepily.

"Hello to you too."

"Look at your watch."

It's three in the morning. "Sorry." Did I wake his wife as well?

"Don't be sorry. Why don't you make it worth my while instead?"

"I've got a list. A better one."

There's a moment's silence, then the sound of a cigarette lighter. "Fine. Bring it to my office at seven."

I look at the list in my hand. Do I know what I'm doing? Have I fully considered the consequences of putting these names on a list and handing it to a cop?

"Ranna?" Hamisi asks when I remain silent.

"Yes?"

"No list can prove you killed Billy. Don't be scared."

He must be reading my mind.

"It's difficult to trust you," I try to explain, wishing I had Alex's way with words. "To trust anyone, you know . . . A few weeks ago you were convinced of my guilt—what has changed? I mean, really changed?"

"You talked to me. Finally. And I've known violence for long enough to know that it comes in every shape and form. The world is a crazy place, full of crazy people doing crazy things, and that's never going to change."

6

During the next few days I photograph Hadhi's pregnant daughter-in-law and a woman who died as a result of a backstreet abortion. Next is the French pilot of Lion Mining. Tom goes with me to write a piece for the BBC website.

I photograph Antoinette Laurent posing proudly alongside her white-and-red Puma helicopter, parked in a shed of the gold mine fifty miles north of Dar. She and her crew saved forty-one people from the flood after the mining company offered the government its services. I ask her to spread her arms as if she's flying. She gives a half-hearted laugh and complies.

I imagine her as Superwoman. A cranky, foul-mouthed, flying Superwoman.

I tell Tom that as we stand next to the Land Cruiser, on our way back, waiting for him to finish his cigarette.

Tom shakes his head. "All these pictures you make up in your head. Can't be good for you."

"Sometimes made up is better than the real world. When I was four, my mother took me to see Tekelar the Magician. He was a short, round man in a black wig and a red cloak. He said he came from Turkey. When he made a bunch of plastic red roses disappear, I immediately saw he'd hidden them in his sleeve. I got up and shouted that he was a fraud.

My mother dragged me out of there by the arm. I was so disappointed. Up until then I believed in magic."

"Was your mum angry with you?"

"Not really. She said she should have known better than to take me to the show in the first place. I was too observant. I told her it wasn't her fault that guy was a bad magician." I laugh as I remember Tekelar's face. "He was furious. I thought he was going to kill me."

Tom hooks his cheap black Bic pen to his notepad. "Were you naughty as a child?"

"My mother says I was unnaturally quiet, and always right, but not unmanageable, no."

"I was naughty. I wrote on the walls. No cute little drawings of Mom and Dad and Rex the dog. No, I wrote. Maybe I did it to drive my mother crazy. She worked long hours and didn't really have time for children."

"So you've always loved words?" I lean against the 4x4, soaking up the sun.

"Maybe. I don't remember. I've been focusing on deadlines for such a long time, I've forgotten there was a time when I enjoyed writing stories."

I think of Tekelar and his red face. The memory is as clear as if it happened yesterday.

"Is it easier to forget words than pictures?" I ask.

Tom rubs his neck while he thinks. I can see he's suffering in the afternoon heat. His face and bald head have reddened in the sun. He drags at his Marlboro. Unlike Hamisi's, his hands are urgent and restless as he smokes.

"Sometimes, yes. Sometimes, no. Some stories stick with you, even if you try and turn it into a dry academic account right from the start. And sometimes you think you've left it behind you, and then you walk into a place and the most unlikely thing brings it all back. The smell of a woman wearing Chanel. Fucking burned popcorn."

I'm about to ask about the popcorn but decide against it. Tom will tell me if he wants to.

"And you?" he asks. "Do you remember all your photos?"

"I don't think so," I say, but I know I'm lying. I couldn't forget any of them, even if I tried.

Tom steps on his cigarette butt. I know he doesn't want to go home. After the rain it's good just to stand in the sun, making small talk. He wipes the dust off his fake Rolex, peers at the time, opens the Marlboros, and takes out another cigarette. Taps the almost empty pack.

"Why didn't it work out between you and Alex?"

I've been wondering how long it would take the Englishman to mention Alex.

"It just didn't."

"That's a *kak* answer." He emphasizes the only Afrikaans expletive he knows.

"It's still my only answer."

"I hoped you'd finally stop your nonsense. You know, give in and love someone." He lights the cigarette. "Since I wasn't good enough for you."

So that's what this is all about. He's still sore about what happened between us—or didn't happen.

"I can't make myself feel something. You know that. It would be a lie."

"You can learn to love someone."

"For me love isn't a process. It just is."

"Who the hell still believes in that kind of bullshit?" he scoffs. "Childish nonsense. Bedtime fairy tales."

"You can't decide what works for me."

He makes a noise at the back of his throat, throws down his half-smoked cigarette, and turns to the car. "Let's go. Before I get too lazy to file this story."

As we approach the outskirts of Dar, Tom turns to me. “Feel like a drink?”

“What about work?”

“Screw work. Your place? Mine’s filthy,” he asks.

“Mine too. Hardings?”

“Perfect.”

Hardings is full. With no parking at the back, I leave the Cruiser on the pavement.

Tom grins. “You could be in for a hefty fine. Or a bribe.”

“Only if someone feels the urge to enforce the traffic laws today. And we won’t be long. One beer.”

I’m both right and wrong. Tom has two Johnnie Walkers, but I ring up the till seven times. For one beer, four single whiskeys, and two doubles. Seems like it’s not a night for beer. Maybe it reminds me too much of Alex.

There’s only one problem: I’m no longer used to drinking whiskey. It goes straight to my head and hands, which feel more disconnected by the minute, as if they no longer belong to the rest of me.

Much later, Tom takes me home, though Maggie has offered me a bed in the storeroom.

Tom battles to get the Cruiser through its gears and off the pavement. The minute one wheel is off, the engine stalls.

“Use . . . put the car in first.”

He glares at me, but I stare straight ahead, at the dark, deserted road. I’m trying to anchor all the things that seem to have slipped their moorings. The building. The Hardings sign gleaming like a yellow moon.

“How do you drive this thing?” Tom starts the engine again. “I’m used to automatic transmission.”

I lean across and grind the gear lever into first. “See, it’s not that hard.”

“If you can find it, yes.”

We pull away, but before we've reached the first bend in the road, the engine stalls again.

"Let me drive," I say, unbuckling my seat belt.

"That'll be the day." Tom pushes the gear lever into second, battles to find first.

"Remember the cl . . . clutch."

He gives me a murderous look.

"Should have slept at Maggie's. Didn't know you can't use a stick shift."

"Ranna. Do me a favor and shut up."

"Sorry." I turn my eyes back to the road.

The gears grind and the Cruiser jumps ahead. Stops. Finally we pull away.

"Well done."

"Ranna."

"Six out of ten. Not too bad for your first time."

"Fuck off."

Ten minutes later we stop at my apartment. Tom has brought the Cruiser to a halt just in time to avoid crashing through the low wall. The engine stalls when he takes his foot off the clutch too hastily.

"Bollocks. Fuck."

"Dammit. *Donner.*"

For a moment he seems to want to shake me, but then he manages a smile.

"I don't know that last one. You've introduced me to *kak*. What's *donner*?" he asks.

"Something like thunder."

"Huh?"

"Yes, I know. It makes no sense in English." I think for a moment. "It's more like bastard. That's it," I say. "That's the word. Bastard. Or wanker, if you're you, you know. All posh and British."

Before I can elaborate, he jumps out and opens the door on my side. "Come. Bedtime."

He helps me out. I stop myself from laughing when I notice how my tall figure towers over his. "I've had too much to drink," I declare.

"What a surprise. Next time, stick to beer."

He leads the way along the side of the house to my blue front door. I stumble along behind him. He holds out his hand for the keys. At the third try I manage to hand him the bunch. At last the door swings open.

"Step," he warns, just before I stumble over it.

"What?"

"Forget it," he sighs. "There's . . . *was* a step."

"Dammit. *Donner,*" I swear, giggling.

He manages to keep me upright and drag me to the couch.

"You're so strong," I say as I collapse on the couch.

"Hmm."

"What does that mean?"

"What mean?"

"Hmm."

"I say it when it's better not to say anything else."

"Coward."

The word is out before I can stop it. I may be drunk, but I feel his body tense under my hands. The next moment he climbs on top of me. His mouth is hungry. He reeks of beer and the peanuts on the counter at Hardings.

"Stop. Tom."

Ignoring me, he pushes his tongue into my mouth and presses his body more urgently against mine.

"Tom! Stop."

His hands wring at my T-shirt and smear across my breasts, my thighs. My crotch.

"Coward, huh?" he snarls.

I think of everything my mother taught me, everything I experienced over the years in strange countries and near-empty bars. I sink my teeth into his lower lip until I draw blood.

He swears and pulls away. With all the strength I can muster, I push him off me. He lands on his back on the threadbare red carpet. When he jumps up, his eyes are wild.

I'm already on my feet, my weight evenly distributed, my head instantly clear.

The expression on his face makes me step back. I clamber up and over the couch until I'm standing behind it, fists ready the way my father taught me the day the nursery school bully hit me.

"Tom, I think you should go."

Is there no weapon close by? Didn't I leave a glass next to the couch last night? Tom is probably just drunk, but I'm not taking any chances.

He stands motionless.

"Tom. Go home. Cool down. Leave. Now. Or I'll call the police."

"Okay," he says at last, still without moving. His eyes remain fixed on me, as if I'm a bright flame in a dark room.

"I'm sorry if I gave you the wrong idea." I try to defuse the situation.

"Did Alex ever know how lucky he was?"

I wrap my arms around my shivering body. "Fuck you, Tom. Go home."

He stands motionless for another moment. Then he laughs brusquely, turns around, and stomps out the front door.

I have no idea how I got to the kitchen. When I return to reality, Nina Simone is singing on the radio and there's a glass of wine in front of me. The bottle on the table is almost empty. I'm on my third or fourth glass, but the alcohol has no effect on me. Instead, my head seems to become clearer with each glass of cheap Merlot.

I put the glass down. Lay my hands flat on the table. The veins on the back of my hands are thick and broad. Leading somewhere. Only I am stranded here. In my helpless bloody body.

I glace at the clock. It's been three hours since Tom left. I push the bottle and glass aside. I'm tired, but it's a different kind of fatigue. More considerable than anything I've ever felt before. Darker. Heavier.

I'm tired of everyone trying to use me as their cheap plaything. Tired of waiting for Hamisi to come up with some brilliant idea. Tired of having to explain myself to cops and lovers.

In the future I'll determine my own fate. Manage my own life. For once, I want to know what it feels like to be the one who makes the rules.

The next day I write down the first names on my personal list of suspects, starting with the man in the white cap at Hardings.

7

The man in the white cap is sitting at the bar, like every other night, drinking beer. I sit down next to him. He looks at me as if I've lost my way but doesn't say a word.

The bottle in his enormous hand is a Tusker. There are no rings on his fingers and no jewelry around his rugby player's neck. Most of his nails are bitten to the quick. An illegible tattoo protrudes from the right sleeve of his red T-shirt. As always, he's wearing the ubiquitous white headgear.

Behind the counter Maggie stares at me as if I've lost my mind. Above our heads Billy Idol screams something about a white wedding.

"Can I have one of those too?" I ask her.

"A Tusker?" She frowns sharply.

"Please."

Next to me the man raises the beer and takes a sip. "Not your usual poison. You always drink Kilimanjaro."

Under the cap his face is red and weary. His eyes, which appear to be light green, seem to regard me with interest, but it's hard to be sure with the shadow of the hat over his face. His eyebrows are thick, his beard at least three days old.

From up close he's younger than I thought. On the right side of forty, even if it's only just. He has an average kind of attractiveness, which I suspect will improve with age. Yet he'd disappear in a large group. If not for his white cap, I wouldn't have noticed him sitting here night after night.

"You're right, it's not my usual poison. But I don't fancy a Kili tonight."

"It's not where you usually sit either."

"Ten out of ten for noticing."

"It's impossible to miss you."

My mouth goes dry. Is he the man who has been making my life a living hell? For someone who's always drinking alone in a corner, he certainly notices a lot. On the other hand, being tall I stand out—whether I want to or not. But how does he know what I usually drink?

I extend my hand. "Ranna Abramson."

"Jaco Steyn." He runs his hand over his beard. "Everyone calls me Jakes."

The name gives away what the accent made me suspect. "You're South African?"

He nods, but his eyes remain lifeless. Too lifeless. As if he purposely avoids revealing anything but a general kind of courtesy.

Maggie puts the beer in front of me. Her eyes flash a warning, but I ignore it. I take a sip of the Tusker. It's warm. Damn, Maggie.

"What are you doing in Dar?" I ask in Afrikaans.

Jakes laughs, and his rigid body relaxes a little. He runs his hand across his jaw again, as if he suddenly regrets not having shaved this morning.

"I work for the brewery. We're installing a new production line. I have three more weeks left of my contract."

"And then?"

"Back to Joburg, until the next contract. Bosses are talking about Benin."

"Sounds exciting. Do you travel a lot?"

He tosses the last of his beer down and wipes his mouth with his hand. "Quite a lot."

"Where have you been?"

"Many places. Too many to name."

"Paris?" I hope it comes across like a shot in the dark. "It's one of my favorite cities in the world."

"Long ago. Honeymoon. Waste of time. It all ended in divorce five months later."

The door opens, and a group of people saunter in. Russian, by the sounds of it.

My heartbeat quickens. "San Francisco?"

He shifts uneasily on the barstool, his face a mask again. "Why do you want to know?"

I try to smile. "No reason."

"You ask a lot of questions." He hesitates a moment. "But I suppose you can't help it. You're a journalist."

"Perhaps."

The conversation peters out into an awkward silence. I finish my beer and look for Maggie. She's standing at a table on the far side of the room. When she looks up, I point at the empty bottle, but she ignores me.

"I'll get you one," Jakes offers.

"Thanks."

He gets up and goes across to Maggie. Points in my direction. Her eyes flicker to me and back to him. She nods curtly.

He comes back, a question mark on his face. "I think she's angry with me."

"Not with you. Me."

He lifts his cap and replaces it. The sun has scorched his ears recently. Maybe while following me? Yesterday, with Tom?

"Why would she be angry with you?"

"Because I'm sitting here, drinking beer with you."

"Nothing wrong with that."

"My motives aren't entirely pure." I want it to sound flirtatious, but I know I'm not very convincing.

His eyes become guarded. “Everyone gets a little lonely. It’s okay,” he says slowly.

I try to laugh, but it sounds nervous and stupid.

“So,” I say, wiping my sweaty palms on my jeans, “you’ve been to Paris. I’m going to San Francisco soon. Is it a nice place for a vacation? I’ve never really liked the French much.”

He pulls the cap lower over his eyes. Looks straight ahead. “I suppose it depends.”

I wonder what I’ve said wrong. I don’t have to wait long to find out.

“Are you really interested in me, or is this about the money that disappeared at the brewery?”

“Money? What are you talking about?”

“Your not-so-pure motives. Don’t play dumb.”

I remember reading something in yesterday’s paper about an inflated tender at the brewery. Of course. The new line Jakes is installing.

I shake my head. Shift on my chair for an impatient Russian trying to lean over the counter to place an order with Maggie. “No. Not at all. That’s not what I meant.”

“Are you looking for a story?”

“What?”

“Something’s going on. I wanted to buy you a beer the first day you walked in here, but you froze me out completely. Remember?”

I try, but can’t. I recall a busy night when two men sent drinks over to my table, but I don’t remember whether Jakes was one of them. If he wasn’t wearing his cap that day, I probably wouldn’t remember him.

“No,” I sigh at last.

I can see he doesn’t believe me.

“Do you really think I’d sit here and tell you everything? Just like that, over a beer or two? Or am I your last chance tonight? Has your boyfriend gone home?”

I want to retaliate, but then I remember why I’m here. Why it’s important.

I look into his eyes. "Why are you nervous? Do you have something to hide?"

He's instantly angry. "What the fuck is going on? I didn't invite you over here. What game are you playing?"

"I want to know why you're following me. Why are you always here when I'm here?"

"What?"

"Don't deny it. You know what I'm talking about."

I know I'm being irrational, but I seem to be standing outside my body, watching myself mess up at record speed.

"Fuck, woman, you're crazy. Go home."

I feel a hand on my shoulder and turn.

Maggie.

I shake her off, annoyed.

Jakes wags a furious finger at her. "You'd better get your friend away from me. She's making me very, very angry."

"Come," says Maggie, her voice soothing. "Please, Ranna. Come with me." She folds her hand around my elbow.

I remain seated. "No."

Jakes knows something. I know he knows something. It's in his eyes. In the expression around his mouth.

"Ranna, please," Maggie pleads. She shakes her head at the man next to me. "And you. Go home. You've had enough."

"What? *Me?*"

"Yes, you. Go home."

He gets up. His hands shake as he peels off two notes from a roll and throws them on the counter.

"There are better places to drink anyway." He pulls his cap down over his eyes and picks up his car keys. At the door he turns to glare at me.

Just before he slams the door behind him, I could swear he flashes me a cocky smile.

8

Hamisi phones me awake the next morning. "I hoped you'd be at the press conference." He sounds tired, as if he's been awake for hours.

"What conference?" I mumble, confused.

I grope for my cell phone. Ten o'clock. Day or night? I turn to the window. Day.

"The one about the Chinese building a new railway line to the interior. The Chinese president is here. He arrived this morning."

Damn! I jump up. Lie back down. The conference started at nine. I do the math in my head. Fifteen minutes to shower and get dressed. Half an hour to drive there. Possibly twenty-five minutes in a dala dala. Those taxis know how to drive.

No. It's too late to get photos. What a way to start the day.

"I gather you missed it?" asks Hamisi.

"So it's not just a rumor. You really are an ace detective."

He laughs. "Let me buy you breakfast. It will make you feel better. There's a place near my office. Will an hour be enough?"

"What's going on?"

"I want to talk to you about your list."

Keeping one eye on my cell phone, I examine my wardrobe. I have one more clean, pressed T-shirt. "Give me forty-five minutes. And order me a black coffee. So long."

"Your list is impressive for someone who's lived in a different country every few years." Hamisi stirs his tea, taps the spoon against the top of the white cup, and places it neatly in the saucer. He waves at someone walking into the industrial-style café.

"What do you mean? Is the list too long now?"

I can't believe it. Not after he told me to go back and add more names to the list.

I think of Jakes. Why didn't I put his name on Hamisi's list? Is it because he doesn't feature more than once, as Hamisi decreed? Or because I suddenly have an agenda of my own?

The policeman in his neat green shirt and black jacket shakes his head. No tie this morning. He must be off duty. "No, it's not that. I just didn't think you'd be able to scrape together thirteen names."

That sounds better. I edge forward on my seat. "Did you find anything interesting?"

"Maybe."

He looks at the piece of paper, frowns, takes his reading glasses from his inside pocket, and puts them on. "The company that always handles your move is interesting."

He taps on the paper with his index finger. "I don't think your mother is the guilty party."

He silences my outrage with a wave of his hand. "I know, I know. I said to put everyone on the list."

"What about the moving company?" I ask. "I know I use the same one every time, but the guys who do the actual work are never the same. I don't think it could be any of them."

"Really?" Hamisi stares at me over the top of his glasses. For a moment he looks like my math teacher at high school. "I told you not to think so narrowly. Somewhere in that company people know where you're moving to next. Maybe they sell the information. Or maybe one of them uses it. Maybe he takes a regular 'vacation' to pay you a visit. What if the first guy who did your move became obsessed with you?"

The words sink in slowly. "Well, okay. It's possible. Who else?"

"Your first editor, who was also your second-to-last editor. He was fired because he freelanced for the opposition. The media pool worldwide is only so big. It can't be too difficult for someone like him to track you down. You changed your name, but you're still working as a photographer."

"Well, it's what I do. Very well, I might add."

"I know. And I know about the award you've refused. But he also knows who and what you are. What you are drawn to. So that's where you're at your most vulnerable—and that makes him a suspect. How old were you when you began to work for him? Twenty-two? Older man, younger woman . . ."

"You may be right," I concede, "but it's unlikely. John has been married for more than twenty years."

"He recently got divorced."

"But Cathy was his whole life."

"Apparently he has a problem with fidelity."

Hamisi folds the list, removes his glasses, and returns them to his inside pocket. He crosses his legs and leans back in his chair. The fingers of his right hand tap irritably on the table. "What's wrong, Ranna?"

"What do you mean?"

"Why are you suddenly so sure all these people are innocent?"

"It's not that. It's just . . . I don't know . . ." As I speak, I figure out that I do know what it is. And it isn't just last night's fiasco with Jakes.

"It just feels wrong," I try to explain. "The more you talk, the more uneasy I get. It doesn't feel right. I love most of the people on that list." I shrug. "Well, a lot of them. And I'm not referring to Hubbard Movers. But John . . . John spent weekends showing me how to take better photos. He understands light and shade better than anyone I've ever met. The power of a magnificent front-page image."

"So you trust him."

I say nothing further.

"Ah," said Hamisi, as if he suddenly understands. "You trust him more than you trust me."

I can't look him in the eye. "I can't help it. I still wonder why you want to help me. I wonder if Billy's death was really murder and not just an unfortunate accident. There have been no more phone calls. You know the man always calls afterward, but this time he's been silent."

"He may still contact you."

"Maybe . . ." I nod gratefully at the waiter, who has placed a second cup of coffee in front of me. "Is there no further information on Billy's death?"

"No."

"Absolutely nothing?"

Hamisi fiddles with the teaspoon again. "I've told you: I haven't found any concrete evidence that you or anyone else killed Billy. I just have this feeling in the pit of my stomach that it was murder. And to me the fingers confirm it. It means I'm prepared to look into your story about a stalker. So no, I'm not trying to prove you killed Billy, if that's what you're wondering. Again."

"But I was—am—your chief suspect."

"Was. How many times do I have to say it?" he says, indignation creeping into his voice.

"Then why does it still feel as if you're just waiting for me to say or do something stupid and give myself away? What if you're just looking for a way to get closer to me?"

He doesn't answer, just looks at me with his inscrutable dark eyes.

"I didn't kill Billy."

"I believe you."

"Are you a hundred percent sure?"

His eyes grow slightly darker. "This is a ridiculous conversation." He tugs at the collar of his jacket and plucks at his shirtsleeves. "I'll phone you with the names I think are worth following up. Until then, avoid contact with the company that moves your books. And with your ex-editor."

"That's no problem. John doesn't even know I changed my name."

"As far as you know."

I motion to the waiter to bring the bill. The conversation suddenly feels stilted and loaded, like the first time Hamisi questioned me. "Fine. I'll do as you say." I take some cash out of my purse. "Thanks for all your trouble."

"We'll see what happens. Maybe we'll get lucky." He takes a deep breath. "Be careful until then." He sounds as if he means it.

"Fine." I place two notes on the table.

He gestures for me to put the money away. "I'll get it."

"It's my pleasure," I insist. I try to smile. "Because you provide such excellent service, you know."

"It's my job."

"No." I shake my head. "It's not your job. And that's why I keep questioning your motives." I hesitate a moment. Should I really open this hornet's nest? "This feels personal to me."

"What do you mean?"

I take a deep breath, suddenly brave enough to ask. Unlike the previous time, when I didn't want to witness Hamisi's personal pain. "Why does it feel as if this investigation has something to do with your life? This thing you have about riddles?"

He doesn't move a muscle.

"You mentioned your wife in an earlier conversation. What happened to her?" I ask.

The policeman clenches his left hand into a fist. Relaxes it. He seems on the point of reaching out and touching me but then places his hand an inch from mine.

"She disappeared one day. She was—is—a teacher. One Thursday afternoon she didn't come home."

"How long ago was it?"

He pretends to think about it, but probably uses the time to steady himself. "Almost ten years."

"I'm sorry."

"Why are you sorry? It doesn't concern you."

"It concerns you."

"Understanding is better than pity. Pity makes me feel helpless."

I nod. "I understand what it's like when one day someone you love just isn't there anymore. When people disappear from your life as if they've simply been erased."

"There's no need to be sarcastic." Hamisi searches for his cigarettes. Takes one out. Puts it back. "I didn't say my situation was unique. Of course you know what it feels like."

"What happened to your wife? Was she abducted? Murdered? Is that why you're attracted to difficult cases like mine? Why you're taking the trouble to help me?"

He shrugs, suddenly looking fragile and sad. "That's enough for one day, Ranna." He beckons to the waiter. "Enough."

9

Few people know when to say "Enough." It's something you learn, mostly the hard way. Something happened to make Hamisi know when to say it. To make him comprehend that it's safer not to let things go beyond a certain point.

What happened to his wife? And why doesn't he want to speak about it? What if that chapter of his history could tell me what I want to know? What if it could finally tell me whether I can trust him?

Charlie Wanga may have some of the answers I'm looking for. He is an old-school newsman. He started out the same way every reporter carved out a career for himself before the Internet was switched on: in the mailroom. Over the next forty years, he progressed from junior reporter to news editor. If anyone will know what makes Hamisi tick, it's Charlie.

At eight the following morning I put my head around his assistant's dividing wall. "Is Charlie in?"

A slim woman with a long, elegant neck and a bright smile looks up from the paper in front of her. Wipes sandwich crumbs from the corners of her mouth.

"Ranna." She rolls the *r* in a way that makes the hard name sound softer. "For you he's always in."

Bee—as she's affectionately known because of her fondness for black and yellow—rolls back her chair and peers around a steel cabinet at the glass box where her boss is seated. "I think you can go in. He's had his second cup of coffee. And he doesn't look too upset about the other papers' front pages."

Any day that Charlie is leading the news and not following is a good day.

I squeeze Bee's shoulder. "Thanks."

"Don't thank me," she laughs. "He may still chase you out. With him, you never know."

She's right. Besides ill humor, it's hard to read any other emotion on Charlie's face.

I knock on the office door that's slightly ajar. He doesn't look up, but keeps leafing through the newspaper on his desk. "Ranna. What are you doing here?"

"How did you know it was me?"

He puts down the paper and taps his chest with two knobby, arthritic fingers. "You're over six feet tall. Besides, there's only one person Bee flirts with like that."

"It's not flirting," I mumble, embarrassed.

He leans back in his red chair that has seen better days and motions for me to sit. He folds his hands behind his head and studies me with expressionless eyes. "So, I ask again: What brings you here?"

"I need a favor."

"Hmph."

"What does that mean?"

"It means it depends. Is it a good story?"

"It's got nothing to do with the news," I lie.

"Nor with the fact that you're a murder suspect? You managed to sidestep that one rather well."

"I'm not a suspect anymore."

It's news to Charlie. Even he can't hide the fact. No one has ever officially called me a suspect—except me, myself, just now. I can see in his eyes he's going to put someone on the story the minute I leave.

Anything fresh on Billy's death is still huge, even though his death was declared an accident.

I place my hands on the polished desktop and begin to negotiate. "Now that I've done something for you, will you do something for me?"

He snorts, but doesn't protest. "Let me hear."

"I want to know more about Hamisi Bahame of the Criminal Investigation Department."

"Ah, the detective who's investigating your case. Or, rather, used to investigate. What do you want to know?"

"I like Hamisi, but I wonder about him. About some things in his past. Call me inquisitive." I weigh my words, careful not to reveal too much. "He might do something for me—a favor—but I need to know if I can trust him."

"What does your instinct say?" Charlie leans forward. He picks up a red pen and begins to draw aimless circles on the open newspaper.

"He seems like a good man. A good cop."

"You're not wrong. He has a lot of experience. Worked in the States for a while, got his first round of training at the FBI after the US embassy bombings in '98. That's why he could get a consultant here to help with Billy Jones's murder. Death. Whatever. Dr. Gomez. And it was necessary."

He hesitates a moment as if it pains him to admit it. "The Tanzanian police are generally short-staffed. They don't always have the resources to solve complex murder cases. And unfortunately a number of cops are underpaid and corrupt. So the brilliant, meticulous, ethical Hamisi was always going to be a star. He couldn't put a foot wrong."

"Wait. Couldn't?"

Charlie looks up from the circles he's drawing on the paper. Clicks the point of his pen in and out. There's the shadow of a smile around his mouth, as if I've passed some kind of test.

"Yes. Up until his wife's disappearance. She took with her his chance of being promoted, despite the fact that he's still one of the best they have."

My heart rate accelerates. My mind switches to fifth gear. "When?"

"When did his wife disappear?"

"No. Sorry." I shake my head. "When was Hamisi in the States?"

A flicker of surprise moves across Charlie's face. "As I said, '98. After that I don't exactly remember. A few years ago. 2008? 2009? When Al-Shabaab started to became more of a threat in East Africa."

"Do you happen to know where he was?"

"The training was at Quantico. Later on he was in California. Los Angeles?" Charlie rubs his cheek where he missed a spot while shaving this morning. "No, wait. Now I remember. The last time he was in the US was in San Francisco, for a murder investigation. An albino Tanzanian boy was murdered by three of his schoolmates. His parents had left Tanzania because they thought he'd be safer in the States."

"Oh." The sound is all I can get out. It could still be a coincidence. Nothing more.

Charlie frowns sharply. "It may not be a big deal to you, but it made headlines over here. You know we still struggle with superstitions linked to albinism."

"No," I protest quickly. "I can imagine. Sorry. I'm just wondering. Everything you've told me points to Hamisi Bahame being an excellent detective. But does it mean I can trust him?"

Charlie nods. "If I could choose someone to work on my case, I'd pick him. He never gives up. Never. Forget the gossip about his wife."

"Everyone gives up at some point."

"Not Hamisi."

"You use his first name."

Charlie puts the pen down. "I know him well. When I still worked the crime beat, he was a lowly constable. That was a long time ago. When I was young and handsome."

"You're still handsome," I tease, but he doesn't crack a smile.

He folds his arms. "What do you really want to know, Ranna? I can see the American trips mean something to you—but it was a surprise. It's not why you're here."

"You're still the most observant newshound I know."

"And you have a silver tongue, but it's time to be honest now," he says tonelessly.

"As I've said: I want to know if I can trust Hamisi."

Charlie picks up the pen again. "That's only half the story."

"I wouldn't lie to you."

"Of course you would."

"The info about his wife helps a lot." I lean back in my chair, cross my legs.

"Many people wonder about his wife."

"You know something." I try to read the expressionless face of the man who will be retiring in two years' time. "Tell me, please."

"Why do you want to know?"

"I told you: I need to trust someone, and I'm wondering if Hamisi Bahame is that person."

"Your reputation says you trust no one."

"Ouch." I place my hand over my heart in mock hurt.

Charlie points at me with his pen. "Why have you never worked for me?"

I remember his offer six months ago.

"It's not you. I just don't know where I'll be in the next three months."

"Alex Derksen has left. Are you going after him?"

The flood of emotion catches me unaware. The grief is familiar, but not the relief. If Charlie knows about Alex, I can't have been as careful as I thought. It means the invisible man probably knows about Alex too, which means it's good news that he left.

I struggle against the sudden lump in my throat.

Charlie looks at my face. "Sorry," he says awkwardly.

"Don't be. It's okay."

He throws the pen down on his desk and leans back in his chair. When he speaks again, his tone is gentler.

"Hamisi's wife simply vanished. Went to work one day and never came back. No one ever heard a word from her again."

"No one?"

"No."

"But?"

"But what?"

"What about the stuff you know but never wrote?"

Charlie knows exactly what I'm talking about. "She and Hamisi had a tempestuous relationship. There were rumors that she cheated on him. Other stories doing the rounds said he was the one who was sleeping around. Clever young girls with university degrees."

He shakes his head. "I didn't believe any of the stories. There was something else that seemed closer to the truth. A friend of Hamisi's wife said she'd confided in her. Apparently his wife had discovered something about Hamisi that made her want to get away. Something that happened in San Francisco. When he returned from San Francisco she vanished before she could tell anybody—including her friend—what it was."

He taps on the table with his index finger. "Up to this day no one knows what that something was."

"When did she disappear?"

"Around 2009 sometime. Maybe 2010."

Interesting.

If what Charlie says is true, Hamisi was in San Francisco at the same time I was there. But does it mean what I think it means, or am I so paranoid that I can no longer distinguish between truth and fiction? And what could Hamisi have hidden from his wife? Did she find out about his obsession with me and leave? Or worse?

Or is it all just coincidence?

I consider my next question carefully. I have no desire to become a headline in Charlie's paper.

"And you? What do you think? Did Hamisi make his wife disappear? Or did she simply leave him?"

The newsman tilts his head to the left, then to the right, as if he's considering his reply. "He's a hard man to pin down. He's one of the smartest people I know. But does that mean he murdered his wife? I don't think so."

"And the fact that he travels so much? It's expensive."

"He inherited money from his father."

"Does he go away often?"

"Almost every year. No one knows where, and he doesn't say. He's becoming more and more of a recluse."

Charlie closes the newspaper in front of him and looks at me with eyes that must have made a hundred journalists shake in their boots. "He's a good cop, Ranna, but like everyone else, he has his demons. No one can really be good at a job like his—ours—without going slightly crazy. So if you ask me, I'd say you can trust him."

"Thanks." I nod, but can't shake off the sudden chill taking hold of my heart.

At home I sit down on the floor, lean back against the couch, and ignore my phone's incessant ringing. Probably Charlie's people, hounding me for an interview.

What should my next move be?

I consider what I know. What to do with the information. Think of everything I don't know.

How did Alex put it? The things you keep silent about are no different from lies. He was right. Why did Hamisi not mention San Francisco? He must have known it would mean something to me.

Is he the man? Did he offer to help me to make sure he can erase his tracks? To find out how much I know?

My mind goes around in circles until I fall asleep on the living room carpet. I dream, but it's a jumble of colors and sounds. Nothing clear surfaces from my subconscious, no sail or life raft.

The sound of my phone wakes me, but I don't answer. I turn on my side and try to doze off again. My watch says I've slept for an hour, but it feels like five minutes. I feel no better, and no closer to an answer.

What's the point of dreaming then anyway?

10

"I'm sorry."

I can hardly hear what Tom is saying. The line is bad, and his voice sounds metallic and distant. I move to the kitchen, where the signal is normally a tiny bit better.

"Ranna?"

"I don't want to talk to you."

"Please don't put the phone down."

"You would deserve it if I never spoke to you again."

"I know."

The memory is there before I can stop it. Tom's smell still clings to my skin, no matter how many showers I take. Why did I answer the phone? Maybe because it's the fifth time he has called. I can't keep ignoring him. Tomorrow we'll be back at the same news conference.

"I'm really, really sorry, Ranna. I don't know what came over me. I'm so incredibly sorry. Please, I didn't mean it. I was drunk. I could have—"

"No, I was drunk." I stop the deluge of words. "Which means you should have been more careful. And you should have known better. 'No' means 'no.' Always."

I hear him running his hand over his bald head. Or is it his chin? One gesture signals embarrassment, the other thoughtfulness. Maybe even untruthfulness.

"I deserve your anger."

"You're right. You do." I stare at the sun setting outside the window.

"Can I make up for what I did? Please. Dinner. Say where." He speaks hurriedly, as if he's scared my patience will run out before he can finish the sentence.

"Tom . . ."

"Please."

"Dammit, Tom."

"I know it's asking a lot, but I'm sorry. Truly sorry."

I know going out with him is a bad idea, but to my surprise something inside me makes me consider his proposal. Something frightening.

I reel at the realization: Tom's actions do not rank as the worst thing that has ever happened to me. In a few days I'll probably chalk it all up to experience and move on. Kick Tom to the curb, pack my bags, and leave.

A wave of nausea washes over me. In the end I'm no better than the stereotypical abused woman.

Never make peace with violence to your person, I hear my mother say. Or to your soul. She allowed it too long, she said. She was sorry.

I've forgiven her. And I can forgive Tom as well. But our friendship will come to an end. I'll make sure the gap between us becomes impossible to bridge.

"Fine." I relent at last. "Coffee. Tomorrow night. I'll meet you on the Skylark's top floor at nine."

A safe, busy, impersonal restaurant, with little time until they close at ten.

The candle flame flickers in the draft from the kitchen window, standing slightly ajar to let in the night sounds. Outside it's raining. A different kind of rain from the deluge that flooded Dar for weeks on end. Tonight the rain is soft and gentle.

It will soon be over.

Next door the plumber and his wife seem to be making the best of a bad situation—yet another power failure. Against my better judgment, I sit thinking about everything that has happened in the past weeks. At least it's better than drinking somewhere. That's got to stop.

Maybe it's time to acknowledge the little bit of my father I carry inside me, before I become just like him. No use running away to end up just like the thing you're running from.

I close my book. *To Kill a Mockingbird.* I never told Alex, but my mother is one of the reasons for my insomnia. She stayed awake to look after me, and I stayed awake to make sure nothing happened to her.

Maybe she's still doing it. Maybe she still gets up at night and hovers at my bedroom door, listening for my breathing. Maybe she's sitting at my window right now, drinking endless cups of coffee and worrying about my future.

She made certain nothing from her old life was repeated in her new life. My stepfather is the gentlest person I know. She advised me to do what she finally did. Marry gentle. Marry decent.

Not even South Africa survived her vow to start over, though it was the hardest farewell for her—even harder than leaving behind her sister. Her sadness was almost palpable. It traveled with her to New York. She could pull up her roots and start over with a new husband, but she couldn't forget her country. Not the colors, nor the sounds. When we left for America, Miriam Makeba and Hugh Masekela came along on vinyl. Irma Stern on canvas.

She never returned. And though the police were unable to make a breakthrough in the case during the six years we remained in South Africa after my father's death, she was still afraid that one day they'd figure out what happened that night, when he smacked her around one last time.

It was time to move on and forget the past.

Easier said than done.

My father taught my mother to always expect the worst. Since the early days of their marriage. It was probably his biggest gift to her, and somehow it was also handed down to me, whether I wanted it or not.

I had to make absolutely sure there was no oncoming traffic before I crossed the street. To be extra careful on the subway late at night. To never go on a date if I didn't have my own transportation back.

Taking into account everything that happened in our family, my mother can't bear the thought of anything happening to me—something I understand, but at my present age, and hers, it has become a bit academic. At sixty-one, she attends classical concerts and makes small talk over martinis in Manhattan, while I photograph floods and dead bodies.

You don't have to accept every inheritance given to you.

I also know that there's one considerable difference between my mother and me. I'm a much better fighter, with much less to lose. I've always been that way.

It means I'll find a way through this mess. Through Tom. Through Hamisi. Alex. This bloody man. Everything. Until I reach a place where I'll be happy.

Or dead.

Tom jumps up when I walk into the restaurant. Shuffles his feet awkwardly. I've never seen him so dressed up. Even the jeans have been replaced with neat khakis. He motions with a white napkin for me to be seated.

The waiter pulls out my chair.

"You look lovely," he says when the waiter has left.

"Thanks," I answer, though I know he's lying. I didn't go to any trouble with my appearance. In fact, the maître d' barely managed to conceal his disapproval at the sight of my T-shirt.

"What would you like to drink?" Tom tugs at his sports jacket and the pink shirt buttoned to his chin.

"Coke."

"Can I order a bottle of wine instead?"

"I'm not staying. I warned you."

"Ranna, please give me a chance to make it up to you. I'm sorry. I'll keep saying it until you hear me. I was wrong. I'm so sorry."

"Why?"

"Pardon?" With nervous fingers he moves the elephant-shaped salt and pepper shakers closer together.

"Why did you have to go and be such an idiot? We've been there. We gave it a try. It didn't last long, I know, but we both grasped pretty soon that we're better friends than lovers. In fact, we were very good friends. Why did you have to ruin it?"

He opens the top button in this shirt. "Maybe I wanted another chance."

A gray-haired waiter in a bow tie approaches, but Tom signals to him that we're not ready to order.

"I have no more chances to give," I say wearily. "In fact, I don't think I'm capable of love anymore."

"You are. Everyone is."

I give a jaded laugh. "Not me. Not now. One day, maybe, but definitely not now."

"Why not?"

I think of Alex, of all the men before him. "I can't explain why. It's too complicated."

"Try."

I put my hand on his, squeeze it, then quickly retreat into my own space. Physically he still leaves me completely cold.

"It's okay, Tom. We've known each other a long time. We won't just throw that away."

He nods slowly, reluctantly.

"But if you pull something like that again, it's the end. I'll put you away in the deepest, darkest hole I can find. And it's not just an empty threat."

"I don't know what came over me. I'm sorry."

"Okay. Enough now."

"Really?"

"Really," I lie.

11

I unlock the front door and throw my phone and keys on the kitchen counter, just to reach for the Samsung again. I missed two calls on the drive home from the Skylark, both from Charlie. He must have called while Heather Nova was pouring her heart out in the Land Cruiser.

I listen to the messages. The news isn't good. Charlie told Hamisi about our conversation. They went for a beer and the subject of Billy Jones came up, and "somehow" they ended up talking about me.

It's the last thing I need. I throw down the phone. I should have known better. Charlie was obviously on a fishing expedition. It was stupid of me not to have seen it coming. Charlie is a journalist. He may have the title of news editor nowadays, but in his heart he's still the guy who broke one crime story after the other before ending up in the glass box.

It means I might as well stop being careful. Things are coming to a head, whether I'm ready or not.

I punch in Hamisi's number.

"Why?" I ask without any preliminary greeting.

"Why what?" He doesn't sound surprised to hear from me.

"Why didn't you tell me you were in San Francisco when I was there?"

"I wondered how long it would take you to find out. You're better than I thought."

"What's going on, Hamisi? Why didn't you tell me?"

"It's not important. The FBI was hunting a killer, a Tanzanian citizen. I gave them a hand and learned a lot in the process. And San Francisco is the only place where our paths ever crossed."

"Is it?"

"What do you mean?"

"Is San Francisco really the only place we have in common?"

"Of course." I can almost hear him shake his head. "Ranna, I didn't say anything because it's not important."

"Not important?" I nearly choke on the words. "How can I trust you if you lie to me?"

"Don't be ridiculous. I'm not your stalker and you know it."

"Do I?"

There's silence on the other end of the line.

"Fuck you, Hamisi Bahame."

I switch off my phone and run a bath. Finally get into bed. Maybe I'll fall asleep if I try hard enough. A few hours under the covers and I may be able to think rationally again.

But it's no use. The green hands on my alarm clock move on to midnight, and I hear every second as it ticks by. In the dark the sound is almost earsplitting. I roll over for the umpteenth time and stare at the clear night outside the window. Hardings is too noisy, and a book seems like too much work. Maybe one of my mother's methods will work best tonight.

I close my eyes and begin to count backward from one thousand. When I reach 512, I give up. Reading is the only solution. I open *Red Light* and sit down next to my bed, at the open window. The air is hot and sticky.

Thirty pages into the book my eyes are losing focus. I stretch out on the floor and am about to close the book when I hear a small sound.

I'm instantly wide awake. It's a tentative, jarring sound. Hadhi hates cats, and there's no garden that can harbor any kind of wildlife. Around here, sounds are more blatant. Doors opening and closing. People talking. Having sex. Watching TV.

The sound I heard was kind of metallic. Like the shuffling of keys.

I put the book down and sit up.

There it is again. Followed by a small, almost inaudible scraping sound.

The front door. Someone is tampering with the lock. A burglar? The man?

Hamisi . . .

But why would he suddenly spring into action?

There can be only one answer: I finally know the identity of the mystery man. It must have frightened him. Or made him angry.

I roll onto my knees and get to my feet. My breathing quickens, but I keep the rising panic in check. I need a weapon. My eyes fall on the clock. Ten past one. Someone should hear me if I scream loud enough. My neighbor is built like a front-row rugby player. He and his wife occasionally borrow coffee. Surely they'll come to my aid if I make enough noise.

But will they be in time? And what if the man flees? Then I may never know who he is.

Stop thinking. Find a weapon.

The front door creaks softly when it swings open.

Quick. Obie Oberholzer's photo book. No. Annie Leibovitz. I grab the book and weigh it in my hands. Feels hefty enough.

Cautiously I peer around the bookcase. The apartment is so small, it's not hard to see him. He's at the front door, bending down. I can't quite make out what he's doing in the dim moonlight.

I wish I could identify him, but a black stocking covers his face. Not even his body or hands, also clad in black, look familiar.

He looks up as he finally scoops up something metal from the floor. The key he used to open the front door?

I pull back my head, adrenaline flooding my body.

The silence is complete.

Surely he can hear my breathing? My heart is beating in my ears. Blood is rushing noisily through my brain. I peer around the bookcase again.

He's gone.

Impossible. I lean out farther to get a better view. The room is empty.

Did he see me and take off?

Cautiously I step around the bookcase, heavy coffee-table book in my hands.

Another step.

Still nothing.

Then a figure rises up from behind a pile of books to my left. Charges at me. I lean back and swing Annie Leibovitz's best photographs at his head. It explodes against his nose. I hear something crack. He groans and covers his face with his hands.

I pull the book back to hit him again, but he anticipates the move and jumps forward.

We fall to the floor, his body on top of me. He weighs less than I thought.

I use the momentum of the fall and roll over, planting my knee on his chest.

Again I hear something crack. "You fucker!"

I jam my fist into his face and put more weight on my knee.

He's struggling to breathe. A wet gurgle comes from his throat.

"Who are you?" I shout.

I go for his mask. Something about him smells familiar. Beer. And something else, something subtler. He snarls, jerks his head out of the way, and bucks his body from left to right, trying to throw me off.

Then he changes tack and digs in his heels. Lifts his lower body off the floor in a sudden, sharp movement.

I try to hold on, but I'm too slow. I fall, landing on the floor beside him. The tiles are slippery with blood. Must be his nose, bleeding.

My hands grope for his mask. Who is he?

As I'm reaching for his face, he scrambles to his feet. I crawl toward him, making a grab for his ankle.

His heel strikes my cheekbone with a massive force. Pain splinters through my face.

He bolts for the door. Throws it open.

"No!" I hear myself scream, but the night has already swallowed him. "No, no, no!"

I remain on all fours, gasping for breath. Shake my head against the darkness threatening to engulf me. Close my eyes. Open them again. Dim shapes begin to come into focus. The couch. The window.

Thank heaven.

But my relief is short-lived. I still don't know who the man is. And what if he comes back?

I stagger to my feet and stumble to the front door. How did he manage to get in? There are no scratches on the lock. Does he have a key?

Hadhi will have to help. I want a new lock.

I close the blue door and sit down on the floor, my eyes on the door handle. I get up, push the couch against the door, and sit back down again.

Get up. Check the door. Sit down.

My hands are shaking. I tuck them under my armpits until the trembling stops. I sit like that until the sun filters through the curtains. Then I get up and go to the bathroom to do something about my face.

I sit waiting for the sound of Hadhi's broom digging into the corners of the building as she sweeps the floors. Kettles boiling. Car doors being slammed. At the first sounds of morning I open the door, walk around the house, and knock on the front door.

She opens almost immediately. Her smile vanishes when she sees my face.

"Ranna! What's wrong? What happened?"

"I'm okay."

"Could have fooled me."

"I am. Promise."

She waves me inside, into the small communal kitchen at the back of the set of apartments. "I'll make tea." She grimaces. "And get some ice for your face."

With a steaming cup of sweet, milky tea in front of me, I manage to speak at last. "Someone broke in last night, Hadhi." I gingerly hold the plastic bag with ice against my cheek. The pain drills right into my head, and I have to clench my teeth not to groan out loud.

"Broke in?" She glances around. "Everything looks okay."

"It was just my place."

"Your place? Who would do such a thing?"

"I don't know."

"What were they looking for?"

"Don't know that either."

"And you? Did they hurt you? I mean, other than this?" She points at my face.

"No. It was just one man, and I managed to scare him away."

"What did he take?"

"Nothing."

She shakes her head. "Then we were lucky. Thank God."

I put the ice bag on the table. "What worries me is that he had a key. How did that happen?"

"What do you mean?"

"Just what I'm saying. How did he manage to have a key for my apartment?"

She straightens her shoulders, fire in her eyes. "You think I gave him one?"

"No, no, that's not what I mean. I just want to know whether there are keys lying around somewhere. Spare keys, you know? What about the previous tenants? Could they still have a key?" I take her hands into mine. "I'm sorry. I didn't mean to upset you."

Her shoulders relax a little, but her mouth remains pinched. "I have a key and you have a key. My key is never out of my sight. I don't know what you do with yours. People hand in their keys when they move. If they have spare keys made, I don't know about it."

"Can you remember who lived here before me?"

"A doctor. No, wait, that was next door. A cop. He didn't stay long, and I hardly ever saw him. He was here for about a month, taking an exam, and he wanted peace and quiet to study. I don't think it could have been him. And you should thank him—if he hadn't left so unexpectedly, you wouldn't have gotten the place."

"A cop? Do you remember his name?"

She shrugs. "I don't. His last name was something like Nyondo, I think."

I sip the sweet tea. The hot liquid burns my throat. It could be a fictitious name, or someone related to Hamisi. Nothing is impossible.

"You're right. It doesn't sound as if it could be him." I push the tea away. "That's all I wanted to know. Thanks."

I can see that I'll have to try harder. Hadhi looks really upset.

"I'm really sorry. I didn't mean to imply you've been careless with your keys."

"Okay. Stop it now." Her mouth softens and her shoulders relax. She gently touches my face. "Let me see what's going on here."

She frowns. Pushes my chin to the right. "Have you phoned the police?"

"I'm not going to."

She lowers her hands. "Why not?"

"I'd prefer not to."

"In other words, I shouldn't ask."

"Right."

"And if he comes back?"

I keep quiet. I've considered the possibility.

"Are you sure you know what you're doing, Ranna?"

"I hope so."

"It's your life, I suppose. And nothing I say will make you change your mind. You're way too stubborn." She gets up, takes my teacup. "I'll call and have new locks fitted on all the doors."

12

There's nothing wrong with the lock. I bend down again and inspect the mechanism from up close. No apparent damage or scratches. My first instinct was correct. Either the man had a key, or he's an ace with locks.

Who was the cop who stayed here for a month? Nyondo? Could be a false identity. Could have been Hamisi. I've been living with Hadhi for the past eleven months. Before that, I rented a room on the other side of the city. Hadhi had a long waiting list.

But if it was Hamisi, wouldn't Hadhi recognize him? She brought him tea a few days ago when he stood out here waiting for me.

On the other hand, she said she almost never saw the policeman who stayed here. And Hamisi could easily have found someone else to oversee the move and receive the key. It wouldn't have been hard for him to find out that mine was the next name on the waiting list.

I test the door mechanism. In and out. Open and shut. Again.

Something is wrong. Something besides Hadhi and the previous tenant. Something has been bothering me ever since last night's sleepless hours. I keep feeling I'm overlooking something.

There's only one way to find out. I fetch the Nikon, close the front door, and take a photo. And another.

It takes three minutes for the printer to spit out the images. I fan them dry and stick them on the fridge door with a magnet. Maybe the images will help dislodge the missing piece of the puzzle.

A flower, I decide. A purple lily. Almost beautiful in its ugliness.

I turn my head to allow more light on my face. Even the soft morning glow can't hide the fact that I look as if someone attacked me with a sledgehammer. The purplish-blue bruise has spread over my cheek and down to my jaw.

Work is not an option. There will be too many questions. And I have too many questions of my own to spend the next two hours at the opening of a railway conference.

I contemplate my image in the bathroom mirror. A thick layer of base will stop passersby from staring, but it's not so easy to hide a broken nose. What will the burglar do about his own face? Whoever attacked me last night is likely to be absent from work today. Or he'll be reporting for duty with a very obvious injury, just like mine.

I smile when I remembered the sound of his nose breaking, but the pain it causes brings me up short.

I wonder whether Hamisi Bahame will be at work today.

I walk up and down the street twice before I find what I'm looking for: a small street café with a view of Hamisi's office at the central police station. I know I could be wasting my time. Hamisi could decide not to come in today, or he may be working elsewhere.

But what if he arrives at the office with a broken nose?

It's important to choose the right table. I survey the plastic chairs and rickety wooden tables until I find a suitable spot. I make sure no one can see me from the white-and-light-blue building across the street, but that I can keep an eye on the front entrance. Unfortunately, it means I'll be sitting in the sun.

I order coffee from a woman with a flawless complexion and braids to her shoulder. When she brings my order and I nod my thanks, she tells me that the coffee comes from one of Tanzania's prime plantations.

She tells me to shout if I need anything else, her eyes locked on my bruised cheek.

Self-consciously I rub my face. "Accident."

She nods, smiles skeptically, and goes back to the counter to resume reading the paper.

Ten minutes later I'm drenched in sweat. Another five minutes, and my face feels as if it's being pricked with a thousand red-hot needles. I search my pockets but don't find what I'm looking for. The painkillers are still where I left them this morning—on my bedside table.

I've just decided to leave when the woman puts fresh coffee, a glass of ice water, and two aspirin in front of me. "You should see a doctor." She points at my face.

"I'm okay. Really."

She shrugs and returns to her newspaper.

"Thanks. You're a lifesaver!" I call after her, immediately regretting it when the sound rolls around inside my skull like marbles.

I swallow the pills with the water and finish the coffee. As I'm putting the cup down, Hamisi comes around the corner.

He walks the way he always does. Calmly, purposefully, with long strides. From my vantage point he looks completely normal. I was hoping for clear signs, like a bright white bandage on his face. Or some indication that he's having trouble walking or breathing.

Maybe he knows I'm watching him. Maybe he has seen a good doctor. Or maybe I didn't hurt him as badly as I thought.

The building swallows the detective.

For a moment I wonder what to do next. Then I fish my phone from my backpack.

I wait ten long minutes before I call his office. A woman answers in a singsong voice.

"Hamisi Bahame, please."

"One moment," she chimes.

Seconds later she's back on the line. "He won't be in today."

Impossible. I saw him enter the building just moments ago.

"Are you sure? He assured me he'd be available today."

"He *was* here, but he left again," the friendly voice replies. "He said he had something personal to attend to. Do you want to leave a message?"

"No, it's fine. Thanks."

I ask for the bill and leave a substantial tip to thank the woman for the aspirin.

Why did Hamisi decide to take the day off? Is it really a personal matter? A medical crisis, perhaps?

A moment later my phone rings. Maybe it's Hamisi.

I come to a standstill on the sidewalk. "Ranna, hello."

There's a moment's silence, before a metallic voice speaks: "You don't deserve him."

I stop in my tracks. A woman collides with me, then another. A middle-aged man in a suit angrily waves me aside.

I wait for the man to end the call, but unlike previous times, when he hung up after his brief message, I can still hear him breathing on the other end.

"Were you hurt last night?" I ask.

He doesn't answer.

"Hamisi?" I try.

"Green really isn't your color," he says finally, and hangs up.

I turn, look around me. People are shoving and pushing against me. I search the streets, surrounding buildings and shop windows. Nothing. I don't see anyone familiar.

I look down at my green T-shirt and the dead phone in my hand.

I hurry back to the café, suppressing a strong urge to get in the Land Cruiser and drive across the border to somewhere where no one knows my name. The kind woman who served me before gives me a quizzical look.

I signal for something to drink. Coffee. I need coffee. I'm trying to get a grip on my rising panic and anger.

He's late. The man is late. Billy has been dead for weeks.

Wait. What if he's not late? What if . . . ?

I take out my phone. Dial the number I know by heart. No reply.

"Come *on*!"

I dial again. Still nothing.

The woman puts the coffee in front of me. I leave it on the table. Get up. Walk up and down. Dial, dial, dial.

At last I hear a voice on the other end. I want to speak, to say hello, but all I can manage is a relieved laugh. Alex is still alive.

13

Charlie's morning news conference takes longer than expected. Bee rolls her eyes when I ask when he'll be finished. He has three appointments afterward, followed by lunch at a hotel with the South African ambassador. Go home, she suggests. She'll phone me as soon as he's back.

I meekly obey, though all I really want is to charge into Charlie's office and ask a hundred questions about Hamisi. I need more information. I must know whether he was also in Paris while I was there.

I spend the time sitting on the couch, downloading and sorting pics from the Nikon.

Bee phones just after three to say Charlie is back at the office.

I immediately call his cell phone. "Hi there. It's me."

"Ranna? Hello." He sounds surprised, then cautious, as if he's trying to work out how angry I am. "You must have got my message. Sorry, my girl. I mentioned to Hamisi that we'd spoken and only figured out afterward I probably should have kept my mouth shut."

"It's okay. I suppose you were just doing your job." I hope I'm a better liar than Charlie. There's no point in being angry. I need his help one last time.

The silence lingers. I can almost hear his instincts coming alive. As if he can smell I want something from him.

"If you're not calling to give me a piece of your mind, why are you phoning?"

"I'll give you an interview about Billy's death. In exchange for something very specific."

"Why would you do that? You're one of the most private people I know."

"Yes or no, Charlie. I'm sure the opposition will say yes." I consider the merits of a close-up shot of the president. Delete it.

"Okay. Take it down a notch. I'm listening. What do you want in return?"

"I want to know everything about Hamisi Bahame. Everything. And don't tell me you told me all of it the other day."

"What makes you say that?"

"You're too smart. You always hold something back. An ace up your sleeve. You'll be the most professional hack in the room until you die."

"You sound like my wife," he grumbles. "She says I'm a much better journalist than I am a husband."

"I believe her."

He swears under his breath. "Okay. But we'll do it question by question. One for you and one for me. The minute I suspect you're not telling the truth, the interview is over."

"The same goes for you. On one condition."

"I don't like conditions."

"I'm sorry to hear that." I close the laptop, put it aside.

"What is it, Ranna?"

"Are you going to tell Hamisi about the interview?"

"It's going to be in the paper. He'll know."

"That's not what I mean. Are you going to tell him we exchanged information? That part won't be in the paper."

"I won't say anything."

"My first police contact still sends me a Christmas card, even though it's to my mother's address." I get up, pace the apartment.

"Ah."

"You and Hamisi are friends."

"Were."

"Really?"

"Yes. But fine, you're right," Charlie concedes. "I do feel a kind of loyalty toward the man."

"Why?"

"I don't know. We've known each other a long time, even if we just have a beer now and again. But Hamisi has changed. Over the past few years—after his wife's disappearance—he's never been the same."

"Why do you still go drinking with him then?" I insist.

"I like him. And he's still a damn good cop. That hasn't changed."

"But you'll manage to keep your mouth shut?"

The newsman in Charlie has the last say. "I won't say a word. I promise."

14

Damn. Charlie's first question is a hard one. I gaze through his office window at a group of fishing boats bobbing in the water. I'll have to answer. It's Charlie's game, and I don't have much choice if I want the information I'm looking for.

I wish my mind was clearer. I hardly slept last night. I lay awake, listening for any small sound. For the turn of a key in the new lock in my front door. For the sound of a window breaking. But there was no sign of the mystery man.

Charlie clears his throat. "If it's too hard, perhaps we should leave it." The pen in his hand clicks in and out.

I close my eyes for a moment. Try to conjure up an image of Billy Jones and his Silicon Valley arrogance. I've been trying to forget for so long. Maybe it's better to soak up everything rather than wipe it out as if it never happened. Maybe it will make me angrier. Stronger.

"Yes, you're right," I reply at last without looking at him. "Billy and I had a thing going. It lasted for about three weeks. That's pretty much how long it took to find out we were better friends than lovers. We'd been friends for ten or more years, but sometimes I forget that friends should remain exactly that: friends. It wasn't the first time I'd made that mistake."

"How did you feel about his death?"

I turn away from the window and point a finger at him. "Isn't it my turn?"

Charlie stops writing and shrugs impatiently. "Okay. Shoot."

I cross my arms and lean against the windowsill. It's important to ask the right questions so that I can get the information I want as quickly as possible. Before this game goes on too long and I give too much away. Or I'm forced to lie. I like Charlie. I don't want to lie to him.

"Why do you suspect Hamisi had something to do with his wife's disappearance?"

"How do you know that, Ranna? That I suspect anything?"

I remain silent.

"Well, now you know," he mutters.

"So, are you going to answer?"

He lists the facts one by one on his fingers. "His wife found out about something. Something Hamisi had done. Something that happened in San Francisco. She told a friend she thought there was something wrong—that there might have been someone else—but she gave no further details. The next day she disappeared. Just like that. It's a little too convenient."

"Who's the other person?"

"Uh-uh, my turn. Why did you and Billy break up?"

"I met Alex at a wedding and . . . it just happened. For the first time it was about more than sex or convenience or need. I wanted to keep it clean, so I told Billy it wouldn't work between us."

I see Charlie biting back his next question. My turn.

"What happened to Hamisi in San Francisco?"

"No one is a hundred percent sure, but rumor has it that the FBI ordered him to leave the country."

"There must be more. Come on, Charlie."

He leans back in his chair and puts his hands behind his head. "There was nothing concrete. Like everything about Hamisi. There were rumors about sex. About young girls. About men. Drugs. You name it."

"What about the wife's friend? Did you speak to her about San Francisco or only to the police?"

"Me first. Do you think Billy was murdered?"

What shall I say? Can't tell the truth.

"I think he could have ended up in the water along with his house, or someone could have killed him," I say at last. "Your guess is as good as mine."

Charlie frowns, unconvinced.

I throw my hands in the air. "What I know and what I suspect are two different matters. I think someone probably killed him, but I have no proof. Hamisi has no proof. If it hadn't been for the rains, things might have turned out differently. Everything might have been clearer."

I look Charlie in the eye. "And you can have the next answer on the house. No, I didn't kill Billy. The two of us had come a long way. He saved my skin on a number of occasions. I would never have hurt him."

"Calm down, Ranna. I hear you." He taps on his desk with the pen. "About the friend. I spoke to her. She said Hamisi was obsessive about his wife. Didn't trust her. Wanted to know where she was all the time, what she was doing and who with. But he himself regularly went away, and no one knew where to. After his wife's disappearance her colleagues reported her missing, but the police never searched for her, despite the friend's belief that Hamisi had done something to her."

"Do you think there was someone else? For him? Her?"

"I'll give you a bonus as well: For her, no. For him? I'm almost a hundred percent sure there was someone. But she wasn't in Dar. Someone would have known. People talk in this town."

His eyes pin me down. "My question." The pen in his hand clicks in and out. In and out.

The sound echoes through my brain.

"Why did Hamisi suspect you of Billy's death?"

"Billy occasionally gave me money. Apparently I'm also in his will."

Charlie's eyes widen.

"It's not what you think," I protest with a smile. I know my answer was deliberately misleading, but I couldn't help it. "He left me something like a hundred thousand dollars—small change for someone like Billy Jones."

I see Charlie writing down the amount. He'll check the number, and I don't blame him. I'd do the same. But what he can never quantify is that a hundred thousand dollars is enough for me to start over, even a second time, and Billy knew it.

I wait for him to look up again. "Last question, Charlie."

"I have many more questions."

"But I'm done. Besides, you have enough for a story. By tomorrow I won't be able to answer my phone. How long do you reckon it will take before CNN knocks on my door? Or the BBC?"

Tom is going to kill me for giving this story to Charlie. In fact, the overall personal cost of this conversation will be massive.

Charlie hoists himself out of his chair, walks around the desk, and comes to a halt in front of me. "Forget about all the journos. Just for a moment. And about me. I don't know what's going on, Ranna, but I know something is wrong." He puts a large hand on my arm. "Be careful—very careful. Hamisi is no fool. Don't cross swords with him."

"I appreciate your concern, Charlie, but I'll be okay. I'm all grown up and I know what I'm doing," I say, though I hardly believe myself.

He shakes his head. Grins. He doesn't believe me either.

"As you wish, Ranna. As you wish." He retreats to a safe distance. Sits on the corner of his desk. "What's your last question?"

"Was Hamisi ever in Paris? And New York?"

"New York, yes. I got a postcard once. And a few copies of the *New York Times*."

"When?"

"Years ago. Soon after he inherited his father's money."

"When exactly? Think of the newspapers—what were the dates on them?"

"About ten years ago. I remember the papers were full of stories about GM filing for bankruptcy." He pushes his hands into his pockets.

Summer. The same time I was there. "And Paris?"

"I don't know."

Damn.

Charlie nods. "Okay. My final question. Did you love Alex?"

"That has nothing to do with Billy's death."

"I'd still like to know."

"Why?"

"He's worried about you. He calls here every now and then to check on you." His eyes seek out mine.

I turn to the window. "Charlie. Don't."

"Ranna. You promised to play along. Did you love Alex?"

"No. I love Alex."

"Why this thing with Hamisi then? Why are you still here?"

"Because sometimes love just isn't enough."

15

Maggie puts a steaming cup of coffee in front of me. Slaps me gently on the arm with the dish towel in her hand. "I'm glad you're not drinking today."

"What happened to being nice to your customers?"

"This is me being nice."

I'm back at my usual table. Jakes in his white cap is nowhere to be seen, but I keep thinking he'll walk into Hardings any moment.

No matter how guilty Hamisi looks, it doesn't mean I can rule everyone else out entirely.

Maggie spots me looking around. "He hasn't been here since your little game of twenty questions." She makes a snorting sound at the back of her throat. "I wouldn't want to look at you again either."

"I had to find out something. It was important."

"You chased away my second-best client."

"Sorry."

"He paid well. Tipped well. I miss him." Maggie lifts her eyebrows and wipes my table vigorously.

I put my hand over hers. "Sorry. I'll try and make up for the tips you've lost."

She throws the white cloth over her shoulder and puts her hands on her hips. "I don't know what the deal is with you and men. I see them with you, and the next minute they're here alone, asking about you, like schoolboys. Tom. Some cop or other. What happened to Alex? He was good for you."

"I wasn't good for him."

"Hmm. I don't know about that. With you, he lost some of his angles. You know, those stiff shoulders. The straight back. He relaxed." She looks at me quizzically. "Are you sure you can't get him back?"

"Maybe I can," I sigh. Am I equally persistent at times? "Who knows, Maggie. Maybe I can work a miracle if I try hard enough."

"Do you have a plan? It's always good to have a plan."

"Maybe."

"Do you have a plan involving *him*?" Maggie knows to drive me into a corner.

"Half a plan."

I realize it's the truth. I want Alex back. What's more, everything I have done in the recent past has been with that single objective in mind.

The only problem is that I'm running out of options. I can think of only one more plan of action. Instead of sitting here, looking for ghosts, I can wait for the ghosts to come to me, to find me, as always.

One last time.

"What's this?" Hadhi points at the photos of my front door on the fridge.

"Just some shots I took."

"I can see that. Why are they here?"

"Long story." I hand her a knife and fork. "Food's ready." I motion at the couch. "Shall we sit here?"

Hadhi takes her plate of bobotie and sits down. She tastes the curried minced beef carefully. "Lovely."

"My mother's recipe, though I improvised a bit."

"I remember. You've been promising me an invitation to dinner for months."

"Yes, sorry about that."

Her knife and fork freeze midair. "If it's finally happening, I presume you're on your way?"

I chew. Swallow. What can I say?

"Yes."

"When?"

"I don't know yet."

"Where?"

"Not too sure about that one either."

She points at the images tacked to the fridge. "The burglary. Do those have anything to do with it?"

"They have everything to do with it."

I go to bed that night like one who fears nothing. Like someone with a plan. With the courage to start over.

I close my eyes and fall asleep.

When I wake, my head is clear and my body rested.

I have to start packing. Where shall I go? Australia, perhaps. Or somewhere smaller. Peru. Northern Canada.

New name. New job.

No, that's too hard. I must make it easier, though not too easy. I must be careful not to do anything that will make the man suspect I'm planning something. It must be a well-known place, yet somewhere people can disappear. Vanish into thin air as if they never existed. Where lots of people stand out, so that in the end no one stands out.

The green hands of my alarm clock say it's already past eight. I've slept for ten hours. No wonder I feel so rested.

I put the clock down and get back under the covers, close my eyes.

During the night I had a dream. It played in my mind like a movie. Clear and precise. Frame by frame.

No. It was more than a dream. It was memories. Something triggered the camera in my head, made me understand exactly what I should do.

I go to the bathroom, take a shower, and brush my teeth. I'm on my way to photograph three new cabinet ministers. The extra cash will be useful, now that I'm about to get on a plane again.

I look at myself in the mirror. The woman staring back at me looks different than the one who stood there yesterday. This one is sure of herself. Purposeful. Is this what you look like when, after so many years, you finally know what you want from life?

ALEX

1

My mother is a small woman. Like a duiker or a sparrow or an ant.

You could easily miss her in a group. She blends in with the color and the noise. Her half-finished sentences hang unnoticed on the fringes of everyone else's noisy dialogue.

Among other people she becomes even more nondescript. Her pale blonde hair, now thoroughly streaked with gray, becomes even paler and the careful tread of her size-five sandals even more cautious. But when she smiles, people notice.

She's standing next to the man with the day-old stubble in the wrinkled khaki shirt, airport passengers pushing past them to the exit. As usual, my father's sunburned legs are wrapped in khaki shorts and brown socks pulled to his knees.

"Hello, Ma." I lean over and kiss her lightly on the cheek. She holds on to me as if she's drowning. Then she lets go, as if she knows it's unavoidable.

"You're home." Her voice is brittle, like old yellow paper.

"Just for a while," I warn.

"It's better than nothing." She points to her left. "Say hello to your father. He's in a hurry to leave."

I turn to the man with the disappointed mouth. The stem of his pipe protrudes from his shirt pocket, as always. "Pa."

"Alexander."

If he wasn't standing next to my mother, he'd be an ordinary man with one light-brown eye not perfectly synchronized with the other. The hands that can completely enfold hers would appear smaller. The same with the shoulders and feet in their brown veldskoens. But next to my mother, he's a giant.

Is that why he's still here? Because she makes him feel more of a man than he actually is? I look for signs of pain in the way she's holding her body, but I don't see any.

My father points at the Avis sign. "I don't know why you couldn't just rent a car."

I don't mention that I offered but Sophia Derksen flatly refused.

"Let's go. It's a long way," I say instead.

He mutters something, puts his hand on my mother's elbow, and steers her through the doors, where a Cape shower is steadily falling.

The farm looks exactly as I remember it. Beautiful and open. The veld is looking good after the recent rains, a multitude of yellow, white, and orange flowers blooming as far as the eye can see.

Sometimes it doesn't matter what you remember about a place, or what happened there. It's still the place where you took your first breath. Something enchanting remains, even if what happened later nearly destroyed all that was good.

My earliest memory is of my mother singing me to sleep. I always slept with the windows wide open and dreamed of the sea. Of the deep blue water swallowing me and spitting me out somewhere else. My favorite Bible story was the one about Jonah and the whale.

At other times I dreamed I could fly. Especially on the nights when my father's words unraveled into silence after too many brandy-and-Cokes.

Silence meant chaos would follow.

The older I got, the easier I found it to read my mother and father. I could probably read people before I could read books. When a muscle over my father's right eye began to twitch, he was angry. When he chewed without closing his mouth all the way, he was almost drunk.

The irony would later become clear: My father made me into the good journalist I became. Because of him, I know what people are thinking. Feeling. What they will do next.

Ranna is the first person I found impossible to read, I consider, as my father unlocks the back door.

No, forget about her.

"I put clean linen on your bed," my mother says as we step into the kitchen.

When I left for university, my bedroom became the guest room, even though there are seldom guests on the farm.

I drop my bag on the tiled floor. Push it up against the cupboards, out of my father's way.

"How long will you be staying this time?" he asks when we sit down at the rickety kitchen table. For as long as I can remember, my mother has been asking him to fix it.

"Francois, don't . . ." she begins.

We both look at her, surprised, but she has nothing more to say.

"Yes? You were saying?" I prompt.

My father won't touch her while I'm here. He stopped beating her in my presence the year I grew taller than him. That was also the year I began to fight back. For my pains, I got the scar under my eye. He wears his on his right shoulder.

My mother peers at my father from under her hair. At me. Shakes her head.

She needs a haircut. Maybe even a touch of color, if she wants. The gray has almost taken over completely. In the past she always wore her hair neatly styled. It was the one thing my father was always prepared to pay for. He grew tightfisted about clothing after they stopped going to church because people were talking.

Have they run out of money? The farm wasn't exactly a hive of activity when we drove up.

My mother gets up, begins to fill the sink with water for the dishes.

"I won't stay long." I finally answer his question. "Two weeks."

I get up, look around for a dishcloth. "The two of us should spend a day in Cape Town, Ma. I missed a lot of birthdays."

Her eyes light up when she looks at me.

"There's no need to waste your money," my father says as he fills his pipe.

"It's my money. And it'll be my pleasure. I'll pay for the diesel," I say over my shoulder.

"The bakkie's brakes have just about had it."

I say nothing. Focus on drying the dishes instead.

He lights his pipe. "Aren't we having coffee, Sophia?"

My mother leaves the dishes and scrambles to fetch cups and put the kettle on.

I wonder why I came. Nothing has changed. Not the rickety yellowwood table, nor the ancient FM radio in the corner churning out country music. Not my mother, and not my father.

Have I?

2

"Alex." I feel a hand on my shoulder. "Alex," the voice says again.

Reluctantly I open my eyes.

It's my mother. She motions with her head in the direction of the hall. "Someone on the phone for you. A woman."

"For me?"

"Yes. Do you want me to say you're sleeping?"

I look at the clock on the bedside table. Ten o'clock. Did I really sleep that late? Since I arrived it's almost all I've done. Eat, run, sleep.

I sit up. "No, I'm coming."

"Your father left early. Don't worry, no one will eavesdrop."

I want to protest, but keep quiet instead. She knows only too well I'm trying to avoid him. He gets up at seven—even later if he drank more than usual the night before—and comes in for breakfast at nine. By ten he has usually left again, got back into his bakkie to go and do whatever it is he does. The farm appears to be falling apart.

I get up, search for a clean T-shirt in my bag. "Are we going to town today?" I ask over my shoulder as I put on my shirt.

The hands that have begun to make the bed stop moving. "If your father says it's all right."

"Must he always give his permission?"

"Don't fight with me. He's not so bad. There has always been food on the table."

I swallow my rising anger, walk down the hall, and pick up the receiver. "Hello?"

"Don't put the phone down."

I recognize her voice at once. "Ranna? Is everything okay? Where did you get this number?"

"You left it in case of emergency at your last job."

Of course. "Where are you? Dar?"

"Johannesburg."

The word hits me like a fist in the stomach. "Why?"

"You mean, why didn't Hamisi lock me up? I'm innocent, Alex. I've always said I'm innocent, and no one has ever been able to prove otherwise."

I try to ignore the accusation in her voice. "No. I'm asking why you're in Joburg. What's going on?"

"I have a few things to do. And I want to see you."

"Don't tell me you've come back to South Africa?"

"I start a new job in about six weeks—hopefully."

"Why?"

"No reason. It was time to come home. But nothing has been decided yet."

"What do you want from me?"

She takes a deep breath, holds it. "A little bit of your time."

"To do what?"

"Talk."

"I tried talking to you so many times, and you refused. There's nothing more to say. We didn't break up about Billy. It was about you and your—"

"I'll try harder," she protests. "Just give me another chance, Alex, it's all I ask. Please?"

I can hear how she hated saying that last word. How she had to stop herself from spitting it out.

"What do you really want, Ranna?"

"I've told you. I want to see you. Explain. Make a better job of explaining."

Again the rapid-fire tone. For a moment I conjure her up in my imagination. How good it would be to see her again. To feel her olive skin under my fingers, her rapid breathing on my neck.

"Fuck, Ranna."

"I'll come to the farm."

"It wasn't a yes."

"It was."

"No."

"Please."

"Ranna."

"Alex. I . . . Please."

I look through the window, at the flat expanse outside. The veld that gets by on so little, like everything in this house. At least Ranna is more. Even though she's more trouble as well. More chaos.

Besides, I know better than to argue with her. She can read my mind like no one else ever could. She's right: it was a yes.

"The farm isn't good."

"I know. Your father."

"Meet me in Joburg. I'll be there in a few days."

I can almost hear her shaking her head. "No. I want to talk to you as soon as possible. In case I don't get another chance."

"What do you mean?"

"I'll explain everything, I promise. I can be there tomorrow evening. I'm leaving now. I'll only stay one night. Then I'm going to the West Coast for a short break."

"Ranna, no. Wait a minute."

"See you tomorrow," she says before I can say anything more.

"Fuck it," I mutter into the dead receiver.

"You father won't like it if you swear like that."

I turn to face my mother. She's holding two cups of coffee. Her hands, wrinkled and spotted, are more proof of how long I've been away.

"Sorry, Ma."

"Is it your girlfriend? Is she coming to visit?" Her eyes are sparkling with excitement. She must have overheard some of the conversation.

"She's just a friend. And yes. She'll be here tomorrow evening. She wants to stay the night." I run my hands through my hair, again longer than it should be. "Will that be okay?"

She nods, pleased. "We've been waiting so long for you to meet someone special."

I don't have the heart to tell her that things between Ranna and me have been over for a long time. That this is just an extended farewell. Nothing Ranna can say will convince me that she has suddenly stopped lying.

3

"Who is this woman?" My father helps himself to more food.

"She worked with Alex in Tanzania."

His knife and fork stop in midair. "I was speaking to Alex."

"Let Ma answer if she wants to," I say, annoyed.

She shakes her head almost imperceptibly, puts her hand over mine. Her arm looks pale and fragile under the bright fluorescent light in the kitchen.

"Listen to your mother," my father says sanctimoniously. "So, who is she?"

"I worked with her in Tanzania."

He waves his knife in my face. "Don't be clever."

I bite back an angry retort. It's not worth it. I have more important things to think of. Like the question that has been gnawing at me since this morning: Should I really expose Ranna to my family?

But what does it matter? She's nothing to me.

Then why am I so excited to see her?

"Alex! Hell, man, I'm talking to you," my father says. "Who is this woman exactly? And don't give me a sarcastic answer again."

"She's a photographer, Pa. We're friends. She's on her way to Cape Town for a vacation and wants to spend the night. That's all."

My mother looks disappointed. "Does that mean I have to make the bed in the study?"

"I don't know what you expected," my father says brusquely. "He's not exactly a Casanova."

I do what I always do, what I have always done: ignore him. I turn to my mother. "So, are we going into town tomorrow? I don't mind going to Tyger Valley mall, or even the V&A if you want."

I try to keep the tone light. She was scared to go today. My father was in a difficult mood.

"We'll be back before supper," I promise. I refuse to look at my father. I don't want him to think I'm asking his permission.

"What do you think, Francois?" she pleads.

My father says nothing. Puts the last forkful of food into his mouth. He seems to enjoy making her wait.

Again I swallow my anger. It's becoming increasingly difficult to remember that the man sitting opposite me is my father. The person who taught me to ride a bike and light a fire so many years ago. When and how did he become this man? This brittle, vicious person? My grandpa was a good man. Or did he just appear that way from afar—like my father?

"Pa. Come on. It will do us both good." My voice remains neutral. It won't help if I lose my temper.

At last he mutters, "Yes, all right. Go, if you must."

"What about this one?"

My mother steps out of the fitting room. She is wearing a dress in a floral print. The fine blue pattern makes me think of a thousand butterflies. And of Ranna. Ranna, who'll be arriving on the farm tonight.

I sit back to get a better view. "It's beautiful."

My mother twirls in front of a full-length mirror, and for a moment she's sixteen again and my father the man of her dreams. She was a Miss Van Heerden, daughter of the town auctioneer in a village north of Wellington, a place very few people know about. Her father went bankrupt three times. My mother and her two sisters, both dead now, grew up poor.

My father was the son of a sheep farmer and was the man who rescued her. She wanted to be rescued. It was long before women knew they could rescue themselves, she once—only once—said mockingly. It was when she turned forty and I was home from university for the holidays.

"Take that one, and the white one as well," I say.

She's tried on thirteen dresses, but I know I must be patient. She won't take anything if I seem in a hurry.

"It's too much. What will your father say?"

"He ought to say you look pretty." I motion for her to make another turn. "You look lovely."

I don't want to say that it's partly because she's out among people for a change. She hasn't spoken to anyone else in a long time. Or done something nice for no particular reason.

"Come," I say, "we're taking them both." I beckon the saleswoman over. "I'm going to tell this lady to help you choose the rest of the stuff. You know, those things boys aren't supposed to know about."

Sarah calls while I'm waiting for my mother, who bumped into a childhood acquaintance outside the shop. "You're back in the country."

"How did you know?"

"Easy."

I think of the array of computers in her living room, where other people have a couch and a TV. "Cell phone," I guess.

"Credit card. What are you doing?"

I look at the wallet in my hands. Laugh. "Visiting my parents."

"Nice."

I don't feel like contradicting her. "Why are you keeping such a close watch on me?"

"You owe me a beer. Or a whiskey. Can't remember."

"Fine. As soon as I get to Pretoria." I hesitate for a moment. There's a touch of uncertainty in her voice that I haven't heard before. "Is anything wrong? Are you okay?"

"My dad is ill."

"Is it serious?"

"Emphysema. All those cigarettes I've been buying him for years."

"Sorry."

She sniffs, exhales sharply. "Shit happens."

I wait until she finds her equilibrium again, then ask, "What else?"

"What do you mean?"

Sarah knows computers; I know people. "What else is wrong?"

"Your girl is in the country."

"I know."

An awkward, surprised silence. "Do you also know to be careful then?"

"Do you really think she's here to hurt me?"

I hear Sarah open a can. Coke, for sure. "That's not what I meant," she says.

"What then?"

"I've read the police reports on all those men who have died."

"And?"

"Something isn't quite kosher. I'm starting to wonder if she's as guilty as everyone makes her out to be. On the other hand, I can't spot anyone close to her who may be a serial killer. I've gone through every possible scenario, and I just don't know."

I think of Ranna and the man she told me about. Could she have been telling the truth all along?

"What are you really saying, Sarah? That Ranna is innocent?" I struggle to hide my disbelief.

She's silent for a moment. "I know what I said, but you make your own decisions, Alex. We've always agreed on that."

Annoyed, I run my hand over my mouth. It's not what I wanted to hear, but she's right. It's my life. My responsibility.

"What did you find out?"

"A few interesting things. I asked around. I was curious. And jealous. You know you're the man of my dreams," she adds in a lighter tone, as if she's trying to cheer me up. "I read through all the police reports and spoke to more cops than I'm comfortable with. Her alibis were good—except for Dar es Salaam."

"Yes? And?"

"There's something curious about all the murders. The fingers."

I remember Ranna said something about fingers, but I thought it was just another bullshit story. "What do you mean?"

"All the men were missing a few fingers. Well, okay, not all of them. The guy in San Francisco lacked only one. The guy in Paris, two—not cut off either. And you know about Billy. Four digits missing."

"What do you mean, the guy in Paris didn't have his fingers cut off?"

"They were bitten off."

I think of the day we found Billy's body. So it wasn't the fish.

"Does that mean the same guy killed them all? It's got to be a man. A woman wouldn't do that. I think."

"Statistically you're right. It's very rare that a woman would do something that violent."

"So, Ranna may be innocent." The realization is a heavy, spiked weight in my stomach.

"Maybe. Maybe not," says Sarah. "The detective who investigated the case in Paris thought she had a partner. He was keen to arrest her. In fact, he did, but he had to let her go. There just wasn't enough evidence, and her alibi was solid."

"She won't have a partner. Ranna is a loner."

"I don't think it really matters, Alex. It's a bit of an academic argument. You should be careful. That's why I called. Ranna may not be a killer, but it doesn't change the fact that men die wherever she makes an appearance. You've got to watch your back." Sarah clears her throat. "And I think the fingers . . . whoever is killing all these men is escalating. He's not playing anymore. This is one crazy bastard, Alex."

4

"Hi. I'm at the gate. It's as stubborn as a mule."

I laugh. I'm not sure whether it's at the sound of her voice or the thought of her tall figure struggling with a sagging wire farm gate. "I'm coming."

"Bring a bandage along."

"What have you done?"

"What do you think?" she asks.

The barbed wire must have nicked her.

Ten minutes later I park the bakkie at the gate. On the other side of the fence Ranna is leaning against a Polo sedan, her face turned to the dry wind, her Ray-Bans the only protection against the late-afternoon sun. Her black hair is shorter than I remember, her complexion a darker olive. Gorgeous, as always.

"South Africa has been good to you," I call out.

"The body remembers, even if the mind forgets."

I open the gate and wait for her to drive through, but she stops her vehicle next to mine. She gets out, walks up to me. She smells of soap and green apples, the familiar smell of lemons lingering in the background.

"Alex." She touches my arm lightly, as if she's afraid I'll disappear.

"Yes?" My breath catches in my throat.

"Please do something before we see your parents."

"What?" I look into her eyes and see something there I've never seen before. The absence of something. Something I never realized was there all along. Fear.

"Kiss me."

"You shouldn't have come." I point at the landscape around us, punctuated with a bloom of orange and white flowers every now and then, turning the normally sparse Namaqualand into a picture postcard. "Not here. Not this place."

I wish I could take my mother to meet her somewhere far from here.

"Here is good," she whispers. "Nothing I see is going to scare me." She leans forward and touches my cheek lightly—first with her hand and then with her lips. "Hello, Alex."

I clear my throat to get my voice back. "Let's go." I point at the farmhouse in the distance. "Drive in my tracks. The road isn't very good."

She gets into the Polo, starts it up, and pulls away. I close the gate and walk to the bakkie. Get in. Search for first gear before navigating the narrow road slowly as to create as little dust as possible.

Fuck. What the hell is going on? Is Sarah right? Could Ranna be innocent? And if she is, what happens then? Do I have the energy to try again? To help Ranna fight this thing that's haunting her?

My mother is wearing one of the new dresses, the colorful one that falls softly to her ankles. She tugs at it nervously and gets ready to shake Ranna's hand.

Ranna doesn't hesitate. She leans over, puts her arms around my mother, and hugs her. "I've heard so much about you, Mrs. Derksen."

Awkwardly my mother pats her on the back. "Call me Sophia."

"Okay, Sophia."

No one else notices, but I see Ranna exhale slowly before turning to my father. I didn't tell her much, but what I said was enough.

"Mr. Derksen," she says.

His eyes skim over her. I've seen men behave in a similar manner before: with too much imagination and too little respect. It infuriates me. For my mother's sake and my own, but strangely enough not for Ranna's. I have no doubt that she'll sort him out if he comes looking for trouble.

"And you can call me Francois," he says.

Ranna doesn't respond, just gives his hand a swift, firm shake, then takes a few steps back as if she can't wait to get away.

She looks at my mother again. "Thank you for your hospitality. I'm sorry to arrive here out of the blue."

My mother shakes her head and runs her hands over the dress, patterned in red, dark green, and mustard. "You must be thirsty. Come in, and I'll make you a cup of tea. Alex can show you where you'll be sleeping. It's in the study. I hope you don't mind."

"Bathroom." I incline my head in the direction of the hall.

"Why?" Ranna is standing next to the single bed in the study, an enormous room with a high ceiling, beige curtains, and a desk large enough for a game of table tennis, a folded T-shirt in her hand.

"I want to disinfect your hands before you unpack."

She studies her left hand and holds it up for my inspection. "Hand. Singular. Do you think I need a bandage?"

The deep red scratch extends all the way across her palm, next to the scar caused by the broken glass in Dar. "I think so. That wire was rusty. If you're a good girl, I'll give you a Pooh Band-Aid."

"Pooh? Like in Winnie?"

"My mother keeps them for the farmworkers' children."

"That's a nice idea." Ranna stares at her injured hand. "She looks like a kind woman. And she loves you very much."

"Not enough to leave him." The words are out before I can stop them.

Ranna puts the T-shirt down but keeps gazing at it. "Sometimes you can only see what's there. It's hard to imagine anything else. Anything better."

"You're probably right. And she doesn't have any money of her own."

"How many times have you offered to help her?"

"Often." I sigh wearily. "Not often enough."

"What did she say?"

"She once said it may be hell, but it's hers. It's the one thing she's got. That, and me."

Something like regret moves over Ranna's face, as if she's sorry she broached the subject.

She holds out her good hand to me. "I definitely want a Pooh Band-Aid. I won't settle for anything less."

5

"She's a real looker. Are you sure she's not your girl?"

My father is standing outside on the stoep, puffing at his pipe. We're waiting for my mother to call us in to supper. Ranna has disappeared to take a shower, promising to be ready in five minutes.

"She was, but not anymore. Maybe sometime in the future again."

My father runs his hand over his clean-shaven face. He smells of Old Spice and Lux soap. I try not to think about the reason for the sudden midday bath.

"Listen to yourself, Alexander. This way and that way. Put in a little effort, man."

"Leave it, Pa."

"She must be good in bed," he persists. "She looks as if she's been around the block."

"Pa . . ."

"What?"

"Just be quiet tonight, please. Don't embarrass Ma and me . . ."

"Doing what?"

"Nothing."

"You've always been a coward," he smirks. "Any real man would have dragged that girl to bed the minute she got here."

"Just be quiet."

He turns to me and taps me on the chest with the stem of his pipe. "Careful how you talk to me. You are under my roof now."

The words are filled with bravado, but we both hear the slight hesitation. As if he remembers what happened the last time he picked a fight with me.

My father holds out the serving dish to Ranna. "Have another lamb chop."

"I can't eat another thing. Thank you." She waves her hand to include both her empty plate and my mother. "That was the most delicious pumpkin pie I've ever had. Was it cinnamon I tasted?"

"There's nothing better than Karoo mutton," my father says before my mother can reply. He gulps down the last of his brandy-and-Coke.

I stopped counting at four.

We're in the rarely used and recently dusted dining room with the windows wide open, paint peeling overhead on the ceiling. We're sitting at one end of a heavy, twelve-seater yellowwood table. Apart from a jackal calling in the distance, the silence is complete. The yellow moon, almost full, is suspended in a sky full of stars.

I breathe a sigh of relief because the meal is drawing to a close. It reminds me of Sunday afternoons before going back to boarding school. Time couldn't pass quickly enough.

Ranna gets up. "Let me help clear the table."

My mother shakes her head. Her hands fumble nervously in her yellow-and-white apron. Her eyes dart from me to my father. "No, leave it. There's still malva pudding for dessert."

Ranna sits down again. "I don't know when last I had malva pudding." She runs her hands through her hair. Smiles.

"It's our pleasure to spoil you."

"It is," my father echoes, but his smile seems fake and contrived.

I know that smile. It usually appears just before he starts criticizing everyone within earshot. It's the short, caustic preamble before my mother becomes the target of his fists.

The barely concealed irritation is already visible in his eyes. Is it because Ranna is doing her best to ignore him?

I look at my mother, but she avoids my gaze. She has noticed it too. Like me, she hopes she's mistaken.

I don't have the energy for what may follow. I keep on hoping he'll remember we have a guest tonight and behave.

"Ranna and I have to talk about work," I lie. "I know her new boss. She wants some advice. Do you think we could have our dessert on the stoep, Ma?" I stand up. "Come and have yours with us."

She hesitates a moment. Pushes the gray hair out of her eyes. "I'll bring it. And some coffee." She speaks without looking at Ranna, as if she's ashamed to have a stranger witness her fear.

Ranna covers my mother's hands with her own. "That'll be lovely, Sophia. Thank you."

I choose the set of wicker chairs farthest from the front door.

"How on earth did you survive?" she asks as she sits down beside me.

"I might as well ask how *you* survived."

It's not a question, and I'm not looking for an answer. I don't want to be reminded of the long nights under my bed while he was beating her. I was three or four when it began.

In time I learned that the night could be your friend, and headed out the window and off into the dark to escape. The first few times my father came looking for me in the bakkie and beat the crap out of me. He gave up later on. Or simply couldn't be bothered anymore.

"You're probably right," she says. "But now it's over for both of us."

"On nights like these I wonder if it will ever be over."

"It only stays with you if you let it."

"Easier said than done. Every time I see him I want to bash his head against a tractor wheel."

"Did he ever beat you?"

"Sometimes." My fingers search for the scar under my eye. "But only until I outgrew him. I take after the men on my mother's side. The last time he tried to punch me, I beat him so badly my mother had to intervene. It felt good, liberating. But then the humiliation set in: I was no different from him. He left the farm and stayed away the rest of that school holiday, returning only after I'd gone back to boarding school. And fighting him didn't make any difference. He went straight back to beating her. No one wins. Ever."

"And today? Is he still beating her?"

"I think so." Why lie to myself? "I know he is."

I keep listening for my father's footsteps inside the house. I don't want him to overhear our conversation.

"Can't you do something about it?"

"No. I've learned that it's not up to me. She has to leave him, and she doesn't want to." I clench my fists in frustration. "Leave it, Ranna. It's water under the bridge. Tell me why you're here. Did Hamisi finally give you permission to leave Tanzania?"

She kicks off her sandals and tucks her long legs under her chin. The cool night air plasters her blue T-shirt against her body. I can't help but notice her breasts responding.

"I didn't kill Billy, so Hamisi had no reason to keep me in Dar. It's like I told you: I didn't kill Billy, even though you don't want to hear it."

"So we're back to the infamous man who got me into so much trouble last time."

"That's why I'm here. And because of you."

Her words, and the sudden tenderness in her tone, catch me off guard so that I don't hear my mother approaching.

"Malva pudding and coffee," she says from the doorway before she walks out and places the tray in front of us.

I take her hand.

"Have yours out here with us," Ranna offers.

My mother runs her hand over her mouth as if she's considering it. Then she waves away the invitation. "No, it's fine. You two talk. I'm going to do the dishes."

She leaves as noiselessly as she came. Ranna's eyes follow her, her gaze dark and brooding.

"What did Hamisi say?" I steer the conversation back to Billy and Dar es Salaam. For now, it's all I'm able to focus on. I'll worry about my mother later. One thing at a time.

Ranna makes no reply.

"Ranna?"

Her eyes return to me. "Hamisi believed me."

"You must have given him more information than you gave me," I say defensively.

How could Hamisi have believed her? From the little I knew I certainly couldn't muster the same degree of faith. No one could.

She shrugs. "You may be right. I was more defensive with you. But to be honest, you didn't give me a chance. Your ego prevented you from listening. Everything I did was to protect you. Every single thing. Like asking you to keep our relationship secret. I didn't want my stalker to find out about you."

"You couldn't prove anything. Do you know what your story sounded like?"

"That's why I'm here. To clear up a few things. To try again. Maybe? You know, if you're willing. I understand that I didn't tell you enough. Trust you enough. All that good stuff. I could have done better. Much better. But if we're lucky I can maybe wrap things up. Move on."

"Whoa. Stop. What do you mean, 'wrap things up'?"

She tucks her hair behind her ears. The familiar gesture makes my heart contract. "The man will probably follow me here. To South Africa."

I look at her in disbelief. "Follow you here?"

"I think I know who he is. When he shows up here, I'll know for sure."

"And then what? He comes here and kills you? Me?"

"No," she protests hastily. "Not here to the farm. I'd never endanger you like that. He always takes a while to work out where I am. After tonight I'll leave you alone until it's over. He won't know we spoke. Besides, I think his attention has shifted to me instead of the men in my life."

"How do you know that?"

"I just know."

"What happened?" I insist, trying to stare her down.

"Nothing."

"Bullshit."

"Believe what you want."

"And when you finally face him? What then, Ranna? What will you do?"

She breaks eye contact, laughs. The sound is uncertain, nervous. "I haven't thought that far ahead."

"Did Hamisi help you devise this bizarre plan?"

"No. Yes. Maybe. He's involved—in a way."

"Sounds familiar. Another straight answer from Ranna Abramson."

She shakes her head, but says nothing. Instead she pours the coffee and offers me a cup. I take it, though I really crave something stronger.

"So what do I do now? What do you want from me?"

She sips her coffee and looks at me. "I want you to say you'll be here when the whole thing is over. I want you to say you still love me. That you believe me, believe *in* me. I want you to know I'm sorry I didn't trust you."

She stops talking. Puts the cup down. Wrings her hands. "That's all. Is it too much to ask?"

How am I supposed to answer her? I'm caught between what I believe and what Sarah told me during our last conversation. I want to trust Ranna, but I can't just forget about Dar and the lies she told me.

And what makes Hamisi's thought process different from mine? Why did he believe her when I couldn't? What does it say about me? About the great love I thought I felt?

Still feel.

Oh, fuck.

"Say something," Ranna whispers.

I remember how I felt the first time I saw her. How I can probably feel again if I allow myself to forget about Billy and Gerard and the others.

There's no such thing as the ultimate, final truth. Facts change, something moves out of position, and everything is suddenly different.

I make a decision I hope I won't regret. "In a week or so I'll be in Joburg. For good. Let's see what happens."

Her coffee cup pauses on its way to her lips. She tries not to look happy. I can almost see her wrap up the emotion and store it for later.

"Slow is good," she agrees. "But give me a month or so. I've found an apartment in Rosebank. If all goes according to plan, I'll be starting as a photographer at Media24 in June."

I pick up a bowl of malva pudding and tuck in. It's rich and soft and perfect. I point my spoon at the other bowl. "Eat. My mother will wonder what's the matter if you don't."

She puts her cup down and reaches for the dessert but stops halfway. Her hand changes direction and searches for mine. She touches my arm. I think of the butterflies on the way to Korogwe. Always butterflies. Light and free.

"Alex. If something is good—if you know it's good—it can sometimes be enough to push you in the right direction. To get yourself sobered up to start over. That's what you are to me—a good thing. A reason to move. Like a law of physics."

"Hmm. I hear you."

We finish our coffee and dessert.

"Tell me about this stalker of yours," I say as she puts down her empty cup. "And I mean everything. That's the one condition I have. I'm not going to live with your silences and lies any longer."

"I will."

"And I want to know what you're planning. I can't let you leave here just to lose you again. I want to know what kind of harebrained scheme you've hatched."

"Okay. Fine. I'll make sure we talk before I leave tomorrow."

Inside the house a door slams. The sound of muffled voices drifts through the window.

I listen, wait until they die down. "Where are you going tomorrow?"

"Elands Bay for a week or so. To gather my thoughts."

"Will you be safe? Will you be speaking to the cops there?"

"Like I said, it usually takes a while for him to work out where I am. And to find a way and an excuse to follow me. This time I want him to follow me, but I haven't made it easy, or he'd smell a rat."

"Do you know what this plan of yours sounds like?" I shake my head in disbelief. "It's madness."

"It's the only way and you know it."

"Let me come with you."

Ranna considers the offer for the briefest of moments. "Too obvious."

"Then we must get you some help. I know someone. He's very good. He was in the police for a long time. The counterinsurgency unit."

"No need. I also have some connections. I'll sort it out. And it's a lot easier now that I can see him coming. I'm almost certain I know who he is."

"Who?"

She shakes her head, inhales the cool night air. "Tomorrow."

"Do I know him?"

She doesn't answer. An uneasy feeling grabs hold of me. A heaviness. Chaos all over again?

"Ranna."

"It's a beautiful night. Why waste it talking about such ugly things?"

I'm about to close my bedroom door, towel and toothbrush in hand, when she appears in the hallway clad in a T-shirt and very brief pajama bottoms. It takes every ounce of willpower not to stare.

"I'm looking for something to read," she says.

"Why don't you try to sleep?"

"I will, but it would be nice to have a book handy in case I struggle to fall asleep."

"Is there nothing interesting in the study?"

"Not really, unless you have a thing for forty-year-old farming magazines. And I'm not crazy about mags anyway."

I point at the dark belly of the house. "Most of the books are in the sitting room. My father reads magazines and my mother prefers love stories and gardening books. Those are your options."

She thinks for a moment. "Gardening."

"Then let's go get you a book on gardening."

I walk past her to the sitting room with its threadbare carpet. My father's hunting trophies are mounted on the wall—as well as the two bucks reluctantly shot by my mother. I randomly choose something from the bookcase and hand it to Ranna.

She weighs the book in her hand. Pages through it. "Three hundred and fifty-six pages on pests and diseases found on rosebushes. Sounds fascinating."

There's no sarcasm in her voice.

I shake my head and my eyes travel over her body, openly this time. I lean in, kiss the curve of her neck. "Try to sleep."

She returns to the study, and I think how badly I want her in my bed.

If my heart was a place, it would be full. Messy, yes. Noisy, certainly. But alive.

6

Ranna's insomnia is infectious. Unable to sleep, I listen for any sign of life from the study but hear nothing. Ranna is probably dead to the world already. The only sound I can track is the shuffling of feet on the worn carpet of the main bedroom. A muted voice. A door slamming.

Usually my father behaves when strangers are around, but tonight he's had too much to drink. Maybe the liquor has clouded his judgment to such an extent that he's forgotten we have a guest. Hopefully the noise won't wake Ranna. My room is next door to my parents', but Ranna is three doors away, next to the sitting room.

I hear my father fumbling with the brandy bottle next to the bed, filling his glass and walking to the bathroom, to which my mother has fled. He knocks on the door, waits a moment, and turns away. The bed creaks as he sits down.

I know that she will stay there until he tries to shout down the door. If she's lucky—along with Ranna and I—he'll fall asleep before it happens. If not, there's going to be trouble tonight. I've made up my mind. I've had enough.

Then I hear a different sound. Something not from the script of my past. A muffled sound from Ranna's room. Can it be? Or is it my imagination? Is she still awake? What if she's heard my father? What if she does something stupid before I can stop her? She knows this particular pattern of violence too well not to understand what may happen between my mother and father tonight. It's a language she speaks fluently.

I get up and hurry to the door. Ten long strides down the hall to the door of the study.

I open the door.

The scene in front of me stops me in my tracks. Ranna is on the bed, her mouth taped shut. A man is sitting behind her. His back is against the wall, and he's holding Ranna in front of him like a shield. One hand is gripping her hair, pulling her head back, and the other is pressing a knife to her throat.

Before he even looks up, I realize who it is.

Ranna was right. There *is* a man. And I know him well.

RANNA

1

Words are Alex's salvation. His escape from the past. He can write himself away from a situation. Explain everything. Rationalize whatever happened.

Pictures are mine. Photos have saved my life so many times. Photos of every kind. Real photos and those you take with your eyes and store for later use. Images stay in my mind, and at night, when I can't sleep, I flip through them and look at what I wasn't able to take in during the day.

Strange how you learn to survive on other people's emotions. Their happiness and grief.

What I don't have is a photographic memory—very few people actually have one. Mine is just a finely tuned visual memory.

In the end, after all the detective work in Dar es Salaam, it was a simple memory that made the formerly obscure suddenly become clear. A moment re-created by means of a photo I stuck on my fridge. The one of my front door. That's the photo that made me wake up that last week in Dar and know who this man is.

I should have figured it out sooner.

Or maybe I knew all along. Maybe I just didn't want to admit that anyone could betray me like that. That I was too foolish to guess his identity sooner.

I weigh the book on roses in my hand. Do I really have the energy to read it? Maybe I should fetch a love story instead. I yawn and look at my cell phone. Hamisi called earlier, but it's too late to call him back now. It's almost eleven o'clock.

I put the book down on the desk. Maybe I should just try to sleep.

I get into bed and lie listening for sounds from the main bedroom. Nothing. But I don't have to hear anything to know what's going on. The oppressive atmosphere permeates the whole house. The clammy, dark shadow cast by Francois Derksen.

I know Alex feels humiliated by my presence. And yet he allowed me to come here. Maybe a part of him wanted me to see how he grew up, so that I'll know everything about him. Where he comes from. Who he is.

Or maybe I matter so little to him that he doesn't care what I see?

And yet . . . he did say we could try again. It's something I've never done before. Just as I've never stopped running.

Maybe it's time to try something new.

2

A soft, insistent sound wakes me.

I know at once what it is. I know it the way you simply know after years of waiting. But I always thought I would be less afraid. Angrier. At the very least more prepared.

In the bright moonlight falling through the open window I see him move closer. Slowly, cautiously. The sound I heard was the bottom of his jeans scraping the floor. A familiar sound. Something I've heard a million times before.

How did he get here so fast? And how did he know I'd be with Alex? I left a trail of false clues, as always, but this time he must have followed me directly, all the way from Dar.

Is that why Hamisi called? To warn me?

Fear paralyzes me. The man's presence here means the rules have changed dramatically. He no longer cares if I know his identity or if Alex finds out. That Alex's parents are here.

He's going to kill us all. Why was I stupid enough to come here? I should never have risked it, thinking he would behave as he has always done.

With his next step, there's a dim flash in the moonlight, and I can make out the knife in his hand.

My breath catches in my throat, but I exhale evenly. Nothing must give away that I'm awake. I must find a weapon. In my imagination I walk through the room. The rose book on the desk. The bedside lamp. The water glass. I have pepper spray and a pocketknife, but they're in my bag in the corner of the room. I haven't yet picked up the pistol a contact arranged for me. I was to pay three thousand rand cash for the firearm in Hillbrow next week. What good is it now?

This is what happens when you get complacent. When you think you know your enemy. The attack in Dar should have warned me that everything has changed, including the speed at which he moves.

I peer at him from under my eyelids. He stops dead.

Now. *Use your size and your weight and charge past him. Get out of the house . . .*

Yet I lie without moving. It will be the end of Alex. Of his parents. I am Tom Masterson's first prize. No one else.

The bed sags under his weight as he sits down beside me. The phantom who pursued me for so long is finally a reality. He smells of beer, cigarettes, and his usual cologne. It's sharp and sweet in my nostrils, like that evening in Dar when he groped me.

He nudges my shoulder. "I know you're awake. I spent so many nights outside your window. I know your breathing when you sleep. When you're afraid. When you're about to come. I know everything about you, Ranna Abramson." He runs his fingers lightly down my arm, pushes his hand into mine.

It's hard not to recoil at his touch. I want to tell him he's wrong, he doesn't know me at all, but the words won't cross my lips.

He switches on the bedside lamp. I search for his eyes in the dim light, but my gaze freezes on the knife in his hand. "Why, Tom? What have I ever done to you?"

He presses the blade against my throat. "Quiet. We can talk later. Hold out your hands."

I do as he asks. He pulls handcuffs from his pocket and clicks them in place around my wrists.

"You don't need to do this. I'll come with you, no questions asked. Just leave Alex and his family alone."

"Alex? I don't think so." He spits out the name. "It was different with the others, you never really cared about any of them."

I want to lie. I want to say I'm sorry for whatever I may have done. Push my body against his and tell him he's the one I've always wanted. But I can't.

"I hope you die a slow, painful death," I hiss.

His eyes grow dark. Deep lines form around his mouth, his face an almost unrecognizable mask. From his jacket pocket he produces a roll of duct tape. He unrolls a length of tape, cuts through it with a single stroke, and tapes my mouth shut.

The sound is loud in the silence—too loud. He and I both know it. I see him grin when we hear a door open in the hallway.

Alex.

No! I yank at the handcuffs, my voice sticking in my throat.

Tom slaps me so hard I taste blood. "Quiet."

He slips in behind me, yanking me back against his body. Positions himself so that we're both facing the door. With his back against the wall, he tugs at my hair until my head is just below his chin. The knife hovers between my breasts.

I dig my nails into his arm until I feel the skin tear.

"Bitch." He slaps me. Again. "Play along or you'll get hurt."

He presses the knife against my throat. I keep struggling, scarcely aware of the pain, until I feel something warm and sticky trickle down my chest.

Alex. I must warn him. I try to slip out of Tom's grasp, but he yanks me back toward him. The knife goes in deeper. A sharp pain shoots through my body.

"You've always had such beautiful breasts," he hisses in my neck just before the door opens.

3

"Quiet," Tom warns, the knife a silent exclamation mark in the air.

Surprise floods Alex's face. It starts in his eyes and moves down to his open mouth. Then comes recognition, and the realization that he has been wrong all along. About Tom. About me. About everything.

I almost laugh at the irony. If Tom kills me tonight, at least Alex will know I haven't been lying.

In a strange way I'm almost glad Tom is here. I've often wondered whether this man was nothing but a figment of my overactive, paranoid imagination. Whether he doesn't exist, and I am nothing but stark raving mad.

The Englishman messed up the night I got drunk and he took me home from Hardings. We'd spoken about where I lived before, but I'd never given him the address. Yet he drove directly to my apartment. He walked past the row of doors at Hadhi's, straight to my door. And he immediately selected the right key from the bunch I handed him.

Tom with all his police contacts. Good old Tom Masterson, who worked with me in Paris. Who must also have been in San Francisco.

The only thing I still don't know is why. It's the most important question. If I must die tonight, at least I want to know why.

The knife moves lower, pushes into the skin on my chest, when Alex takes a step forward.

"Stay where you are," Tom says in a soft, flat voice. "And be quiet."

We all stiffen when Francois Derksen begins to shout. "Where are you, Sophie? Come out of this fucking bathroom, you bitch!"

He seems to be beating on the bathroom door, with his hands at first, then with his fists.

"Come out! You can't be brushing your teeth all this fucking time!"

Alex tilts his head to listen, concern on his face.

"If that was my old man I would have sorted him out a long time ago," Tom sneers. "I can't believe big, strong Alex turns out to be such a bleeding wuss."

Alex makes no reply.

Tom scoffs. "Take a look at your brave lover."

He lets go of my hair for a moment and pulls off the tape so that I can answer. I taste blood on my lips, inside my mouth. "Who the hell are you to talk? You're the biggest coward I know. Sneaking around in the dark. Attacking me. Killing Gerard. Peter. Billy."

The knife's blade taps against my forehead. "Shut up. Don't be a stupid little girl now."

Alex takes another step forward.

"Uh-uh, stay right there," says Tom. "You don't want Isabel to get hurt, do you? We haven't even had a chance to chat yet."

"Chat about what?" I ask.

"You know."

"No, Tom. I don't know. I have no idea what's going on."

"Of course you know. You're not stupid."

I shake my head. "I really don't."

The hand in my hair clenches into a fist. He turns my head so that I look him in the eye. "Very well. Let's play this little game of yours. Let's show Alex who you really are and why we're all here tonight."

"Please fucking do," Alex hisses.

"Quiet, wonder boy," says Tom. "You don't want your girlfriend to get hurt now, do you?" His attention turns back to me. "Tell me the names of the men in your famous photo series—the one for which you got that shiny award."

"Which men? The firemen?"

"Yes."

"It's been years. I don't remember their names."

"Try."

I think back to the night of the fire. The images are still fresh in my mind. I close my eyes and see everything. The smoke. The flames. The fear of the trapped children. The bulky men in their oxygen masks repeatedly charging into the flames to save just one more child. Afterward I asked their names for the captions.

Very well, the captions. I conjure the first photo in my mind. The one of the two men with a child in each arm. "There was a Teasdale. Kennedy." The men resting next to the fire truck nearest to the scene. "Peters. Kelly. The one that got hurt . . ."

I look at Tom, astonished. "Impossible."

"Don't pretend you don't remember. I know you don't forget anything."

"Elliot Masterson?"

"Correct." He spits out the word. "My father was the fireman who lost his job because of your photos."

"What do you mean? They were all heroes! Every one of them."

Tom's face becomes twisted with rage. "They were! But your photos showed my father doing something he would never have done. You did something to those photos. You manipulated them to make them more sensational, so that you could win your fucking award."

"I didn't change any of them. Not one pixel."

"My father lost seven fingers in that fire. He was a hero. You changed the photos. That's why you refused to accept the World Press Photo award. You knew what you'd done."

"I refused the award because Peter died. Because the police wouldn't leave me alone. I wanted to get away from San Francisco. From you."

"No, no, no." The hand in my hair shakes my head in rage. "You refused because you changed the photos. You made it look as if my father had frozen, as if he was too scared to enter the building, as if he injured himself on purpose so that he wouldn't have to go inside the fire. You were afraid someone would find out."

I remember the man in the photos. Elliot Masterson. A shortish man standing at a window, staring at the flames as if he was hypnotized. He must have stood like that for five minutes before my attention shifted to the first child rescued from the flames. When I saw him again much later, the paramedics were bandaging his hands, and I assumed he'd been injured in the fire.

The series of photos were in all the papers, winning the World Press Photo award a year later.

"Tom." I try to calm him down. "I didn't change any of the photos. Your father was just like all the others—brave and strong and doing what they knew had to be done."

"His colleagues didn't think so. After you sent the photos, they plastered the extra copies all over the walls of the station. They said he should resign because they didn't want a coward as a colleague. He lost everything. His self-respect. His job. Everything. Three months later he hanged himself. I had to beg my mother to send money from Manchester to bury the man she once loved."

"I thought you lived with her? That you never knew your father?"

"They got divorced when I was young. I spent vacations with him—when we could afford it. He worked shifts and couldn't always look after a child. I later moved to San Francisco to be closer to him."

I dig deep for any semblance of empathy. "I'm sorry, Tom. It's not a good way to grow up."

"No. You're not sorry. You don't even remember the people whose lives you ruined with your photos."

"If you were so upset, why didn't you talk to me? And why not take it out on me? Why hurt the people around me?"

"I wanted you to suffer the way my father suffered. If his life was hell, yours had to be hell too." He presses the knife up against my breastbone. "And I succeeded. You cried your eyes out at Gerard's funeral."

The memory makes me gasp. The words grow thick in my throat. But I swallow the tears that threaten to overwhelm me. I must remain calm, quiet. Look for an opportunity to get away.

At the other end of the hallway, Francois is still hammering on the bathroom door, but the sound is softer. Less persistent. The brandy is taking its toll.

Nothing seems to put Tom off.

"Billy. Gerard. Peter." He lists the names of his victims. "They didn't know who and what you were. You didn't deserve them. You deserve being alone. You deserve rotting in a corner in your own piss and blood."

The blade finds a new place, higher up my neck. Pierces my skin. The pain is sharp, immediate.

"I'm sorry, Tom," I plead. "Really. Why don't we talk about this? You can help me understand what I did wrong."

"Tom, calm down," Alex chimes in, his voice soft and cautious.

Dammit. Not now. Alex should keep quiet. I look toward the door and try to warn him with my eyes, but he ignores me.

"Let her go," Alex insists.

He holds out his hands as if he actually expects the Englishman to give him the knife. He takes a slow step forward.

His eyes flicker toward me. Back to Tom.

I see what he's doing. Every time Tom has seemed distracted, he has shuffled closer. He's already considerably closer to the bed without Tom or me having noticed.

"I wouldn't worry about Isabel if I were you." Tom spits out the words. "Worry about yourself instead. You're the one who fucked up everything. Before you arrived in Dar she was a miserable drunk."

"I don't think so. She was pretty happy. I think the real reason for your anger is that Ranna didn't want you. You had your chance, remember?" Alex measures the distance between him and me with his eyes. "And you couldn't make it work. Probably couldn't deliver what a woman like her needs." He glances at Tom's crotch.

Rage takes over Tom's body. His hand begins to tremble. The knife jerks wildly. I feel blood pouring down my neck, hot and sticky. I smell copper and wet earth. The pain is overwhelming. Everything goes dim, turns black. I shake my head. Clench my teeth.

I must focus. Concentrate.

Alex takes another step forward, more hurriedly now.

"No," Tom warns. He swings the knife in Alex's direction. Back to the painful wounds at my throat. My chest. "Stay there. I'll cut her fucking heart out."

"Ranna can do so much better than you," Alex persists. "You're a good-for-nothing whiner. A pathetic little boy who couldn't get over it that a woman didn't want him. That his father was a coward. Poor Tom."

With each word Alex shuffles closer.

"I'm warning you!" Tom shouts.

"You're too gutless to do anything. Just like your father."

I see something in Alex's eyes. A signal. A message?

Suddenly I know what he wants.

I wonder what price we will pay.

I feel Tom's attention shifting to Alex.

Now.

I jerk my head away, free from his grip. From the corner of my eye I watch as Alex takes the last few steps to reach Tom.

I push away from him. Fall off the bed. Crawl across the floor to the door.

"No!" I hear the Englishman call out behind me. When I turn he has a gun in his right hand.

I turn. See how Alex grabs Tom's arms and forces the barrel up, toward the ceiling. He tries to bend Tom's body back, but the Englishman is strong, berserk, his eyes wild. Slowly but surely he's getting the better of Alex.

I see the knife half under the bed. Don't think, I tell myself. Just do it.

I kick myself away from the door and slide forward. With my cuffed hands I grab the knife and scramble to my feet.

I bury the knife in Tom's shoulder. My hands slip on the bloody hilt, but I force it in. Again. And again.

"Ranna. Ranna!"

Alex's voice slices through the buzzing in my ears. I look at the knife in my hands. Shake my head incredulously. What just happened?

Tom is kneeling between Alex and me, dazed. He slaps at his shoulder with an uncertain hand.

"But I love you." He coughs. Wipes blood from his lips. Looks at it. "Isabel?"

Slowly he topples over.

The knife falls from my hands. I close my eyes. When I open them, Tom is still there, on the floor.

At last.

I speak the words aloud.

"At last."

Again and again, only stopping when Alex shakes my shoulder.

"Ranna. Stop. It's over."

"What?"

He cups my chin, and forces me to look at him. "Are you okay?"

"Is he dead?"

He turns to Tom, bends down, feels for a pulse. "Almost." He searches the Englishman's pockets for the keys of the handcuffs. Finds them. Frees my hands.

"We've got to call an ambulance."

He hesitates a moment. “Is that what you want?”

“What do you mean?”

“You know what I mean.”

He’s right: I know. How long has Tom held me prisoner in my own skin?

“The ambulance won’t come in time.” I make the decision.

“Probably not. It’s a long way to the farm.”

I look down at Tom. Alex’s feet are covered in blood, I notice with a feeling of disbelief.

Alex grabs my wrists and pulls me towards him. “Come here.”

His hands are all over my shoulders, my chest, my throat. Touching, checking if I’m okay. He kisses my neck.

“It’s over.” He kisses me again. “It’s all over. I love you.”

But he’s wrong. It’s not over. Not even remotely.

It’s only the beginning.

PART THREE

ALEX

1

The blood on Ranna's body scares me.

Perhaps this is how you know you love someone: Their blood makes you taste something like fear. Thick and salty. Hard to swallow. When you see it, your mind jumps back to what you said to hurt them. Forward to the mornings you still want to wake up next to them. The Christmases and anniversaries you want to spend with them.

My hands can't let her go. I examine each wound. How deep. How painful.

I don't look at Tom. His pulse was weak and irregular a moment ago. It won't be long. Ranna aimed for his heart and found it.

Perhaps he'll finally be happy, now that he'll live forever in her head. Because he will. I know he will. Perhaps even more than when he was alive.

Ranna stiffens when someone knocks on the door. I know at once who it is. Only one person moves so silently. When I open the door she's standing there, a hunting rifle in her hands. She's pale, but her hands and her gaze are steady.

Chaos. Again.

Ranna follows me to the door and positions herself behind me, her hands on my shoulders.

"Ma," I say cautiously. "Are you okay?"

"Yes." She points to Ranna. "And you?"

Ranna nods. "Yes."

I take a slow step forward and push the barrel of the rifle aside. I know the weapon will be loaded and ready.

My mother doesn't resist, but her eyes still hold mine. "I heard a noise. At first I thought you were . . . you know . . ." She swallows the words and motions at Ranna with her head. "Clearly I was wrong."

"Pa?"

"Out like a light. I've been putting sleeping pills in his nightcaps for almost three years now." She smiles, as if her honesty is liberating. "If I hide in the bathroom long enough, he drinks himself to sleep. Then I can go walk in peace."

"Walk? In the middle of the night?"

Her grip on the rifle relaxes slightly. "It's the quietest time of day, and God knows, I crave silence. Your father is noise. Always. Constantly. Shouting. Shouting. Shouting."

I feel Ranna's body move behind me, her head growing heavier. Her breathing in my neck. Rapid. Unsure.

I have to take a closer look at her wounds.

My mother looks past me at Ranna. "Are you sure you're all right?"

"Ma, it's okay, really," I assure her again. I put my hands on hers and try to pull the rifle from her grip, but her fingers remain clenched around the .308.

"What's going on in here? I think you better explain."

"Ma. Everything is okay," I repeat because I don't know what else to say. "We're okay."

"What happened, Alex?" Her voice is steady. "And don't tell me again that everything is okay."

"It was . . ." I search for words to explain but decide against it. "It may be better if you don't know."

I look over my shoulder at Ranna. She steps back, her eyes scared.

"Child!" my mother gasps.

I turn. Oh, fuck.

Ranna's chest and throat are bright red. For the first time I notice that her cheek is swollen. Tom must have gotten to her face as well.

"What happened?" my mother asks sharply.

"Nothing," says Ranna. "It was an accident."

My mother's head swivels in my direction.

The realization hits me like a hammer blow.

"Ma! How could you think that?"

Ranna shakes her head, her eyes wide. "No, no. It wasn't Alex."

"If it was . . . If he's like his father, I'll shoot him."

I look at the small woman in the thin white nightdress, wondering if she means it. She is certainly more than capable. She taught me how to shoot during the school holidays. She can knock a one-rand coin off the kraal wall at almost a hundred feet.

"I'd never do that," I protest angrily. "I can't believe you'd think it."

She ignores me. Looks at Ranna for confirmation.

"It wasn't him. I promise."

The rifle doesn't move.

"Sophia. Really. Not Alex. You know that."

My mother lowers the rifle. "Yes. Okay. You're right. Of course. Sorry."

She puts the safety catch on and props the rifle against the wall. "Are you going to tell me what happened here?"

"No," I say, still angry.

"It's . . . it's hard to explain, Sophia," Ranna adds.

She comes to stand next to me in the doorway, as if she wants to stop my mother from seeing what's inside the room. But she can't do anything about the smell of blood in the air. More blood than Ranna has on her T-shirt.

My mother knows the smell of blood intimately.

I put my hands on her shoulders. "Please trust me, Ma," I plead. "It's better you don't know."

"Why?"

"It just is."

She folds her arms as if she's cold. Keeps looking at me with questions in her eyes.

"Ma. I promise. You don't want to know. Trust me. This time I do know better."

She pins me down with her eyes. "And what if your decision ruins your life? You must be absolutely sure what you're doing is right. Not just for now, this moment, but later as well. A few days from today. A year. Years into the future."

I can see she speaks from experience. And she's right. But Ranna and I don't have too many options.

"I know what I'm doing, Ma." I feign an assurance I don't feel. "Remember that time I told the reverend about Pa? You were furious. You said I should have trusted you. That you knew what you were doing." I indicate the room behind me. "This is the same."

"And do you think I made the right decision back then?"

It's not the answer I was expecting. "Whether it was right or not, it was the decision you made. And I respected it."

I could swear her eyes are amused, despite the graveness of the situation. "Then I trust you, my boy."

She turns away, walks down the hall, and looks back at me. "Just answer me this: Why?"

I take Ranna's hand. Swallow, the acid taste of truth in my mouth. "Because no one would believe us."

2

Tom is remarkably light. I take off my T-shirt and hoist him onto my shoulder. Hand the T-shirt to Ranna. "Clean up after me. And grab another shirt for me to wear."

She jogs to my room, comes back with shirt in hand.

The moon and stars light up the landscape. We leave the house, making as little noise as possible. I know what my mother said, but Francois Derksen is a bastard. What if he wakes up? Maybe he's gotten wise to the sleeping pills in his brandy.

My mother has gone back to their room, having insisted on making tea first. We couldn't refuse, though sipping sickly sweet Five Roses was probably the last thing we wanted to do while my mother expertly tended to Ranna's wounds.

A few feet from the house I turn and look back. The lights are off, but I think I see a chink in the curtains of my parents' bedroom.

Ranna's eyes follow my gaze. "What is it?"

I shift Tom's weight on my shoulder. "Nothing. Don't worry." It will be dawn in an hour. We have to hurry.

"Your father's bakkie or the Polo?"

"The Polo. We might not be back by the time he's ready to leave."

When we reach the silver sedan, I motion at the trunk with my head. "Can you open it?"

She does as I ask, but holds up her hand. "Wait."

I'm amazed at how calm she sounds. "What?"

Tom is getting heavy.

She opens the rear passenger door and comes back with something in her hand. "Here. An old sleeping bag and some garbage bags. For the blood."

"Good thinking."

She spreads the bags in the trunk and places the sleeping bag on top. It's a struggle to fit Tom's body into the cramped space. I finally force his shaved head down to his knees. It won't be long before rigor mortis sets in. You learn a lot covering the crime beat.

Gently, softly, I close the trunk.

Ranna fumbles in the pocket of her jeans and hands me the key. "You drive. You know your way around."

The T-shirt in her hand is stained red. "Did you mop up everything?" I take the T-shirt from her and wipe my chest before putting on the fresh shirt she's holding out.

"I think so. But we'll do a proper job when we come back. And we have to find Tom's ride here. I can't see a car or bike. Maybe he hitchhiked to the farm."

"I'll take a bike around the farm later, but yes, let's hope so."

"It will definitely make it much easier."

Still the perfect calm in her voice.

"You okay?" I ask.

She nods.

"Ranna?" I take her hand in mine. Squeeze it. "Are you all right?"

She looks away. When she looks back at me, her eyes are brimming with tears. "I am, yes. I think I am."

"You know we're doing the right thing. Nobody will believe us, given your past. And especially not when it comes to Tom. He had a spotless reputation working for the UK media." I can't believe the betrayal. The talks I had with him in Dar es Salaam about Ranna.

"I know. But you can still walk away."

"I don't want to. And I'm the one who didn't want to call the ambulance. I am as guilty as you are." I open the sedan's door, grimacing. "And believe me, I can live with that."

RANNA

1

We drive in silence. At last we stop at a white concrete picnic table next to the two-lane road. Someone's half-eaten ham-and-cheese sandwich lies on the table. I touch it. Still fresh. I look around but don't spot its owner in the veld or near the road.

I wonder what Alex's plan is. Does he have one?

"What do we do now?" I ask.

He doesn't say anything. He hasn't spoken since we loaded Tom's body into the Polo. He doesn't seem shocked, I think. Just preoccupied with finding a way to get rid of Tom's body.

Sophia said if Francois is sober enough to ask, she'll tell him we went to buy milk and bread. "Don't forget," she warned before she disappeared to her room. "Don't come back without bread and milk."

I promised to remember. Now, half an hour later, we're sitting beside a road that seems to go on forever. The solitary line of gray tarmac cuts the horizon in two. The only sign of life is two crows hovering above the railway line next to the road. Where does one find bread and milk around here? And at this hour?

"Ranna."

I turn to Alex. He motions for me to get back in the car.

He starts the engine and pulls away. I roll down the window. For a moment I detect a faint promise of the ocean in the air, but it soon vanishes. I roll the window up and turn to Alex. The sun will soon rise, and time is running out.

"What now? What's your plan?" I ask again.

"I'm not entirely sure."

He got back into the car as if he had something in mind. As if he knew how to make a dead body disappear.

"We can't drive around forever," I say.

I roll down the window again and pull my hair back in a ponytail, only to remember I have nothing to tie it with. I release my hair. It fans out around my head in the cool breeze flowing through the car.

Cautiously I touch my throat, my chest. Sophia cleaned the wounds while we were having tea, but I can still feel the knife hovering there. And I still smell blood. On my hands, in my hair. A bath would be bliss. Or a shower. Even a farm dam would do.

I look at Alex's hands. They are miraculously clean, except for a rusty brown stain on his wrist. I put my hand over his that is gripping the wheel. It's time to think past the blood.

"Alex. You know you don't have to do this. I can do it alone. I've always managed in the past." I squeeze his hand when he doesn't appear to be listening. "I could easily tell the police I killed him. It's the truth, after all."

"I'm just as guilty. I didn't believe you. I was a complete idiot," he says angrily. "Besides, like I said, you wanted to call an ambulance. I left him to die. To think Tom and I were friends in Dar. I even asked him advice on how to handle you."

"Alex . . ."

"Don't." He waves his hand, clenches it into a fist. "You don't owe me anything."

"That's what you say now, but the time will come when you'll blame me for screwing up your life."

"I won't. Let it go."

"Alex . . ." I try again.

He takes his hand from the steering wheel and places it on my knee. "I'll never blame you for what happened last night. I promise."

"Never is a big word."

"I can do big words."

A few miles farther he turns onto a road that seems to lead to the railway line. I look at the landscape. The sun is a red ball hovering at the horizon. I look to my left and to my right, but there is nothing, no one, to be seen.

Alex seems to read my mind. He drives a short distance and stops next to the tracks.

"This is as good a place as any. There's no one here." His fingers tap restlessly on the wheel.

I look in the direction of the tarred road, the dirt road behind us. At the railway line. "Are we going to dig a hole?"

"I was thinking of the train."

"Why the train? Why not a hole in the ground?"

"Jackals. Farmworkers. Birds. And the soil is hard. Tom's wearing old clothes. If we position him so that the train takes off his hands and head, people will think he was a drunken tramp. They won't be able to identify him for a while. We've emptied his pockets. Killed his phone. You can get rid of his stuff on your way to Elands Bay." He looks at me questioningly.

"Sounds good," I agree.

"The only problem is that I've no idea when the next train is due."

"Are there still trains here at all? Didn't they stop running years ago?"

"No. There must be at least one a day. The iron-ore train is definitely still running. I know that for a fact. It's a heavy long-haul train going to the Saldanha port. It won't be able to stop in time for a body on the track." He points at the railway line. "And we can put it right there, at that bend, where the train driver won't be able to spot it until it's too late."

I open the door, throwing caution to the wind. "Let's go then. I doubt we'll find a better place."

We carry the body to the tracks. I turn away while Alex positions Tom's body. There's an audible crack as he forces the Englishman's neck down onto the steel.

"Is it a sin if you kill a bad man?" I ask as we walk back to the car.

Alex shrugs. He's surrounded by a silence I could have captured with my lens. A dead no-man's-land.

"I don't think so either," I say as we get back into the Polo.

2

When we return to the farm, Alex parks the car in the shed. "I'll clean the study and burn the sleeping bag in the veld. You do the car. After that we can do a quick sweep to see if Tom left a vehicle anywhere near here."

He's doing me a favor. The study's tiled floor is covered in blood. The trunk is a lot cleaner. I probably should have volunteered to do the room, but I simply can't face it. Blood seeps into every joint and groove. You battle to get it out. I know.

Impatiently he touches my shoulder when I don't answer right away. "Will you clean the car?"

"Of course. Yes. If it's okay with you."

He hands me the keys and glances suspiciously in the direction of the house. A carrier bag containing the bread and milk swings from his finger. We drove all the way to the nearest service station to get it.

"Do you think your mother knows?" I ask.

"Don't worry about her."

"It's hard not to. What if she decides to talk? What if your father makes trouble?"

He touches the scar under his eye, catches on to what he's doing, and gives an angry snort. "She's told so many lies. To the doctor. Doctors. The whole town. To me. She won't say anything. She understands."

"This as well?"

He nods. "I'll fetch bleach and some old rags. You'll have to work quickly; my father will be back for breakfast before long."

The sharp smell of chlorine burns my nostrils every time I lean forward. The sleeping bag and the rubbish bags weren't much use in the end. I've been scrubbing for an hour and can't see any more blood, but I keep going at the carpet with a brush.

Tom's blood.

Tom is dead.

What does it mean?

Everything. Simply everything.

But what do you do when you're suddenly released from prison? And why don't I feel any happier?

Because my prison has been my home for a very, very long time.

I wipe the sweat from my brow. Look at my watch. Behind me the door of the shed swings open.

"Almost done!" I call out.

"Done doing what?"

I turn.

Francois Derksen puts his pipe back in his mouth. My breath catches in my throat. I look down. The water in the bucket at my feet is pink. I crumple the rag in my hands and awkwardly position myself in front of the bucket.

"What are you doing?"

"The car . . . just cleaning it before I leave," I manage to say.

"The trunk as well?"

"We went to town for bread and milk. The milk leaked in the trunk. It's going to smell awful in this heat."

He comes closer for an inspection. I move again, this time putting myself between him and the car.

"Pa!" Alex calls from outside.

Francois doesn't budge. I tug at the bandanna I've placed around my neck to hide the knife wounds.

"Pa!" Alex calls again. "Ma says breakfast is ready."

Francois's eyes remain fixed on me.

Hurried footsteps finally cause him to turn. Alex is at the door. "Ma says come, the food's getting cold."

Francois frowns, then finally turns and walks out.

Alex sits next to me on the bed in the study, stroking my neck, my back. "Try to catch a quick nap. Lunch is in an hour. Everything is cleaned up, and there is no sign of a vehicle anywhere. Tom must have arrived here by foot. Probably hitched a ride from Cape Town. You can relax."

I stare out the window. At the sun, high above the horizon. Then at the floor where Alex cleaned up Tom's blood. The room smells of bleach, but I can't change rooms without raising Francois's suspicion.

Alex puts his hand over my eyes as if he wants to force them to close, but I push it away. "I won't be able to sleep."

"Why not? Tom's dead. You're safe."

I shake my head. Touch my throat. I cleaned the wounds again, with unnecessary vigor. "Am I really safe?"

He leans forward, kisses me. "You are."

"I'm sorry he came here. I didn't know . . ."

Alex runs his hand through my hair. Kisses my neck. The spot between my breasts, where Tom's knife will leave a scar. "I know. I know you'd never do anything to harm me."

"Do you believe that? Do you really believe that?"

He gives a slight smile, but a yawn catches him unawares. "Yes, I believe it. Sleep now."

3

"Stay another day. It's so nice to have interesting company for a change."

I see Alex's back stiffen when his father speaks, but he doesn't say a word. Sophia, silent as usual, dishes up our late lunch into white porcelain bowls.

"I want to get to the coast. I can't wait to see the sea again." I'm sitting at the kitchen table, trying to smile.

"But—"

"Food's ready," Sophia announces before Francois can continue. She sets three serving dishes on the table.

"Thank heaven," Alex mutters. He briefly squeezes my leg under the table.

I nod almost imperceptibly. I understand. Eat and leave so that this bloody day will come to an end. We'll see each other back in Johannesburg.

I jump when I feel a new hand on my leg.

Francois. Dammit.

"Help yourself." He points to the generous spread on the table. "You're the guest. And such a pretty one too."

I turn slightly on my seat and move my legs until they touch Alex's. The kitchen table shifts. I glance up guiltily.

Sophia is holding out the serving dish filled with mashed potatoes. Her gaze is flat and hard.

"I didn't . . . I mean, I don't . . ."

"Don't what?" Alex's eyebrows are question marks.

"No. I mean, thank you. It looks delicious."

I fill my plate, eat mechanically. What if Francois Derksen makes trouble? If Sophia changes her mind? What happens if she decides to call the police?

"Drive carefully." Alex is leaning on the roof of the Polo, the sun in his eyes. He ducks down to face me through the open window. "Call when you reach the hotel."

"I will," I say, glad lunch is over and that I can finally leave this place.

"I'll finish up here, then I'll be home."

"Is that so?"

I laugh, and he laughs with me. There's no home. Neither of us knows what a proper home is. Yet he mentions home as if it exists. Could exist. It feels good.

I tug at his shirt, and he leans into the car. His kiss settles somewhere in the region of my hips. I moan at his touch.

Laughter lines crinkle his eyes. "Go now. And don't worry."

I think about Tom on the railway line. "Do you think the train . . . ?"

"Don't. Forget about him," he says. He hits the roof of the car with an open hand. "Go."

I turn the key. Nothing happens.

I try again. And again. My newly bought secondhand car stutters and jerks but fails to move an inch.

"I don't understand why the thing won't start." Alex runs his hand through his hair in a helpless gesture. "I don't know enough about engines to know what could be wrong."

"You've always been a bit soft," Francois calls from the stoep.

"Then why don't you come and fix it?" Alex raises his chin as if he's squaring up for a fight.

"You said you'd take care of it."

"That's not what I said," Alex mutters before sticking his head back under the hood. "I said I'd take a look."

How on earth did Alex last so long under Francois Derksen's roof? And what about Sophia, who still has to live with him? I look at where she's sitting next to her husband, darning socks. I would've gone completely off my rocker. Or ended up in prison.

I push my sunglasses up over my hair so that I can look Alex in the eye. "It's okay. We'll find someone to come and fix it." I rub his shoulder. He relaxes slightly. "I don't expect you to fix everything. You know that, don't you? Not even one day when we're married."

"Really?"

"Really."

"The married thing too?" His eyes are mischievous, his father forgotten.

"Definitely. We'll have a long list on the fridge with the names of people who can fix things. Everyone except a plumber. That I can do myself."

"I'm impressed." He takes his cell phone from his jeans pocket. "But seeing that you don't know squat about engines, I'll call the garage in town to come and tow the car."

Sophia must have overheard. "Leave it!" she cries. "I'll phone Jan Frederik. He can always do with some extra cash. And it'll be quicker. It's probably just something small."

I look at Alex.

"She's right," he offers.

"That's kind of you, Sophia!" I call back.

And then I kiss Alex. Properly. In plain sight of his parents.

We're having coffee on the stoep. Or rather I'm having coffee. Sophia is sewing, and Alex is checking his emails, probably making plans to get to Johannesburg sooner. Earlier, when I got up to go to the kitchen, I saw him send a message marked "Urgent" to his new news editor.

Francois has gone off—something to do with sheep—and I tried my best to hide my pleasure.

I watch as Jan Frederik, a thin, pale man in his early forties, disappears under the hood of the Polo. Sophia has told us he's an accomplished artist who paints mostly watercolor landscapes. One of them hangs in the study.

Jan Frederik came to Namaqualand all the way from Knysna in search of silence. Silence, car engines, and painting are his passions, she explained—in that order. He seems to fascinate her.

Something about him reminds me of Hamisi. His nails are clean and neatly trimmed, his T-shirt perfectly pressed. It's hard to believe he works on car engines for a living.

Jan Frederik straightens up, his hands on his hips. "Where did you fill up the last time?" he calls out.

I put my cup down and hop over the stoep wall. On my way to the Polo I catch sight of his toolbox. Amazed, I stare at the red metal box. Every shiny, spotless tool is numbered.

He clears his throat next to me. "Gasoline?" he asks impatiently.

"Oh, yes. The car is new. Well, secondhand, actually. I bought it in Joburg. I've only filled it up about three times."

"Well, the last time someone made a mistake. There's diesel in your gas tank."

"Impossible. The last time I filled up was two hundred miles from here, and I don't imagine I would have reached the farm if there was diesel in the tank. And we have used the car since then. This morning, in fact. Alex and I took a short drive. Besides, I know the car takes gas."

"Are you sure?"

"I wouldn't forget something like that. And like I say, the car was perfectly okay just a few hours ago."

"Well, there is diesel in your gas tank, and it's an odd thing to happen, because the nozzle of a diesel pump doesn't fit in a gas tank." He walks to the side of the car, points to the fuel tank.

"I have no idea how it could have gotten there," I say despondently. "It wasn't me."

"It takes a while before the diesel has an effect, but I doubt you would have been able to drive two hundred miles. So it must have happened more recently. Are you sure you didn't fill up again closer to the farm?"

I shake my head. Then it dawns on me I may know who could have added the diesel. Maybe Tom didn't want me to leave the farm before he could execute his plan.

"No. I didn't," I say at last.

He takes a neatly folded black handkerchief from the back pocket of his jeans and wipes his hands. "So how did it happen then?" He insists on an answer.

I don't know what to say. I can't really answer—not with a dead body on the railway tracks.

"Can you fix it?" I change the subject.

"It's going to take a while."

I think of Francois Derksen. I would really like to get out of here as soon as possible.

"I'm supposed to be on vacation. The hotel has been booked. Can't we think of something?"

He shrugs, glances toward the stoep. "I suppose we could. I can lend you a car while I fix this one. Alex can drive through later and collect the Polo. Or you can come and collect it yourself later. Unfortunately, I'll have to charge you."

"No problem. Thank you, Jan Frederik." I put out my hand to shake his, but he ignores it. "It's kind of you. I appreciate it."

His neck flushes red. "Don't mention it. Anything for Mrs. Derksen."

He wipes his hands one last time, folds the handkerchief, and puts it away. "I'll bring the car tomorrow. It's an old Jetta I sometimes lend to clients. It's not as clean as I would like, but I suppose it'll do. Unfortunately, I don't have anything better. Keep it as long as you need to."

"Thanks. Really."

He nods stiffly and begins to wipe down his tools and put them away. I return to the stoep. Another night with the Derksens. Oh, joy.

Alex closes his laptop. "What does he say?" His mother has gone to the kitchen to make more coffee. Francois has thankfully also disappeared.

"Diesel in the gas tank." I sit down next to him. "Looks as if it was done on purpose."

"But the car was fine this morning?"

"Jan Frederik says it takes time to take effect, but not too long. And it's been quite a while since I filled up."

"So it didn't happen at the filling station. Do you think it was Tom? Did he want to stop you from getting away?"

"Maybe." I sigh. "Maybe it's worse. Maybe he had help."

Alex shakes his head. "This kind of thing—this focus on you—it's usually one man's obsession."

"But what if he had someone helping him? He must have gotten to the farm somehow."

"I'm almost one hundred percent sure he hitched a ride. Or maybe he paid someone to bring him here. We didn't see any unknown vehicles on the farm or in the vicinity, and we drove miles this morning. So yes, he may have had help, but if he did, that person is long gone." He rubs his hand up and down my back, trying to soothe the doubts. "Believe me."

"But what if he saw what we did to Tom?"

"Ranna, it's unlikely there was a second man. I'm convinced Tom worked alone." He takes my hand in his own, forces me to look at him. "Everything will be okay. It's over. Leave it now."

I try to push my anxiety aside. Alex is right. He has to be right.

I smile half-heartedly. "Unfortunately, it means I'll have to spend another night, if it's okay."

"Of course. Please."

"Won't your mother mind?" I glance in the direction of the front door.

"Not at all."

"Thanks."

He gives a mischievous laugh. "It's my pleasure entirely."

"It means we can clean the room again tonight. Before your mother . . . you know . . ."

"Don't worry. It's clean, I promise. The sheets, the bed, the floor. Everything."

"Are you sure?" I place my hand on his knee, squeezing it.

"I can't do anything about the ghosts, Ranna."

"What do you mean?"

"Tom can no longer hurt you. Never again. Don't allow him inside your head like this."

I look at his earnest face, his suntanned hands. The jeans legs, slightly frayed around his tanned feet. I have always loved his runner's legs. "What about you? Is Tom . . . is he inside your head?"

"Why would he be?"

"Because I know you." I smile. "You're the original good guy, remember?"

"I'm okay. Really."

"And what if we have a huge fight one day and Tom pops up? If you're angry and disappointed and you feel like you want to walk out on me and never come back?"

"If you know something may be a problem, then you can see it coming and stop it, can't you? We'll see it coming and we'll deal with it," he insists.

"Promise?"

"Promise."

4

It's colder than last night. I rub my arms and draw up my legs up under my chin. I'm sitting alone at the far end of the stoep—the same place Alex and I sat last night. I'm grateful for the silence. The only sounds are the occasional cry of a jackal and the tin roof of the old farmhouse creaking after the day's heat.

Supper was much like last night, except that it was a braai. Plenty of meat. The stark dining room. The small talk. The veld flowers on the table, somewhat wilted tonight.

But it was also different. Sophia was more restless, her eyes less apologetic and her back stiffer, more tense. Francois drank less but set my teeth on edge with his lame jokes and endless innuendos.

I can't wait to get away.

Francois and Sophia have long since withdrawn to the master bedroom. Alex went to bed an hour ago, reluctant to leave me on my own. I promised I'd have just one more cup of coffee before going to bed, but one turned into three.

I know it's not only the silence that keeps me out on the stoep. Any space is preferable to the room where Tom bled out last night. The photos in my head won't allow me to forget anytime soon, no matter how often Alex and I speak about it. The dam wall in my chest remains. I want to scream and shout, but it's as if I'm mute. Frozen. As if I don't know what to do now that Tom is gone. I've never lived for the future. How do people do it? Plan beyond next week? Make five-year plans?

My cell phone rings, interrupting my thoughts. I stare at the screen. Unknown number.

I know Tom is dead, but still my breathing quickens.

"Hello?"

"I know it's late, but I had to call. Tom disappeared a few days ago. I checked the flights. He's in South Africa. Take care."

Hamisi. I give a sigh of relief. "I know. Hello. How are you?"

"You know?" The line from Dar crackles as if someone is crumpling paper. "What happened?"

"We sorted it out."

"We?" I hear him light a cigarette. "You and Tom? Just like that?"

"No."

"What then? You and Alex? What did you do? Talk to him?"

His voice is filled with disbelief. I don't know what to say.

"Ranna . . . Do I want to know what happened? When you hatched this harebrained scheme of luring Tom to South Africa, I warned you to be careful. That things might go south very quickly."

"I know. You've been fantastic. But now you don't have to worry anymore. Everything has been . . . it's been resolved. That's all. That's a good word. Problem solved."

I hear him hissing out the smoke between his teeth. "You scare me when you talk like that."

"I've never scared you. Not once."

"Perhaps, then, I've always feared for the people close to you. What you might do. Since the first day we met."

"What I might do? What does that mean?" I shiver as a sudden gust of wind sweeps across the stoep.

"Exactly that. The things you might do to solve your problems."

"If no one is willing to help, you learn to solve your own problems."

"And how long have you been doing that?"

"Doing what?"

"You're being difficult tonight. You know what I mean." He coughs. Apologizes.

I think for a moment. Should I be honest? "Long. Too long."

"Sounds like the truth." I hear him sip from a glass or a cup. Is he drinking water? Coffee? Something stronger? "Maybe it was never Billy and Tom that I saw in your eyes. Maybe it's always been someone else. Something else. From farther back."

I don't reply. Some things should never be spoken aloud.

But the policeman doesn't give up so easily. "Who is it, Ranna? Who's chasing you? Why do I think Tom isn't the end of everything?"

Yet again I curse Hamisi Bahame's tenacity. "It's nothing. No one. It's your imagination playing tricks on you."

"Are you sure?"

"You're the one who doesn't say a word about your wife. About what happened. What it did to you."

"Why are we talking about me now?"

"It's high time we do," I say. "There are so many things you've never told me. Things I've had to discover for myself."

"I should have known you would go digging in my past. Charlie says you're one of the smartest people he knows. And the most stubborn."

"I had to know whether I could trust you."

"And now?"

"Now I trust you completely."

"Despite my past?" asks Hamisi.

"I'm living proof of the fact that everything is not as it seems."

I could swear he's smiling. "Probably. My history is no different."

"I sometimes wonder whether your past isn't darker than mine."

"Maybe. Maybe not."

"Tell me about your wife." I stare into the sky, watching as the full moon slips free from a wisp of cloud.

"Why? So we can . . ."

The connection falters, comes back to life.

"Ranna?"

"I'm here."

"I say again. Why do you want to compare battle scars?"

"So that I know. So I can understand what's driving you."

"Sounds like a pretty selfish reason to me."

"It is," I admit.

Again the almost audible smile. "What do you want to know?"

"Your wife. What happened to her?"

"The question isn't necessarily what happened to *her*."

"What is it then?"

"It's who I am."

I frown. "I don't understand."

Hamisi ponders his answer for a moment. "I'm not the man my wife thought I was. Nor the man I thought myself to be a long time ago. When she discovered the truth, she disappeared."

"Disappeared, or ran away?"

"Ran away. I guess the humiliation was too much for her. Maybe I would have preferred her to disappear. That way it would sound as if it wasn't my fault." He lights a fresh cigarette. "I want to locate her, apologize. And see my child. She was three months pregnant when she left."

Humiliation? Who I am?

I try to piece together the puzzle. Hamisi's cryptic, careful words. Hamisi at Hardings. Hamisi on my couch in Dar. Hamisi in San Francisco.

Of course.

"It must be hard."

"Harder than you think. This isn't the States or Europe. Three men were sentenced to death in Malawi a few years ago. If human rights groups hadn't appealed to social media and aid organizations, they'd be dead. Two women died in Uganda. Stoned. And it's not much better here. If I couldn't get away now and again, I'd lose my mind. I'm one of the lucky ones who can afford it."

"Why stay there? There are better places in the world, as you know. Places where no one asks so many questions about your private life."

"I know. But your home is your home. I actually don't mind the rumors about young girls. Seems it's more acceptable than men."

"People have always had double standards. It will never change."

Hamisi coughs, clears his throat. "Sorry. I really must stop smoking." I hear him stub out the cigarette. "Maybe things will change one day."

"If we're lucky."

I think of Alex and Tom. Of how I've been forced to pretend. To keep silent and lie.

"Did you love her?" I ask.

When at last he replies, he speaks so softly I can hardly hear.

"I did. Very much. In my own way. I don't understand why she had to disappear. Why she just couldn't talk to me when she discovered the truth. But maybe it would have been too much to ask to raise a child with someone like me. What if I made a mistake someday? Became careless? It would have endangered her and the child. And what if her family ostracized them? Left them to fend for themselves?"

"It's no good torturing yourself with maybes, Hamisi."

"It's all I have left—what I can imagine in my mind."

The line falters again, fades, crackles with static.

"Probably a sign that it's time to go," says Hamisi. "Will I see you again?"

"I hope so."

We say our goodbyes, and I tuck the phone back into the pocket of my jeans. Wonder what I would have done in Hamisi's place. Probably the same. I rest my head against the back of the chair. Swallow the acrid taste of too much caffeine at the back of my throat.

There's no way I'll sleep tonight. Maybe I can just wait for morning out here. It's quiet and peacef—

I turn my head, searching for the sound that startled me. Hear a dragging noise.

Footsteps. From the direction of the front door. A soft, uncertain tread.

I jump up, but before I can turn, I feel strong hands on my shoulders, forcing me back into the chair.

"Shh," a voice says.

I turn ice-cold. Blood and adrenaline rush to my brain, my hands. The starry night turns white before my eyes, comes back into focus.

"It's late for a woman to be out here on her own."

Francois's words sound moist as they stumble over this tongue. His breath smells of brandy-and-Coke.

Slowly, reluctantly, he removes his hands from my shoulders.

I jump to my feet. "I was just going to bed." I gather my things from the stoep wall. Book. Cup. Sandals.

Still he doesn't move. He's dressed in rugby shorts and a white T-shirt.

Leave everything, I decide. I may need my hands.

I put it all down. The night air is thick against my skin, as if it has congealed and time has stopped.

"Why don't you stay awhile and keep me company?" He rubs his hands together and smiles, but the gesture does nothing to put me at ease.

I am so glad that Alex doesn't take after his father or resemble him in any way. His inquisitive dark eyes and his strong hands are his mother's. The rest must be from other relatives. And they couldn't be more different in their approach to women.

"Thank the bloody stars."

"What?"

Did I say it aloud? "Nothing. Good night, Francois."

I don't have the patience to be polite. And he doesn't deserve it. I step to the left to get past him.

He grabs my arm and jerks me to a stop. "Is my son such a useless little boy?"

"What do you mean?"

"Well, you're out here on your own, aren't you? And he's in there. Anyone can do the math."

"Take your hands off me."

"Don't be like that. It's a simple question."

I shake off his hand. "Leave me alone." I stretch to my full height, using every inch to tower above him. "Besides, Alex is a better man than you'll ever be."

His face darkens. "You better watch your mouth. You're a guest in my home."

"This dilapidated ruin?" Anger pushes up in my throat—an anger greater than it should be, but I can't help it. I tap Francois on the chest. "You don't care. Not about your house. Your farm. Sophia. Alex. They mean nothing to you. All you care about is the next drink."

He draws back his hand and slaps me in the face.

I see it coming but let it happen. My cheek, still aching after the incident with Tom last night, stings from the blow.

"Is that the best you can do?" I mock him.

"No. This is." He rams his right hand violently between my legs. Pain shoots up into my stomach, my chest. "This is the only language a slut like you will understand."

I swoop forward. Swing my elbow at his face.

Something cracks. I use my height, lift my knee, and ram it into his stomach. He gasps and staggers back. Blood is oozing from his nose, trickling into the stubble on his chin.

He leans forward, hands on his knees, panting for breath. He licks his bottom lip, spits onto the floor.

"I'll teach you to be grateful when a real man takes an interest in you," he pants. "I make sure you stay longer, and this is the thanks I get."

"The car? It was you?"

He doesn't answer. Straightens up, sneering. Beckons with his hand to me. Grabs his crotch. "Come and get it, Ranna. You know you want to."

I spread my weight evenly between my feet. I don't want to talk, I want to fight. Rage burns inside me like lava. I'm furious about Tom. About nearly losing Alex. About my mother. My father. I want to break this miserable old man in two with my bare hands.

"Oh, I do want to come and get it," I mock him. "I want you so very badly it hurts."

He lowers his hands, a surprised look on his face.

I lift my fists. "Come on, Francois. Don't be shy now. Or are you scared?"

Fear stirs in his watery eyes. Years of alcohol abuse have slowed him down considerably, and I have at least four, five inches on him.

"Come on, you bastard."

Something dark is simmering in my veins. Something reckless. Something tired of sitting in a corner, waiting. Sick of running.

I close the gap between us. "Come on, Francois. Hit me."

He aims a lazy hand at me, as if he wants to slap me.

"Make a fist, Francois, or I won't fall."

His fingers automatically clench into a fist. Then he looks at his hand, as if it's not a part of him. His fingers relax. "I don't hit women."

"You bloody liar. Do you think no one sees who and what you are?"

I step forward and tap him in the chest with every word I speak. "You're nothing but a worthless coward. You're not even worth my time."

I turn, pick up my book, and walk past him.

I hear his footsteps on the cement floor behind me. I duck to the left to dodge his fist and turn. I step forward and punch him in the face, putting all I've got behind the blow.

He wobbles and collapses to his knees, his hands covering his face. I pull back my fist again. He ducks, trying to get out of the way, and falls to the floor.

I crouch down in front of him. "Alex is a much better man than you, Francois. Stronger. Kinder. He'll always be. Shut your mouth about him. And keep your hands off your wife. I'm going to be a regular visitor from now on, you see," I whisper, as if we were old friends. "And Alex may be too decent to take you on, but with me it's a totally different ball game." I smile. "I might just be crazy enough to kill you."

It's barely light when I get into the shower, dress, and hurriedly pack my things. I wish I could skip breakfast, but that will probably upset Sophia. Besides, I have to wait for Jan Frederik and the Jetta.

Francois isn't at the breakfast table, but no one mentions his absence. I wonder whether Alex or Sophia heard anything last night. It seems unlikely. There is, however, the shadow of a smile around Sophia's mouth. I wonder if she knows that she looks ten years younger when she smiles.

I'm pouring my second cup of coffee when there's a knock on the front door.

Sophia gets up. "That must be Jan Frederik with the car. He called to say he'd be here around eight."

They talk at the front door before coming to the kitchen. At first I think the mechanic is wearing the same clothes as yesterday, but on closer inspection I can see I'm wrong. The jeans and T-shirt are fresh, though the color and brand are identical to yesterday's.

He takes a spotless white folded handkerchief from his back pocket and wipes his hands before shaking Alex's hand briefly. He waves at me. "I brought the car," he says, gesturing over his shoulder. "And I made sure it's clean."

"Thanks. It's very kind of you. Mine should be clean as well. I spilled some milk, and it reeked in this heat. I hope you don't mind the smell of bleach."

I finish my coffee and walk to the study to collect my bag. I want to hit the road before Francois Derksen makes an appearance. I certainly don't want to have to explain to Alex what happened to his father's face.

5

The scenery along the road to Cape Town is breathtaking. As there's no longer any reason to hide out on the West Coast, I booked a room at a small hotel in the Bo-Kaap for a few days. I wish Alex could come along, but Sophia will never let him go before his promised two weeks are over.

It's hard to forget her face when I kissed her goodbye. She looked me in the eye and thanked me as if she really meant it. She told me to take care of Alex. He's a good man, she said.

She made no mention of that night—as if she is content not to know.

She's right about Alex. I'm smart enough to know what I've found, and I plan to look after it for the rest of my life.

I only wish I could do something to help Sophia, convince her to leave Francois and the farm. But every person's salvation is in their own hands. That's a lesson I learned the hard way.

I take a detour along the coast in order to gather my thoughts. At a service station I dump Tom's wallet into a trash can and wedge his phone underneath the tire of a sixteen wheeler.

At a deserted rocky beach near Jacobs Bay, I pull to the side of the road and throw Tom's pistol and the knife we killed him with into the sea. One by one they disappear under the white foam. Each one sets me free.

Finally.

My hotel has only seven bedrooms. It's reasonably priced, and the food is fantastic. I eat everything I've found only lame replicas of over the past few years. Roosterkoek, bobotie, sweet potato, snoek. I walk along the beach and answer my phone without hesitation.

But sleep is still eluding me, and when at last I doze off at night I dream of blood. Tom's blood on the floor. Blood on my hands. At my throat. On Francois Derksen's face.

Alex's call on my third day in Cape Town does nothing to improve matters.

"They found him."

I put down my cup at once. "I suppose it was inevitable."

"It was a bit sooner than I'd hoped, but it's okay. There wasn't much left of him."

"How do you feel?"

"Better than I thought I would. He was already dead, after all."

"You just remember that. It's important."

Three days later, as I'm about to walk through the hotel's front door, the Nikon in my hands, I spot him in the foyer.

Everything about him says cop. The cheap haircut. The swagger. The way he studies his surroundings. I've seen enough cops to know them immediately.

This one looks a bit more jaded and tired than some of the others I've known, which is bad news. The near-lifeless eyes mean he will work long hours, because there's nothing and no one to call him home, just like that relentless detective in Paris.

He'll make a lonely photo. Isolated and insulated, even in a room full of people. As if he knows he's different. As if he's wondering whether anyone knows what he has seen. What he has done.

As if he fears what he's capable of, just like me.

He watches as I cross the room. Walks over. "Ranna Abramson?"

"Yes."

He shakes my hand. "Sergeant Boel de Jonghe. Vanrhynsdorp Police."

The town nearest to the Derksen farm. I nod while I review the events of the past few days. Why is he here? Did Alex say something? No, impossible. Sophia? Or did we leave something behind at the railway line that has led him here? Alex didn't say anything about a police investigation when we spoke last night. And how did the cop know who I was?

Boel de Jonghe coughs and folds his hands awkwardly, as if he doesn't know where to start. On one hand he wears a discolored gold wedding band—to my surprise. There are old scars on the other hand and the inside of his arm. Vertical scars. The way you cut when you mean business.

I find it strange in a man. Especially a policeman. One of the first news photos I ever took was of a captain in the New York Police Department with striking blue eyes. The photo was taken just after he had placed his service pistol under his chin in the middle of Times Square and pulled the trigger.

The violence you know is usually the violence you choose to exercise.

This cop's eyes are as gray as the dry landscape he probably comes from. He doesn't seem at home in the city—his eyes wander outside too often, as if he'd rather be under the open skies. He keeps flexing his biceps as he looks from me to the door. Somewhere in his past he must have been a bodybuilder. Now all that remains of the enormous muscles are the upper arms like rugby balls, the surplus skin crinkling in the crook of his elbows. I'd guess he's somewhere in his forties.

"Can we talk somewhere?" he asks.

"About?" I swing the Nikon over my shoulder. It suddenly seems unlikely that I'll be taking any photos today.

"About the . . ." He considers his reply. Chews on his bushy black mustache. "Jan Frederik Fouché is the only man who can keep my 1972 Ford Capri running. He called two days ago to say he found something interesting in the trunk of your car. The car he's fixing for you?"

He looks past me at the desk clerk, who is craning his neck to eavesdrop on our conversation. "Can we talk somewhere else, please? If you don't mind?" he asks.

Can it be something that fell out of Tom's pocket? Out of mine? An icy cold settles in my chest. It doesn't sound good.

"Very well," I concede. "There's a coffee shop around the corner."

Boel de Jonghe likes cappuccino with thick foam—in a cup. I would have thought him the black coffee type. In a mug, with lots of sugar.

I'm right about the sugar. I watch as he empties four packets into the cup, then struggles to get his index finger through the ear. Finally he gives up and wraps his hands gingerly around the white china, as if he's holding a communion cup.

I'm suddenly reminded of communion with my mother and father when I was very young, before my father grew so angry. He was strong, in a civilized way. Was Francois Derksen like that once? And Tom?

My black filter coffee tastes as if someone made it last night and left it to stand. I stir it listlessly and wait for Boel to start talking.

"Tell me about the blood Jan Frederik found in the back of your car," the cop says after he has dropped the complimentary biscotti into his coffee and clumsily fished it out.

Blood. "What blood?"

"Come on, Ranna. May I call you Ranna?"

"Sure."

"The blood?" he repeats.

"I bought the car secondhand. I don't know anything about blood."

"That's strange. Jan Frederik said you told him that you cleaned the trunk after you spilled some milk there. But being the perfectionist he is, he had to make sure you did it properly before he returned the car to the Derksens. It was only when he took out the spare tire that he saw the vaguest hint of blood hidden between the tread. Don't you find it strange?"

The spare tire. I focus on my coffee, sip the bitter liquid. Curse Francois Derksen's nosiness. If he hadn't come sniffing around the shed, I would have looked at the spare tire. I took it out and cleaned underneath, but I didn't inspect every bit of rubber.

I do what I always do. Keep quiet.

"It would be better for you to cooperate, Ranna. I had a hard time finding you after Jan Frederik told me about the blood. I was going to ask Alex Derksen where to find you, but Jan Frederik didn't think it would be a good idea. Apparently you and Alex are . . . fond of each other. He said Alex's father might be able to help. And he was right. Francois Derksen gave me the name of this hotel. Francois doesn't seem to think you're a good match for his son." He gives a smug smile. "Evidently he saw you clean the trunk. Thoroughly. With bleach, it appears."

So that's how Francois Derksen is taking his revenge. Safely, from a distance. The bloody coward.

I make no comment. Blood on its own means nothing. Boel de Jonghe can't do anything with it.

"Are you really just going to sit there and say nothing?"

"What do you want me to say? I don't understand. You've come all the way from Vanrhynsdorp to speak to me about a few drops of blood in the trunk of my car?"

He sighs, exasperated. His upper arms become rocks as he clenches his fists.

"It's more than blood, Ranna. On Monday a boy looking for two lost sheep found something interesting beside the iron-ore railway line. It appears to be a man in his thirties or forties, though he is so badly mutilated that fingerprints aren't even an option. His face is in an equally bad state. In fact, parts of him are probably still scattered all over the veld, despite the forensics and K9 teams trying to put all of him together. Whoever placed him on the tracks did a good job. They knew what a freight train at full speed can do, especially the Sishen–Saldanha iron-ore train. Do you have any idea how long that train is? More than three hundred forty wagons on a heavy-haul line carrying hundreds of tons of ore to the port." He shakes his head. "Of course you do. You media people know everything, don't you?"

I have to stop myself from shivering. The same thought keeps running through my mind: If only I had cleaned that trunk properly. If only Jan Frederik wasn't such an obsessive-compulsive man.

But there's still a gap in Boel de Jonghe's case, and he and I both know it. Nothing links the man beside the railway line to the blood in my Polo. He's here on a fishing expedition—hoping I'll let something slip, just like Hamisi Bahame in Dar es Salaam.

"It sounds as if a drunk landed on the rails," I offer. "Pedestrians often get killed by trains in this country. Or they commit suicide by train. You should know. It's very unfortunate."

He nods reluctantly. "It's possible," he concedes. "But it would be an incredible coincidence, wouldn't you agree? Someone dies on a railway line not too far from the Derksens' farm, you happen to be a guest on this very farm, and blood is discovered in the trunk of your car."

"I think you're wasting my time. Are you tired of sheep theft and Friday-night domestic stabbings? Were you looking for an outing to Cape Town at the state's expense? That promotion that keeps on eluding you?"

"Uh-huh. Careful," he warns, waving two stubby fingers in the air. He finishes the last of his cappuccino and signals to the waiter that he wants another. "Maybe you're right. There's no apparent reason to connect these events, but my gut tells me someone—someone who knows the area—drove to the railway line with a body in the trunk and placed this unfortunate man in such a way that the train would destroy most of the evidence. I can't help but wonder why. Who is this man that someone had to get rid of him in such a way? Maybe I'll have most of the answers I'm looking for when we identify the body. And you should know that we *will* identify him."

I believe him. Fuck it. I believe him.

And this time I'm guilty. This time I did kill a man. It was self-defense, but who would believe that?

"Are you still not saying anything?" Boel takes four packets of sugar from the bowl and arranges them in a square on the table. "You don't have to. I think the blood in the trunk will tell me everything I need to know. I think it belongs to the man on the tracks."

"Sounds like a waste of time to me," I say offhandedly.

Boel leans across the table. "I'll have the DNA results shortly. Then we'll know. I've phoned a few friends, pulled a few strings to speed up the process."

He stacks the sugar packets one on top of the other to form a wobbly tower. "So, tell me, Ranna. Don't you think it would help your case—your case and Alex Derksen's—if you told me everything now? No one really knows what goes on in someone else's life. What drives them to do what they do. Maybe there was a good reason for what happened."

"Whoa right there." I stop him. "Why are you talking about my and Alex's case?"

"A handsome guy. A beautiful woman. A loving couple. You were a guest on the farm. The body was found only a few miles away. You don't know the area, and dragging a dead body around requires some heavy lifting."

"Sounds to me like you're making a whole lot of assumptions."

"Not really. It's always the same story. The words may differ, but the story's the same. Last year I had a case where a man beat his lover to death with a clothes iron because she'd infected him with HIV and he'd passed it on to his wife. We love. We're abandoned. Betrayed."

"Not all stories end like that."

The waiter brings Boel's cappuccino. He adds the sugar from the packets.

"Maybe not." He touches his discolored wedding band absent-mindedly. "But most do."

I want to hit him, hurt him. "It may be true for you, but not for me. I love Alex."

There's a spark of emotion in his gray eyes, something like regret, but it disappears instantly.

"All it means to me is that Alex would do anything for you. And vice versa."

I laugh. I remember the bar in Dar, our last conversation before Alex left. The fact that he wasn't prepared to live with half-truths. So, no. Not Alex. He wouldn't do anything for me. Tom was the right thing to do. That's all.

I finish my coffee in a single gulp. Put down the cup. "I must go."

"Must?"

"You're right. I want to go. I'm bored with this conversation." I get up and sling the Nikon over my shoulder. "Besides, the morning light won't wait. You blink and it changes."

Boel touches the ring on his finger again. "We'll talk again—soon," he says. "As soon as I have the DNA results. Until then I want to know exactly where you are and where you're going."

"Understood," I say, and leave him with the bill.

6

I photograph Table Mountain from every angle. Travel to Woodstock to capture a group of homeless people sitting around drinking in Albert Street, harassing tourists on their way to the Biscuit Mill. At my request, a toothless woman gives me a wide grin and promptly offers me a sip from her bottle—for a fee.

No thanks, I gesture.

A rich blond man looking for someone—or something—turns his head away when he sees the camera. Just for fun I snap his BMW X5 as it speeds off.

I keep myself busy, but a single thought keeps surfacing: finding everything I never knew I was looking for, just to lose it again. Can't I simply be happy for once? Have a life consisting of more than books and empty beds?

Alex called a few hours after I left Boel de Jonghe in the coffee shop. He made no mention of the police or anyone who had been to see him. I said nothing about de Jonghe's interrogation. He may be monitoring our conversations, waiting for me to rush to the farm or say something incriminating on the phone.

I know there isn't much time, and there's nothing I can do about it. It won't be long before the policeman gathers enough evidence to talk to Alex. How much time do we have—a day? Two, at most?

Suddenly it feels as if Tom Masterson has risen from the dead, mocking me from his grave. As if he is still keeping me captive in my skin.

Last night I dreamed I was in the desert. A dream like my photos—bright and overpowering, the images drenched in color. I was running knee-deep through thick sand until I was completely out of breath. Until I melted away in the sun and seeped into the sand.

When I woke up, I was panting, my lungs and throat on fire.

Later this morning I wondered about the dream. What it meant. What I imagined it meant.

Maybe you never escape your past. You try and subdue it. Force it into a corner. And just when you think you've put a leash on it, you fuck up. And history repeats itself.

I dial the only number I have on speed dial.

"I need a favor," I ask before even saying hello.

A door slams. Alex's voice sounds distant, as if he's in the bathroom. "Ranna? Is that you?"

"Yes. Where are you?"

"Putting away the laundry. Is the signal poor?"

"Yes." I move to the window of my hotel room, in search of better reception.

"Can you hear me?" he asks.

"Barely. How are you?"

"Counting the days. My father's being difficult. I think he's up to something. Can only be bad news." He sighs. "I can't wait to get away from here. I miss you."

"I miss you more."

"Is everything all right?"

"Yes, but I need your help with something." I look at the top of Table Mountain, hidden among white clouds driven on by a relentless southwesterly wind. "Work."

"Work? You're supposed to be on vacation."

I try to laugh. "I know." How can I ask him without arousing his suspicion? "It's just, I'm looking for someone with IT skills for an investigative story the paper is working on. They asked if I could help. Seems my reputation precedes me. You said in Dar you know someone like that, remember?"

"What skills exactly?"

"A passport trace. Someone they want to do a front-page story on. I have to take photos next time he sneaks into the country." I bite my lower lip until I taste blood. This lie is harder than I imagined. "I can't say any more, unfortunately, it's a sensitive story, and you're going to work for the competition. Can you help me?"

He doesn't even think twice. "I think so, yes. I know someone who can help."

"Really? Who?"

"Sarah Fourie. I'll speak to her and find out if she's willing. If she agrees, she'll call you. It doesn't work the other way around." He hesitates. "Only thing is, she's not cheap."

"It's okay. I think the paper will pay. Seems like it's urgent."

"I'll tell her."

"Thanks. You're a lifesaver."

I hoped it would be Sarah Fourie. The night Alex told me how she'd dug around in my past, I heard something. Not in what he said, but in how he said it. Something only a woman can hear. In the silences between the words. The careful consideration given to finding the next right word.

Alex is strangely attached to Sarah. What's more, it seems Sarah Fourie will do anything for him.

I hope I'm right.

I wait. The day drags on while I think and drink too much. Maggie would hate to see me like this. In the early evening I take the Nikon and use the soft light to take some beautiful scenic pictures of Lion's Head and the beach at Blouberg that I know will make me homesick one day.

I have a few enlargements made of my favorite photos. Of Alex in Dar, the first morning he woke up in my bed. Of his furious back when he came searching for me among the butterflies.

I put them in an envelope and leave it on my hotel bed with a note: *For Alex. Thank you. I love you very much. I'm sorry . . .*

Along with the envelope, I leave two sworn statements, one for Alex and one for Boel de Jonghe. They are identical because I know Boel will check. I leave a separate letter for Alex, which I ask the hotel manager to send via courier in two days' time. It must arrive on the Derksen farm before Boel shows up, my statement in hand.

I have one more thing to do. I use the public phone in the hotel foyer.

Hamisi answers at the first ring. "Ranna! Good to hear from you."

"Same here." It isn't a lie. I like Hamisi Bahame and I'll miss him.

"What can I do for you?"

"A favor, please."

"Is everything okay?"

No, I'm tempted to say. Everything is not okay. On the contrary. Could things be any worse? I swallow hard against the sudden lump in my throat. "I can't say much or I'll make you an accessory."

"Ranna? What are we talking about? Tom?"

"Yes."

"What happened?" His words are hurried, his voice worried.

"I can't really say much, Hamisi."

"But you need a favor?"

"Yes." I wait for a second or two as a couple get into the elevator to go to their room. "In three days' time I want you to phone a policeman in Vanrhynsdorp—it's near Alex's parents' farm—and tell him you're looking for me. Say you have a few more questions about Billy Jones's death. You've found out I was on the farm with Alex, and you're phoning the closest police station. Tell him about Billy, and about Peter and Gerard. And be cryptic. He doesn't have to know about Tom. About the stalking. Tell him you're worried about Alex."

There's a moment's silence. When Hamisi speaks again, he sounds despondent.

"Why? Ranna. . . This is madness. Just talk to the cops. Let me talk to them."

"There's no evidence . . . Shit. I can't debate this, Hamisi. There is no time."

The hotel's front door opens, and a businesswoman walks in, small silver suitcase rolling beside her.

"What's going on?"

"I can't tell you. For your own sake."

"What are you doing, Ranna?"

"The right thing."

"Why does it feel so wrong then?"

"I wish I knew."

Sarah calls later that night. Her voice is huskier than I imagined. I can hear she hates making the call, but curiosity has prevailed.

"Alex asked me to contact you."

She doesn't pretend not to know who I am. I think I'll like her.

"I need your help."

"Why?" She doesn't sound surprised.

"I can't tell you on the phone. Can I meet you somewhere?"

"Maybe. Where are you?"

"I'll be where you are in three days," I say cryptically.

I know she's in Pretoria, and it won't be a problem to get there.

"Okay. Tuesday at noon at the hotel Alex told you about."

I know the place she's referring to. The Palace.

"See you then," I say, but the line is already dead.

Shortly afterward Boel de Jonghe phones. Reluctantly I take the call. I must know how his investigation is progressing.

"So, Ranna used to be Isabel. Interesting."

Dammit. He dug that up reasonably quickly. "Not really. I didn't like the name."

"And Isabel's father shot himself."

"All the more reason not to like the name."

"What will I find if I dig deeper, Ranna?"

"Everyone has a few skeletons in the closet. I suspect you're no exception."

"I can't wait to see what else is hidden in yours," he says before hanging up.

Early the next morning I pack my things. I hang the "Do Not Disturb" sign on the door, collect my camera bag and the rest of my luggage, and take the elevator down to reception. The clerk at reception doesn't seem surprised when I pay for another week, nor when I say I don't want to be disturbed. I'm working on an academic paper, and I'll be at it night and day. I'm just popping out to the laundromat.

I eat a final meal at a small restaurant in Kommetjie. The sea is the same color as the clear blue sky—calm and peaceful. The beach is a brilliant white, a single trail of footsteps disappearing into the distance.

I drive to the airport and park Jan Frederik's Jetta on the top level in the farthest corner from the terminal entry. I leave a tourist brochure for Hong Kong under the seat, along with a printout of a confirmed reservation for two weeks' hotel accommodation. I put a hat on my head and sandals on my feet and take a taxi to the city.

Six blocks before the train station I pay the driver, get out, and walk the rest of the way. I board a train heading north. Hopefully it'll be the last place Sergeant Boel de Jonghe comes looking for me.

I make certain again that my laptop and cell phone are switched off and remove the SIM card from my phone. I made my last call to Alex last night. It was supposed to be short and sweet, but in the end I couldn't stop talking.

Don't think about it.

Forty minutes later the train leaves for Johannesburg.

8

If the Palace Hotel & Bar was ever a place where the in-crowd hung out, it must have been long ago, before the houses in Church Street morphed into car workshops, parts dealers, and other Mr. Fix-It businesses. All that remains of its glory days are a bar counter made of solid yellowwood and a carpet that might have once opulently muffled the sound of every footstep that entered here. Now every stiletto heel and black-soled shoe hitting the threadbare material sounds like a gunshot.

I sit on the veranda, despite the chill in the late-morning air, drinking my second Castle. It's eleven, which means I'm an hour early, exactly as I planned.

People who plan ahead live longer. It was the second and last useful thing I learned from my father.

I would have liked to be less conspicuous, but it's difficult not to stand out in the Pretoria West establishment. I'm taller than everybody else at the Palace and the only woman not here to earn a living. Every time I look up from my beer, the buzz dies down and everyone returns to staring at the bottom of their glass.

No doubt the curiosity of the Palace's patrons will soon eclipse their wariness, probably long before Sarah Fourie arrives.

I take another sip of my beer, which is lukewarm by now.

"Hell no," someone finally calls out. "We can't let a pretty girl sit out there and drink by herself."

The booming voice belongs to an old man in the middle of the line of drinkers at the counter. He climbs down from his barstool, hitches up his black leather trousers, and comes hobbling over through the sliding glass doors.

A few more years and his right hip will probably disintegrate completely.

I wonder which of the six motorcycles in the street below belongs to him. I'm guessing the ancient Harley with the flaming black-and-orange paint job.

His hands look as if they once knew how to fix things. And break them. A long time ago, before he began to move like cold syrup. His face is cracked with age, unshaved gray stubble hiding in the deep lines that crisscross his neck.

He stops in front of me, rests his left hand on thc table to steady himself. The other is holding a full glass. Something-and-Coke. Rum?

"Hey, girlie, I'm talking to you." He smells of old tobacco and gasoline.

"Don't worry about me. I'm waiting for someone. And I don't mind drinking alone."

"Well"—he turns, jabbing a thumb in the direction of the line of men at the bar—"we think you look lonely. Come join us."

I smile. "I'm okay. But thanks for the offer."

"You know, if you insist on sitting here alone, some rude asshole is bound to come over and bother you, and we don't want that, now do we?"

"Like you."

"What?"

"Some rude asshole like you is going to come over and bother me."

I regret the words the moment they slip from my mouth.

"Are you trying to be funny?"

Oh, hell. In for a penny, in for a pound. "I thought it was quite funny, yes. Ironic, you know."

"No need to be nasty, girlie. We were just being nice."

"I'm not nasty. But I don't know about you. If you make a habit of drinking too much, it starts to show in your face, you know. Especially the nose." I stare openly at his enormous nose.

His face turns red. The hand holding the glass begins to shake. Some of the dark liquid spills over the rim and onto the table.

It's the first time I notice his hands. There's an old prison tattoo between his thumb and forefinger.

I wish I'd seen it sooner.

One of his comrades gets up from his barstool. He's even older, probably pushing seventy.

What is this place? A retirement club for alcoholic bikers and ex-convicts?

"Stop this nonsense." The gravelly voice cuts through the din in the room.

Must be Sarah. It's the same distinct voice from our earlier phone call. I search for her among the forest of leather-clad men. See a short, slender woman exit the kitchen and walk around the bar counter.

The voice is almost too big to belong to someone who could be on the cover of *Cosmopolitan*. It's full and rich and deep for such a petite woman.

She navigates cautiously through the testosterone, then stops to glance around her.

Everyone averts their eyes.

When she reaches my table, she puts her hand on the old man's shoulder. "It's okay, Uncle Tiny. She's here to see me."

"I thought the woman was a no-show. You've been waiting since this morning."

So much for being early. Outgunned by a tiny redhead in camo pants.

The old biker looks me up and down. "Are you sure it's her?"

Sarah nods. "It's her. I know what she looks like. Tall. Dark hair." She raises her eyebrows. "Bitchy."

"Bloody rude woman." The old man looks me up and down. Turns and walks away.

"Family of yours?" I ask.

Sarah doesn't answer. She pulls out a chair and sits down. Her green-and-brown camouflage pants are a perfect fit. Same with the tight pink T-shirt. Everything looks expensive, made to order. She's probably just over five feet tall. Her bright-red hair is short and spiky, covering the top of her pixie ears. Her body has the lean, muscled stance of an athlete. I would guess she's a runner. Short, angry bursts of speed around the block.

Her photo will be a reddish-orange light pulse.

Her foot taps impatiently on the floor.

I finish the Castle, put down the glass. "Thanks for agreeing to see me."

"Alex asked me to do you a favor." She lights a cigarette, drags at it, her eyes a mix of hostility and curiosity. "Only thing is, he said it's about a story, but as far as I can see you are only starting your new job next month. And no one from the paper called you about a story, Isabel."

"I prefer Ranna."

"If you say so."

I spin the empty beer glass slowly between my fingers. Swallow my pride. "I need your help."

She laughs, but her body remains tense. Under her chair her feet are positioned like those of an athlete in the starting blocks.

"Why would I help you?" she asks.

"For Alex's sake."

"I'm listening." Her feet move. Take on the stance of a boxer. "Make it quick."

I realize why she agreed to see me. Yeah, she's doing Alex a favor, but there's more. She wants to protect him from me. She has wanted to protect him from me all along.

"It's complicated."

She gazes at me without expression. Gets up and goes to the bar. Jumps onto the counter, leans over, and jumps down again, Coke in hand. She returns to the table and opens the can. Sips without offering me anything to drink.

"Tell me."

"I have to disappear. And Alex can't know."

She puts the can down, frowns. "He'll be hurt if you just up and leave."

"I know." I look her in the eye. "But I have no other choice. It's better this way. For him."

"Why?"

"Someone's dead. I'm going to confess to his murder and disappear so that no one can point a finger at Alex."

"The body near their farm?"

Of course she knows about Tom. "There's a little bit more to it, but that's about right, yes."

"And where would you run off to this time?"

"Maybe Gambia. Even Lagos will do."

"Dangerous places for foreign journalists."

"I know how to disappear. And I can look after myself."

She finishes the Coke and lights another cigarette. There are small calluses on her fingertips. Does she play the guitar? Spend a lot of time on her laptop?

Again she weighs me with her eyes. "What kind of help do you want from me?"

"I need documents. A new name. A passport."

"Money?"

"I have enough. But a new bank account would be great."

"Yeah, right. You inherited money from your father. Your mother got nothing. And there's Billy's money as well."

I stare down at the fists in my lap. Wish I had the Nikon with me.

"Don't you miss him?"

"Alex?" I ask.

"Your father."

"No."

Sarah runs a contemplative thumb across her bottom lip, cigarette between her fingers. "I dug up everything I could find on you, but there's one thing I still don't understand. Why you did it."

"What do you mean?"

"You and your mother claimed your father committed suicide. You were eleven. Was it to protect yourself or to protect her?"

"I don't know what you're talking about."

"Of course you know. I had a chat with the cop who investigated your father's case. He never believed it was suicide, but he couldn't prove otherwise. The distance was right. The entry wound was right. And your father had a long history of violence and depression. But something between you and your mother made the cop wonder. A love-hate thing he couldn't understand."

Love and hate. Sarah has no idea.

I shrug as if I couldn't care less. "What does it matter? It happened so long ago, I can hardly remember anything."

"It matters because I want to know who you are, Isabel. I want to know if it's worth risking my neck to help you."

All of a sudden I regret our meeting. Of course Sarah would put a price on her help, and sometimes you pay with more than money.

"Why do you only call your mother on her birthday?" she persists.

"That's not true."

"It's what your phone records say."

"We don't need any more contact. I love her."

"But you're angry with her."

"I don't recall asking you to dig around inside my head."

Sarah stubs out her cigarette in the ashtray. Crosses her legs. She's wearing heavy motorcycle boots. One of the bikes out front must be hers. Probably the bright yellow Suzuki.

"Why are you so angry, Isabel?"

My fists untangle and I rub my eyes. I'm finding it hard to focus.

"Isabel. Answer me. Why?"

"I'm angry—was angry—because my mother should have done it a lot sooner." I give in. "She should have done something. Anything."

"And when she didn't want to, you did?"

I close my eyes against the bright afternoon sun. Memories wash over me like flotsam. "You don't know anything about my life."

"The detective, remember him? Reyneke. Jaap Reyneke. He says he always thought you did it, but that you were way too clever to be caught. He said you were never a child. The hundreds of books in your bedroom were mostly detective and true crime stories—much too advanced for an eleven-year-old girl. Your mother was all over the place. She could never have planned anything like what happened in the study that day."

"Once my father kicked my mother so badly that my unborn brother died. I was six."

There is silence while Sarah lights another cigarette. "Sorry," she says at last.

"No, you're not."

I blink away the tears. The last thing I want to do is cry in front of this woman.

Sarah looks away. Shifts in her chair uneasily. "Look, I didn't mean to upset you. I just had to know. For Alex's sake. I owe him. He comes first."

"That's why I'm here. Because of Alex. It's all about Alex."

"Then explain to me why you want to disappear on him, Isabel?"

"Please! Just stop. My name is Ranna."

"Okay. Ranna. What have you done?"

"I'm not going to tell you. It's not important. And the less anyone knows, the better. I'm here because you care about Alex—enough to help him. I suspect you may even love him."

She remains silent, but the flush in her neck betrays her. I wish I could pack a greater punch, but I know too little about Sarah Fourie.

"I must disappear and you must help me. It's all you have to know."

Sarah points the cigarette at me. "And I repeat: Alex will be hurt."

"If I stay, it will be much worse, though he may not understand it at first."

"And that's the truth?"

"Yes. The complete and utter truth."

She drags deeply at her cigarette and blows the smoke into the blue sky. At the edge of the horizon, somewhere to our right, between the tall buildings of the inner city, a thunderstorm is brewing.

"Fine." She gives in at last. "I'll help you. But on one condition. I'm going to give you a secure phone along with your new identity documents. You call Alex just before you get on the plane. Say goodbye. Or it will eat him alive. Don't just disappear."

I shake my head. No. No way.

She grinds out the cigarette. "I'm not asking you, Isabel. I'm telling you."

9

I'm counting people in an attempt to forget why I'm at the OR Tambo International Airport in Joburg with a passport stating my name as Quinne Sophia Daniels.

Sophia. Clearly Sarah wants me to remember this fucked-up chapter in my history.

Seven hundred and three.

Four.

Five.

A woman and three whining kids.

Nine.

I have to call Alex. In twenty minutes I'll be boarding a flight to Dakar, Senegal. Once there, I have to continue on by car, bus, or taxi, Sarah said. "Your docs are good, but it's always better to be careful."

The phone in my pocket is ringing. Only one person has this particular number.

There are no pleasantries. "Call Alex," says Sarah.

Seven hundred and fourteen.

"I will."

"Do it now. He's furious. The cops are making his life a living hell. A Sergeant Boel de Jonghe went nuts after he got your statement. The one you left at the hotel? Things don't look good."

"What has de Jonghe dug up already?"

"The blood in the Polo's trunk? The DNA is a match with the body they found on the railway tracks. What's going on, Ranna? Did you really kill someone? The man who was chasing you . . ." There's a moment's silence. "Did Alex help you?"

"It's all in the statement I left for de Jonghe. I left Alex a copy as well. And I sent him a letter. Please make sure he keeps to the story in the statement. I tried to explain everything in the letter."

I suddenly fear Alex will do something reckless. "He must do what I asked, Sarah. It's very important. I killed Tom Masterson in Joburg and left him on the railway tracks on my way to the Derksens' farm. Alone. It's the truth—I killed him. Alex must stick to the story and say nothing more."

"So this Tom was the man—"

"Yes."

"It'll be hard to prove Alex's innocence."

"There's nothing to prove. He *is* innocent. Besides, de Jonghe will dig deeper into my past, and a Tanzanian cop will help him do exactly that. He'll find out about the other men and think what everyone else thought. In the end he'll tell Alex that he is extremely lucky to still be alive."

"Will the cops believe you carried the body on your own?"

"I'm tall and strong. Tom was a normal guy of average weight."

"Fine," says Sarah. "And you're sure Alex will be okay?"

"Yes. If he sticks to the story. And, besides, you're here. You can look after him. Make sure he's okay." There's a bitter taste at the back of my throat. It could be jealousy, but I don't want to give it a name. "I have to go, Sarah. My flight is about to board."

"Okay. Remove the SIM card when you've finished. Take the phone apart and throw it in different trash cans. Flush the SIM down the toilet."

"Will do."

There's an awkward silence.

"Thanks, Sarah," I venture. "Thank you very much."

"Anything for Alex," she says.

Anything for Alex, I think as I kill the call.

I show my boarding pass to a young Indian woman wearing a blue pantsuit and a false smile. An electronic eye scans the paper, and she hands it back to me.

27A. Window seat. Good for taking pictures.

I call Alex's number. He picks up almost at once.

"Hi, Alex."

"Fuck, Ranna. I've been looking for you for days. Where are you?"

"You don't want to know."

"Sarah phoned. Ranna, you can't." His voice is filled with anger and something verging on despair.

"I must. It will keep you safe. Your mother needs you."

"Ranna. Please. Don't. We've been through a lot. I love you."

I think of that first day at the wedding. It was already true then. For both of us.

"I know."

"Then why? Why run away again?"

I don't say anything.

"Ranna." His voice is urgent. "Stay. Please."

"I'm sorry it worked out this way."

"Ranna, don't do this."

The last passengers are disappearing down the gangway. Time to go.

"Alex. Stick to my story as I explained in the letter. And clean the study again. You never know. Talk to your mother. Make sure she doesn't say anything to incriminate you." I make an attempt to laugh. "And try to forget me. Even forgive me, if you can."

"I can't. I won't."

Forgive, or forget?

"Goodbye, Alex."

I switch off the phone. My fingers tremble as I take it apart. My eyes burn.

I shake my head. No. Not now. Not here. Maybe tonight. Maybe some other night when sleep eludes me again.

ALEX

1

I stare at the words on my computer screen. *I'm really sorry I can't be of more assistance, Alex. As I told the South African police, I've not heard from Ranna since she left Dar es Salaam. I don't know what more to say.*

Hamisi Bahame is lying. He helped Ranna concoct her fantasy story about Tom's death for the cops. I know it. Is he scared the police might be tracking my emails? Possibly. But surely he would have noticed that I've created a new false email address? I even bought a second laptop the police hopefully won't know about, encrypting it with software Sarah developed, hinting as much in my email to him.

No. Hamisi doesn't want to help me. He doesn't want to help Ranna.

Ranna doesn't want to help Ranna.

Fuck them.

I stand up from the desk. My Joburg apartment is only slightly bigger than the one I had in Dar. I don't need much. A bed, microwave, TV. I've been working sixteen-hour days at the newspaper since I left the farm.

I pace the cramped space between the bed and small desk, the latter parked in front of a window overlooking Rosebank's hustle and bustle. Sit down again.

Get up again.

Hamisi was my last hope. I don't know where else to look.

To be honest, I don't know why I started the search in the first place. What would I do if I found Ranna? Kiss and make up?

No way.

Then why go searching in the first place?

I look out the window at the gathering clouds. My watch. I have to meet Sarah in an hour.

I slam the computer shut, white-hot anger boiling up inside me for the millionth time. I stare at the laptop.

"Fuck it," I say out loud, the finality of it all hitting me in the stomach.

I swallow the acrid, bitter taste of disappointment. Pick up the laptop, open the window, throw it to the empty parking lot below, and watch as it smashes into pieces. I wait for the vaguest hint of satisfaction, anything bordering on happiness or pleasure, but only the disappointment remains.

"Great," I mutter. "As if I don't have enough shit to deal with."

The air is so cold I breathe white clouds as I jump from my pickup, jogging the two blocks to the Palace Bar & Hotel. Pretoria is almost never cold. And this driving rain is completely unseasonable. This place is always some degree of dry and warm.

Reminds me of Dar before the rains came.

I bloody hate Dar.

I step into the Palace's lobby, running a hand through my wet hair. It needs a cut.

I find Sarah at a table for two that would normally overlook the city center but now stares at a bank of heavy gray clouds.

"Alex." She slams her laptop shut. Gets up. Her small frame is wrapped in a black leather coat and checkered scarf. "I'm glad you came."

I lean down to kiss her cheek. She smells of sugar, smoke, and the faint whiff of gardenias. She must have helped her mother in the garden this morning, probably against her will.

I shrug off my jacket and hang it on the back of the chair. Push up the sleeves of my sweater, hot from the run to the hotel. "Did you find her?"

"No, not yet, but I will, eventually."

I almost sigh with relief. I wipe an errant raindrop from my forehead, look at my soaked boots, a memory stirring in the back of my mind that I kill immediately. "I think we should leave it."

We sit down at the table for two.

Sarah frowns. "I've only been looking for, what? Seven weeks? Give me some time. She has an excellent passport, and she's obviously picked up some new tricks." She rolls the string of silver earrings in her right ear between her fingers, a sure sign that she is pissed off.

"It's nothing to do with you." I look at the bright umbrellas rushing by in the street below us. The line of minibus taxis stopping to pick up people from the small workshops and other blue-collar businesses in Pretoria West. "Ranna doesn't want to be found and we're . . . I'm wasting my time trying. And for what? I'm done."

Sarah's green eyes squint at me, as if measuring my resolve. "You love this woman."

"Not anymore."

"Bullshit."

A waitress walks by. I order a whiskey, gesture to Sarah.

"Rooibos tea," she says, her fingers playing an irritated tune on top of her black computer. "With lemon and honey."

"Come on," I joke. "It's five in the afternoon."

"I'm not going to drink with you."

I shrug. "Then I'll do it alone. Any news from the police?"

"Don't change the subject. Focus. We're talking about Ranna."

"She's gone, and even you would agree that it's a good thing. Admit it. She's a runner. Things get ugly and she bolts. Not exactly relationship material."

Sarah crosses her legs in the tight faded jeans. Instead of the heavy motorcycle boots she favors, she's wearing bright red Converse sneakers.

I look at her properly for the first time since I sat down. Her eyes are bloodshot, exhaustion dragging down her shoulders, slowing the restless hands obviously craving a cigarette.

I reach out, silencing the hand tapping out her frustration on the laptop. "You know it's better for me to just let her go. The police aren't going to charge me. They couldn't find anything to prove that I was involved in Tom's death. My parents both swear they have never seen Tom—not on the farm or in town, which is true. Jan Frederik says the same, and that detective, Boel de Jonghe, trusts him completely. The cops did, however, find the knife Tom was killed with, close to where Ranna told them it would be. They were bloody lucky. It got snagged on seaweed or something. They're even hopeful they can recover evidence from it with some new forensic technology. No sign of the gun, though." I shrug as if I don't care. "So Ranna may be in trouble, but I'm free and clear."

I look past her to the clouds, the rain that seems to intensify with every passing minute. No way I'm going back to the office today. Besides, this rain has killed most criminal intent for the day, it seems. The newsroom has been deathly quiet since this morning, prompting me to call it quits just after twelve. "It's done. Finished. Why not drink to that?"

She sits back in her chair. Fishes a pack of cigarettes from the pocket of her jeans. Zips down her coat, unfurls the scarf from her neck. "I'll stop the search if you are convinced you know what you're doing."

"Ranna is old news."

Irrelevant. No longer interesting. Of little value to anyone.

A faint smile tugs at Sarah's mouth. She spins the cigarette between her fingers. Waves at a passing waitress.

"A whiskey," she orders. "The good stuff. Top shelf. Single malt."

When our drinks arrive I hold up my glass. Outside thunder and lightning have added to the rain's intensity. Traffic is at a standstill, red lights snaking from the Palace Hotel to the inner city.

"To whatever happens next?" I say.

Sarah nods. Touches her glass to mine. "To whatever happens next."

Acknowledgments

I have traveled to Tanzania on occasion, but I am not a regular visitor to the country. I took some liberty around the city of Dar es Salaam to suit my story arc. Tanzania is a beautiful country with warm, hospitable people, as is its neighbor Kenya, and I would recommend a visit to East Africa for anyone's bucket list.

I have many people to thank for making this book possible, including the excellent team at Amazon Crossing—Gabriella Page-Fort, Nicole Burns-Ascue, Jacqueline Smith, and Lauren Laxton—Rachel Fudge, Phyllis DeBlanche, Janita Holtzhausen, the Odendaal siblings, Marisca Harris, Esta Calitz, and Anneke Hanekom, as well as my parents, Andries and Susan Venter, and my sister, Erika Venter. It takes a village . . . you guys would know.

About the Author

Photo © 2017 Rudi de Beer

Irma Venter is a journalist and thriller writer. She loves traveling, Labradors, good coffee, excellent whiskey, and expensive chocolate—and not necessarily in that order. She writes books about strong women, interesting men, and that fascinating space between right and wrong. She lives in South Africa.

About the Translator

Elsa Silke grew up in Simondium, a village near Paarl in the Western Cape province of South Africa. She studied for a BA at the University of Stellenbosch, majoring in English and French. She later returned to the University of Stellenbosch for an honors degree in English and in 2004 was awarded a master's degree in translation. Since then she has been working as a freelance editor and translator, chiefly of literary texts. She is a four-time winner of a South African Translators' Institute prize for outstanding translation, each time in a different category or language combination: the fiction category in 2006 for Karel Schoeman's *This Life*; the nonfiction category in 2009 for Chris Karsten's *Charlize: Life's One Helluva Ride*; the children's literature category in 2012 for Linda Rode's *In the Never-Ever Wood*; and the fiction category in 2015 for Paula Marais's *Shadow Self*. She has two sons, a daughter, and five grandchildren, and she and her husband live in the Strand.